PRAISE F

Pretty CROOKED

"Filled with mystery, high-tension heists, and flirting with an enigmatic bad boy, *Pretty Crooked* kept me hooked right up to the action-packed ending."—Tera Lynn Childs, author of *Forgive My Fins, Sweet Venom,* and *Oh. My. Gods.*

"Intriguing characters, high adventure, good-hearted heists, and plenty of romance. *Pretty Crooked* has me pining for Willa's next adventure!"—Jennifer Echols, author of *Forget You* and *The One That I Want*

"Tantalizing. For fans of Sara Shepard's Pretty Little Liars books."—ALA *Booklist*

"This debut keeps readers zooming along as a formerly poor girl plays Robin Hood when she strikes it rich."
—*Kirkus Reviews*

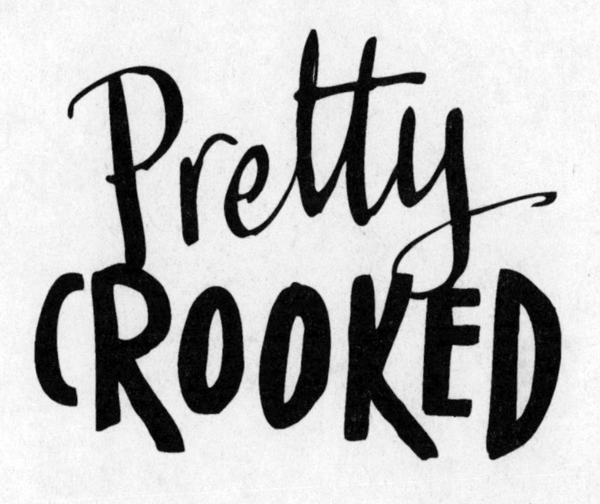
Pretty
CROOKED

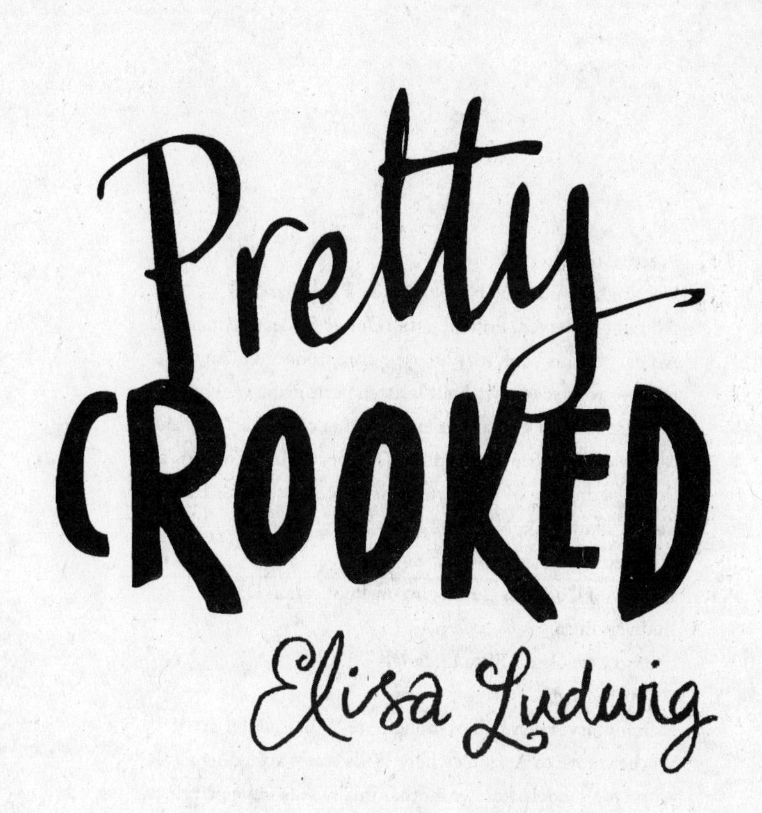
Pretty
CROOKED
Elisa Ludwig

KT
KATHERINE TEGEN BOOKS
An Imprint of HarperCollinsPublishers

Pretty Crooked

 For information address HarperCollins Children's Books, a division of HarperCollins Publishers, 10 East 53rd Street, New York, NY 10022.
www.epicreads.com

Library of Congress Cataloging-in-Publication Data
Ludwig, Elisa.
Pretty crooked / Elisa Ludwig. — 1st ed.
p. cm.
Summary: High school sophomore Willa and her artist mother move to Arizona where Willa starts attending an elite prep school after her mother finally sells some paintings, and Willa attempts to even things out by stealing from the rich students and giving to the poor ones.
ISBN 978-0-06-206607-7 (pbk.)
[1. Social classes—Fiction. 2. Wealth—Fiction. 3. Stealing—Fiction. 4. Preparatory schools—Fiction. 5. Schools—Fiction. 6. Arizona—Fiction.] I. Title.
PZ7.L9762Pr 2012 2011016555
[Fic]—dc23

Typography by Torborg Davern
14 15 16 17 18 CG/RRDH 10 9 8 7 6 5 4 3 2 1
❖
First paperback edition, 2014

TO JESSE—the Marian to my Robin Hood, the Clyde to my Bonnie, and the thief of my heart.

PROLOGUE

GO GO GO go go go!

The chant was in my head, because I didn't have enough breath in my lungs to make sound. I was too busy pushing my bike up a killer beast of an incline, churning my legs against the pedals like my life depended on it. Which it did. Ordinarily, I might relish the burn in my chest, the rubbery feelings in my thighs, the butt-whupping high of a challenging ride. But this situation was anything but ordinary. In the thick dark of the desert night, I was fighting against gravity and space, and my body was losing.

For the millionth time, I was reminded that my vintage cruiser wasn't built for this desert terrain. Someday, when I got my driver's license, I'd speed through these back roads no problem, just like Aidan in his dad's Porsche. That is, if I actually made it out of here.

Still, I kept moving, breathing hard, and leaning forward to urge my old bike on. The wind whipped against my hoodie, taunting me with its ease. Coyotes called to each other in the distance, their high-pitched whimpering like balloons losing air. Or was that the sound of fate catching up to me?

I am so completely dead, I thought.

As I approached the top of the hill, the view opened up to a thick carpet of shrubs on either side of the asphalt, the silhouettes of craggy mountains in the distance, and the inky evening sky hovering over it all. Here and there were the lights of houses tucked into the darkness, but beyond that, there was little sign of life. The emptiness I'd loved so much about the Arizona desert now seemed less like a promise and more like a threat.

Doubt was creeping in. How long could I keep this up? Even if I managed to escape, where was I going and what would I do when I got there?

I thought of Tre, how he'd made me promise to be careful. *Believe me when I say that what you're doing is just not worth it, Willa,* he'd said. *You'd get kicked out of Prep. I'm sure your parents would never forgive you.*

All of the possible consequences flashed in front of my eyes. The disappointment on my mom's face. The disgust on Mr. Page's as he told me I was expelled from school. Cherise shaking her head. Tre telling me he'd told me so. And there was Aidan, with his knowing smile—though for some strange reason, I felt like he, out of everyone, would understand why I'd done what I'd done.

But none of this could really happen to me, could it? I'd been so lucky so far. I just needed a tiny bit more luck to tide me over.

Please, God, I thought. *Please just let me get away—just this once—and I promise I will never screw up ever, ever again. Just do me this one solid, God.*

But even as I thought it, I knew that I didn't have much pull with the Almighty. My mom was a pseudo-Buddhist and when she'd taken me to churches, it was to look at the architecture. It wasn't that I didn't believe, but my relationship with God, casual as it was, probably didn't count for much when it came time to beg for favors. Not even now.

I was so deep in thought I hadn't noticed that I'd hit the peak of the hill; the road had plateaued and I was on flat ground. It should have been cake. Something was wrong, though. My legs knew it before my brain did, because they were keeping pace yet I wasn't gaining ground. It felt like I was *slowing down,* riding through quicksand.

Maybe it was fear or lack of oxygen, but in that moment my brain was slowing down, too, looping backward. I could no longer think about what came next. I could only think about how I had gotten to this point. How I ended up alone and trembling in the desert. How I'd come so close to losing everything.

ONE

TO THE LOCALS, it was probably a weird sight: a short blond girl in a miniskirt and laced-up boots, riding through the desert on a bright orange 1970 Schwinn Suburban on an early September morning. Maybe that's why cowboys in SUVs and tractor-trailers shot past me, honking and shouting things.

Okay, I was new here. How was I supposed to know there was no bike lane?

The Schwinn was my most prized possession—I'd bought it at a garage sale and tricked it out with chrome fenders, a crushed-velvet seat, and a headlight for night riding. It was also my only way to get to school. So there was nothing to do but embrace my own personal freakiness and smile with pride as I pedaled.

Eat my dust, cars.

The thing was, I wouldn't have wanted to travel in any other way. The view from my saddle was outrageous.

Close to the ground, going twenty miles an hour, I could see everything—the cacti like giants' hands, the succulents studded with clusters of orange and yellow and pink blossoms, the funny furry blobs of tumbleweed. The air smelled like sweet incense. Giant hawks swooped overhead. And on the horizon, always, were the ghostly shapes of mountains, layers of blue and amber like colored sand in a jar. I was fifteen years old and I'd lived in lots of places over the years—twelve by my count—but none as gorgeous as this.

Paradise Valley, Arizona.

Leave it to my mom, the painter, to find it. She'd been moving us around whenever inspiration struck. Every so often, she would announce that we needed a new start. There was a certain look in her eye—you know, like how some people get all glassy when they get a fever?—and as soon as that set in, she'd be online, looking for the next place for us. It was only a matter of hours before she started weeding out old lip glosses and stacking clothes on her bed.

This time was different, though. An amazing stroke of luck, really. We'd been living in Castle Pines, Colorado, for almost a year. One day, a few months back, I came home from school to find my mom on the front step of our bungalow. She handed me a smoothie and told me the good news: A few of her paintings had sold at an auction for big money. Big, big money. A windfall, really.

We'd giggled together as she wrote down the number on a piece of paper. So many digits. I couldn't believe it. This was the break we'd been waiting for all these years. We could afford a much nicer place now, she'd said, and she knew just where we could go when our lease was up in August. She went online to an Arizona real-estate site and showed me a listing for the house on Morning Glory Road.

"Morning Glory," she'd said, tilting her head, so that her silver earrings jingled slightly. "It just sounds fresh, you know?"

I would be starting sophomore year in yet another school. But it was going to be a private school this time, she insisted. She had it all worked out.

So here I was, riding to that private school. I guess that's what it's like for people who win the lottery. One minute you're eating ramen bricks and the next you're meeting with an interior decorator. We'd been in town for a few days and I was still slapping myself to make sure I wasn't hallucinating. This fancy place? Us? Here? For realz?

It just felt like a very pretty mistake, like any minute my mom might be like, *"Psych!"*

Now, scoping out the incredible landscape, I was more than willing to be mistaken.

Lawns and trees started filling up the brown patches as the road led through the center of town, which was not really much of a town at all, I could see now—just a thickening of houses. These were sprawling Spanish-style buildings, their stucco walls in bleached-out whites, peachy pinks, and lemon-curd yellows, each spread out fetchingly over the land, and every single one of them with a pool.

Suh-weet.

A red Jeep slowed down next to me so that it was neck and neck with my bike.

"Hey, sexy," a balding guy yelled out the window.

"It *is* a sexy bike, isn't it?" I called back. "You should see my head tube!"

Then I flipped him a gesture I learned on a crime show. Hopefully not a gang sign.

As if on cue, I saw the school entrance from the street, a small white square on a post: VALLEY PREPARATORY SCHOOL, FOUNDED 1952.

As I pedaled up the driveway, the school buildings, all modern concrete and glass, loomed ahead, flanked by rock formations glowing golden in the sun—a scene as picture-perfect as the website promised. Neatly lettered signs pointed toward the Upper School campus, the Lower School campus, the Fieldhouse, the Weston A. Block Art Center and Galleries, and the arboretum, a thirty-acre expanse of natural plantings with a man-made pond. It wasn't so much a school, it seemed, as a luxury educational complex.

I gawked, taking it all in. I mean, I'd seen those photos on the site, but it was something else to be here in person. Inspiring, actually.

In front of the Upper School entrance was a line of

fancy cars: BMWs, Jaguars, Range Rovers. Behind me, at the Lower School entrance, parents were escorting kids in little blazers with plaid skirts or striped ties up the front steps.

This was the place, no doubt about it. More money than the US mint.

And I was going to be a student here. I could barely believe it.

I rode closer, my heart rattling like I was going to bust an artery. Then, a flash of white . . .

Shiny white. The side of a VW cutting me off.

I fell backward, but not before grabbing hold of my horn and honking it, a long blast like a ship going down. Then I *was* down, down on the ground.

"Oh my God," the girl driving the car called out, after she'd screeched to a halt. "Did I just hit you?"

"Not technically, no." Still on the pavement, I felt my extremities for fractures or fabric tears.

She turned off the car and hopped out. She was black, with a pouf of curly hair streaked with highlights, and she was wearing a denim blazer over gray skinnies. "Are you okay?"

"Just a little shaken up, but I'm fine," I said, coming out of my crouch to stand up. Legs supporting torso: check.

"I'm sorry. It's just—no one really rides bikes around here. I just wasn't expecting—I didn't see—"

I shook my head and tried to smile. "It's okay, really."

"Do you want me to take you to the nurse?"

"No worries," I said, doing my best impression of someone who, like, hadn't been hit by a car. The last thing I wanted was to go to the nurse's office on the first day of school.

"Are you sure? Because you could be in shock or something." She leaned in and stared into my face, as if examining me. Her brown eyes were earnest, and subtly emphasized with silvery shadow. "I'm a doctor's daughter. I know about this stuff."

"Seriously." I smiled and wiggled my fingers so she could see. "I appreciate it, though."

She shrugged, holding out her arms helplessly. "If you're sure . . . Well, I guess I should just go park my car then."

I waved her on. At that point I was more embarrassed than anything else. Did my entrance need to be so dramatic? Did the very first person I meet here have to be the one who almost killed me?

Smooth, Willa. Really smooth.

I secured my bike against the rack, where it was, as the girl had noted, the only one. I patted the seat, as if to reassure it that I would be back soon.

On the curb, I adjusted my favorite sleeveless black top, straightening its row of mother-of-pearl buttons. My fingers prickled with nerves—my usual first-day jitters spiked with a surge of fight-or-flight adrenaline.

Never mind. I'd escaped the Jetta unscathed. Onward and upward. Right?

Entrance, take two. And, scene . . .

I took a deep breath, trying to regain my composure before joining a swelling flow of students on the brick-paved walkway. I could hear kids greeting one another excitedly, talking about their vacations.

"We did the Maldives," a tall, tanned girl to my right was saying. "You should totally come with us next summer."

The nodding girl next to her was carrying a Chanel purse and wearing a white silk blouse, her blond hair tied back in an elaborate knot. "I heard that yacht race was amazing."

I followed them through a gated archway into a central courtyard where bougainvillea flowers spilled out of hanging planters, a fountain gurgled cool water, and students were standing around in twos and threes, probably waiting for the bell to ring. I'd been to a lot of schools over the years, sure, but none that seemed quite this *rich*. It was just dripping off of them—not just their clothes and jewelry and bags, but their teeth and skin and hair.

Even the kid lying on a bench at the courtyard's far end looked perfectly groomed, like his tattered henley shirt and longish mop of surfer hair could've come from a catalog or something. Preppy hobos—could that be a trend?

For the second time this morning, I felt out of place, and now it wasn't just the bike. It was the way I looked. I cared about fashion as much as the next girl, but I'd always bought vintage and sewn whatever needed updating myself. My style was my own—after all, not just anyone could rock a shoulder-padded faux-fur jacket. And, well, in public school, where there were all sorts of fashion statements and disasters on a daily basis, no one had ever seemed to care what I wore. But now I could feel eyes on my nondesigner skirt as I crossed the courtyard. Eyes of the very worst kind.

Girl eyes.

Okay, maybe I was a little afraid of girls. Most of my friends at the other schools had been guys. It was just easier, as a new person, to find dudes to hang out with. The girl cliques were almost never looking for new members, while guys were like social ShamWows—they could just keep absorbing new kids into the fold. There was no jealousy, no hating, no jockeying for status. No questions, either. I suspected it would be the same here, so I was keeping my eyes open for any obvious dude-friend candidates.

I continued on through the double glass doors to look for my locker. Though the campus stretched over two hundred acres, Valley Prep was small, especially compared to my last school. The website said that there were only 150 students in every grade, so everyone knew everyone, or at least it seemed that way as I dodged around more girls hugging and squealing, "Oh my God!"

I opened my lonely, hollow locker and stared into

it, trying to stay positive. The first day was always the hardest, but it was only one day. Right now this was a bunch of strangers, but eventually I would know who they all were, I reminded myself. Their names, their siblings, who hooked up with who, and which of them made freshmen cry. Eventually, all the unfamiliar pieces would come together like little pixels to make a picture.

This thought calmed me, as did a quick swipe of lip balm. I checked myself in my compact mirror. My hair still looked good, artfully tousled, even after the fall. Cheeks, still freckly. The touch of mascara I'd flicked on to set off my hazel eyes was still unsmeared.

Okay, now get on with it.

I allowed some girls to pass, then looked both ways before crossing the path.

The one thing I've learned is that starting up at a new school is kind of like a stealth operation. You watch. You wait. You look for your opening. But only then do you make any moves.

"Hey, hang on," called a voice from behind me. At first I assumed it was meant for someone else, but when she called out again, I turned around. It was the girl from the parking lot. She was listening to her iPod and carrying a brown leather backpack. "Where are you headed?"

"Homeroom, I think?" I unfolded the schedule I'd gotten in the mail and read from it. "Davenport."

"Me too." Matching dimples framed her pink-glossed

smile. She gestured for me to follow her. "I'll take you there."

"You don't have to—"

"Yeah, I do. It's kind of a rule with me." I could see now, as we fell into step, that it wasn't just the smile—her entire face radiated openness and warmth. "After I almost kill someone, I like to offer my escort services. Besides, if you're not careful you'll end up in the Claymation lab or the robotics team headquarters. The tech geeks will eat you alive."

I laughed. "I *do* have recurring robot nightmares."

"You see?" We rounded the corner into another wing of the building and I was immediately glad she was with me—I knew I would be totally lost otherwise, walking around with that dreaded new-kid squint. A stream of people greeted us—well, her, really—as we walked past, and she was friendly to everyone. She held the door open for me in the stairwell. "So you're new."

"Is it that obvious?" I asked.

"No offense or anything, but, yeah. When you've been here forever like I have, you can spot 'em pretty easy. And that bike is kind of a giveaway."

"How long is forever?"

"I'm a lifer. I started Prep in kindergarten."

"Wow," I said. "That's a long time in one place." I was thinking, of course, of my own North American tour of educational institutions.

"No joke." She sighed. "We had to wear those little

skirts and everything. Glad *that's* over. Now it's just the stupid dress code—no T-shirts, no hats, no slutwear. But I can work around that."

She unbuttoned her blazer to show me a T-shirt with the words *Hella Kitty* on it.

"Crafty," I said. Maybe this was a girl I could actually get along with.

We found the classroom and sat down at an oblong table. She pulled out her earbuds.

"What were you listening to?" I asked her.

"Old school. *Midnight Marauders* by A Tribe Called Quest. Q-Tip is an effing god. Wanna listen?" She handed me the headphones and I slipped them in my ears. Involuntarily, my head started to swivel.

She pulsed her own head with approval. "That's my jam. It'll colonize your brain. When I DJ, it's the first track I play to get it started."

I looked around, feeling self-conscious about dancing in homeroom. "You better take these back," I said. "I might do something I regret, like pop and lock."

She laughed, throwing her head back as she wrapped her headphones around the iPod and deposited it into her bag. "Hey, we need some b-girls in here."

The homeroom teacher came in, a stout woman with short, graying hair and round glasses. She introduced herself as Ms. Davenport. Then she started going over the rules of homeroom: official policies on lateness, gum-chewing, hat-wearage.

"Sorry again about the whole parking-lot thing," the girl whispered. "I'm Cherise Jackson, by the way."

"Willa," I said. "Willa Fox."

And then the alarm went off.

When I say "went off," I mean full-scale audio assault. Like the chimes of the apocalypse.

Mass pandemonium followed as everyone in the classroom stood up and ran for the doorway, including a panicked-looking Ms. Davenport, who was calling after us, "This was not scheduled, people. This is not a drill."

I stumbled out into the hallway, where the lights were strobing and the parade of moving feet made a thunderous sound. The line was anything but single file, which made me wonder if they'd ever done a fire drill in the history of the school.

Cherise was beside me and we were practically jogging to the exit to avoid getting stampeded. "All of our parents' tuition money . . . up in flames!"

"You think this is it?" I panted. "But I just got here."

"Well, it was good while it lasted, right? At least you didn't have to write any papers."

Eventually, we spilled out into the front parking lot. Already two cop cars had pulled in, lights flashing, followed by an ambulance and three fire trucks. More sirens wailed in the distance. Apparently, Valley Prep was pretty well protected. Not that I would have expected any less. Ol' Weston A. Block knew what was up.

In the crowd, people were chattering and peering back at the building nervously. There were no obvious signs of fire, but if it wasn't a drill, something had to be going on. A lab explosion? Poisonous gas? A bomb threat? That had happened at one of my old schools and we'd all gotten two days off.

"I heard someone lit up a tree in the auditorium," a kid behind me said.

"Man, how come I wasn't invited?" his friend said.

I craned my neck to catch sight of Cherise. I'd been trying to follow her but she'd disappeared into the crowd. Someone grabbed my elbow. I whipped around, thinking it was her.

"Looking for me?" the guy attached to the hand on my elbow asked.

It was the shaggy-haired kid with the polo shirt I'd noticed that morning in the courtyard. "Uh, do I know you?" I said.

"I don't know. Do you?" he said, breaking into a grin and flicking his hair out of his face. I could see now that his eyes were a greenish-gray color, accentuated by his blue henley. He had strong features, a not-quite-straight nose, and a soft-looking mouth that contrasted with a geometric jawline you could cut ice on.

Utter hotness.

I inhaled, without really breathing.

C'mon, brain. "Well, I've heard a few things."

"What kind of things?" His voice was deep but also

round at the edges, like melting caramel.

"You know. Things," I said, trying to be mysterious while desperately trying to summon up some wit.

Seriously, Willa? Is that the best you can do?

"From who? The Glitterati?" he asked, tilting his head to gesture behind me.

I followed his gaze to two pretty, perfect-looking girls. They had their phones out and were laughing with the air of people who know they're the center of attention.

"Forget what they say about me," the hottie added. I turned my gaze back to him. "It's all vicious lies."

"Whoever they are," I said, disoriented by the alarm, by the strange place, by this specimen in front of me. "Whoever *you* are."

"Well, you're definitely new to VP if you don't know who the Glitterati are," he said with what looked like an ironic smile. "Everyone knows who they are."

"And what about you?"

"I'm pretty famous, actually." He flashed his baby greens at me.

"And you are . . . ?"

"Aidan." He stuck out his hand, which was firm and dry. Unlike mine, which I was sure felt like a sponge at this point. "Wait. Let me guess. You're Chloe? No, Samantha. Jasmine?"

"Willa," I said, trying to ignore the fluttering in my chest. This Aidan character was having some sort of weird impact on my nervous system. I snuck another glance in his direction. Maybe he could be a friend . . . or something.

"Well, Willa, welcome to my party," he said, grinning.

"Your party?" I squinted at him in confusion.

He gestured all around us. "Exactly."

Perhaps the radioactive rays of Aidan's hotness had scrambled my neurons, because I apparently no longer understood the English language.

"Here they come," he said, watching the three policemen that were now running toward the building. A fire truck had pulled up to the Upper School entrance and a fireman hopped out, approaching the doorway. "Right on schedule."

I looked at him and pointed to the ambulances and cop cars. "Wait a minute. You mean, *this* is your party?"

He grinned, looking proud of himself. "Isn't it magical?"

Hold the phone, hormones.

Was I supposed to be impressed? By a fake fire alarm? What was he, in third grade? Because I'd seen that hot-paper-towel trick before. "Isn't that illegal?"

He shrugged. "Senior year only comes around once in a lifetime, you know? I've gotta find a way to make a mark."

"Which is to get yourself suspended?"

"I won't. That's the pathetic thing. My dad is one of

the biggest donors to the annual fund." Again with the dashing grin.

"And your message is what, exactly?"

"I don't need a message. My actions speak for themselves."

I gave him a sarcastic thumbs-up. "Way to stick it to the man."

"Hey, I got everyone out of their boring classes."

Ugh. Only a grade-A narcissist wouldn't care that he was making us all look like idiots for his own thrills. Knowing that he'd never get in trouble because Daddy could buy his way out of it.

"You can thank me later." He winked and walked away.

Thank him? *Pfft.* For making me stand out here and sweat? I'd been thinking maybe I could hang out with this guy, but now I knew he was way too cocky. I watched him wander over to some other kid, who was giving him a high five. Probably congratulating him on his prank.

"You can all go inside now," announced a man in a suit. I assumed he was the principal, or someone of equal authority. "We've checked it out and everything's fine."

Like a vision in denim, Cherise emerged from the crowd and came over to where I was standing. "There you are. I see you met Aidan Murphy. An essential part of the VP experience."

My bewilderment had to be showing on my face. "What's his deal?"

She raised a shoulder in half a shrug. "Besides flirting with every new girl that comes through the school?"

"Besides that."

"*He* thinks he's special, that's for sure," she said, fluffing the ends of her hair. "But everyone seems to lust after the guy, or at least every freshman and sophomore girl at Prep."

"I can see that, I guess." You'd have to have cataracts not to. We made our way back toward the door, along with everyone and their mother.

"Well, he's hot, of course. But my theory is that it's because he's rich. He oozes the slickness."

"Isn't everyone here rich?" I asked.

"Well, there's rich and then there's my-dad-is-CEO-of-MTech rich," she explained. "It's a whole other level."

"MTech? *The* MTech, of virus-killing software fame?" I'd seen a whole documentary on the company on TV not that long ago, about how it had revolutionized computer security and how its CEO—Aidan's dad, apparently—was regarded as a genius in the field, the Steve Jobs of the future.

"That's the one." I could tell Cherise had more to say on this topic because she had pinned her lips together in a tight smile. But instead she said, "Homeroom is probably over by now. What do you have second period?"

"Earth science."

She pointed to a standalone building with solar panels on its roof. "That's over there."

"Thanks for looking out for me," I said, feeling a swell of affection toward her. This girl was definitely cool. Of all the people to be almost killed by in the parking lot, I'd clearly picked the right one.

"No problem." She smiled slyly and clapped a hand on my back. "Welcome to Prep, young Willa. We have a lot to teach you."

TWO

THE PLACE ON Morning Glory had to be the swankiest house I'd ever seen up close, let alone slept in. Over the years, we'd pretty much run the gamut of low-rent living. Sometimes it was an apartment tower, other times a trailer, and for one cool and rainy Oregon summer, our car. Our last place, the Colorado house, was a small brick bungalow with two tiny bedrooms and a mildewy bathroom ceiling.

We were free spirits, my mom said. Artists didn't worry about mold. We went where the wind blew us. I kind of did worry about the mold and I was pretty sure she was more of a hippie than I was, but whatever. We were together, the two of us, and that's what mattered.

But this place was something else. Long and low, it was shaped like a squashed *u* and capped with a funky Spanish tiled roof. There were two tall palm trees in front and a neat little covered walkway from the driveway to the front door. A row of giant glass windows streamed light from the backyard through to the front. It looked like something out of a magazine, or one of those true-crime shows where someone gets murdered and no one can believe it because the neighborhood is so nice.

After school, I walked my bike up the driveway and leaned it against the garage door. I was still using the front entrance like a guest, and I still got a tickling feeling across my shoulder blades every time I came home.

Once inside, the AC hit immediately, the cool air rushing around me like a doting servant. Yeah, the free-spirit lifestyle was overrated.

The place came furnished, but nicely, with clean-looking chairs and couches—unlike so many of the places we'd put up with in the past. I walked through the huge sunken living room into the den with its wall-sized stone fireplace and sliding glass door leading out to the pool. Our own pool. Sparkly, turquoise water rippling and beckoning me for a swim any time I wanted it. As soon as I finished my homework, I was so going to start working on my tan.

"Mom?" I called, and marveled at the echo of my voice bouncing through the multiple rooms. We could actually lose each other in this place. That was a first.

No answer. I walked into the kitchen, where there was a gigantic island, all-new appliances, and a terra-cotta tile floor. As always, she'd left a snack out on the counter. Smiling widely, I grabbed one of her famous raw cashew cookies and sank my teeth into it. It was soft and sweet. Was it possible that even the food tasted better here? It was paradise, after all.

A laundry room and the master bedroom—it was called a "suite" on the Realtor's website—were a few steps beyond the kitchen, with the laundry room opening into the garage. The bedroom had a little area for dressing, two closets, and a gigantic bathroom—we could've fit all of our possessions in there easily, especially now that she'd gotten rid of a few more lip glosses. We didn't have much to begin with, though—my mom made sure we didn't spend a lot of money on wasteful things and she was always telling me to keep it manageable—i.e., not to buy more stuff than we could haul to our next destination.

My bedroom had only one closet, but it was a huge walk-in lined with built-in shelves and little organizer cubes, plus an adjoining bathroom with an enormous glass-walled shower. The tile was marbled and the showerhead hung from the middle, offering a rainlike sprinkle that had already done wonders with my hair.

I flung my bag down on the bed and sank in next to it, unlacing my boots and wondering what exactly it was they put in this mattress to make it so soft and firm at the same time. I felt like a princess, pampered and comfy under my smooth expanse of perfect white ceiling. So far, Arizona and I were getting along just fine.

"Mom?" I tried again.

"In here, sweetie," she called.

I found her in the middle bedroom, the one she said was going to be her studio-slash-office. She'd wasted no time in making the studio her own, apparently, because she was standing in front of her easel, wiping a brush on a rag. She was wearing old jeans and a ratty T-shirt—her usual uniform for painting. Her blond hair was messily tied back because she was too impatient to dry it.

I had the same blond hair, though mine was longer and just a tad wavier. Even though she was taller and more graceful, people always knew we were related—the hair, the hazel eyes, and the round freckly cheeks were giveaways.

"I know I was supposed to be unpacking today, but I looked out the window and that light just smacked me in the face. I couldn't let it go," she said. "I mean, look at that."

I looked, grinning from ear to ear. We were seriously crushing on this place.

Then I took a peek at her latest creation. "That looks great," I said.

Like all of her paintings it was abstract, a landscape with blurred patches of bright jewel colors. The ground melded into sky like dyed cotton. She said it was all energy, and that's why you could never really truly pin down anything living on paper—just the "feel" of things. I loved looking at her work because it was like peering into her brain and seeing how she filtered the world.

"So? How was it?" She rubbed her hands together. "I want to hear everything."

I wasn't sure where to begin. "Amazing? I mean, they have everything. Did you know they have a movie-making lab? And a radio station and a skating rink?"

She cocked a sneaky half smile. "You don't even want to know all the hoops I had to jump through to get you in there."

"You're right, I don't," I said, giving her the side-eye. Sometimes her methods for doing things were, shall we say, a little *suspect*.

"And the people?" She sat on the desk and leaned forward, resting her chin on her hand.

"I met a few. A girl who seems pretty cool. Then there was this guy—I don't know, he was kind of intense."

"A guy?" she said, raising an eyebrow.

"Not like that," I quickly countered. I don't even know why I brought it up. There'd never been anyone "like that." We'd moved around so much I didn't have the chance to get to know anyone in a boyfriend capacity. Sure, I'd had some infatuations. They were usually sweet, laid-back, shy types. This Aidan character was none of the above. The hawt factor alone put him into another category.

"But a friend?"

"I don't know. Maybe."

My mom had never really dated much, either. It was kind of weird unspoken territory between us.

I knew the basic story—I'd heard it a thousand times: She'd gotten pregnant with a high-school boyfriend and dropped out to have me, even though her parents disapproved and eventually disowned her. The guy—you know, the one whose genetic material I carry?—was out of the picture and enrolled in the military by the time she ran away from home, and he was never heard from again.

"We just went our separate ways," was my mom's explanation.

Beyond that, she hardly mentioned him. I wanted to know more, of course—not in an I-must-seek-you-out-when-I-turn-eighteen kind of way, but more of a vague hope that someday our paths might cross. The thing was, in the day-to-day, he'd never been there, so it's not like I missed anything.

It had always been the two of us. Not your typical American whatever, but my mom always did what she could to make it work. We didn't really need anyone else, as far as I was concerned. We had our own *Gilmore Girls* thing going on.

"I've totally lost track of time in here. . . . Well, I should get back to work, shouldn't I?" I followed her out into the living room as she gestured to the boxes lying around. "This stuff isn't going to unpack itself."

"I'll help," I said, kneeling down and reaching into a box for some books.

"So, I'm thinking that we could put that photo I took

of Tillamook State Forest over the couch here," she said, making a frame with her fingers. "And maybe the Navajo rug would go well in the den? I'll leave out a few paintings we can hang, too."

"Yes, yes, and yes." I was excited to hang my mother's paintings around the new place. For years, she'd been struggling to get some attention for her artwork. Her dream had finally come true—this house was proof of that—and she deserved to revel in it.

"Oh, I also did a little more research today. Do you know that there are like ten ski resorts within a ten-mile radius?"

"We don't ski," I reminded her, as I stacked up the books next to me. "Which I'm pretty sure made us the freakiest people in Colorado. Is that why we had to leave? You can tell me the truth."

My mom giggled. "No, we were the dump*er,* not the dump*ee,* I swear."

"Mom, are you sure we can, like, afford all of this?" I asked, glancing out to the pool. It was such a dramatic change for us. For the past few days I'd just been swept up in the excitement, but suddenly I was worried she was going overboard.

"Of course, sweetie," she said, beaming at me. "This is what we've been scrimping and saving for, all these years: a beautiful new life. We're just lucky, with the market, that Arizona is so affordable now. And Valley Prep is a great school—it's supposed to be one of the best. You'll be all set for college."

"College," I repeated, like it was a new word. I pulled out some sheets of newspaper from the box and flattened them. I'd been so busy picturing our new lifestyle—Whole Foods groceries, all the cable channels, maybe even salon haircuts—that I'd blocked out the fact that my mom had something else in mind. Valley Prep was supposed to prepare me for the future.

Gulp. No pressure or anything.

"I had you so young, Willa—not that I would trade that for anything in the world—but you know, I didn't get to do this stuff or have any of these opportunities you have. The Valley Prep website said one hundred percent acceptance rate. Who knows? You could even go to an Ivy League school if you wanted."

"Let's not go crazy," I said. "That's a lot of paintings."

The future was never a good subject for me. The present—this one, right now, with this incredible stuff all around us—was where it was at. I stood up and bundled some of the newspaper before carrying it into the kitchen. By the trash can, a door slid open to reveal a three-part recycling bin.

"Did you see this?" I called out, laughing in disbelief. "Even the garbage has a cute little nook in this place!"

"I saw that," she yelled back. "There's no place to compost, but I'll have to figure something out."

"Not near the pool, please," I said, imagining a rotting pile of food clippings growing on the patio.

She appeared in the doorway with a wink and a smile. "I was going to just throw it into the water. You think that's a bad idea?" She gestured me toward her room. "Come in here. I want to show you something."

She led me to her closet. Most of her clothes were already unpacked and hanging neatly. On the floor where she'd lined up her shoes was the small silver safe she'd always kept with us. She didn't trust banks, so whatever cash she had was kept in there. Like I said, she's kind of a hippie.

"I'm going to give you the combination. I want you to feel at home here, and I want you to start being more independent, so if you need some money, you can take it. Within reason, of course."

I nodded slowly, taking in the information. This was new. I'd never been trusted to open the safe myself before. It felt good, to be treated like an adult. But a little scary, too, to have that responsibility. I wasn't sure I was ready for it.

"And there's this." She handed me a small red satin envelope.

"What is it?" I asked, feeling its soft weight in my palm. But I knew. It was my moving gift. Every time we'd uprooted, my mom had given me a little something—a crystal perfume bottle or a beautiful piece of sea glass. Never anything expensive; just a small token I could hold on to or look at when I was feeling down. I'd saved them all and kept them on my dresser. Even when a new place seemed tough, the moving gifts always made me feel more hopeful, and they reminded me that she had my back.

Tucked inside the envelope was a necklace, a delicate gold chain with a cloisonné bird pendant. I recognized it right away, because I'd been obsessed with it when I was little. She used to wear it all the time and I'd spent what seemed like hours studying its bright intricate patterns. To a kid, it had always seemed like a magic charm, the kind you'd wave to summon a fairy and make all your troubles go away. I no longer believed in magic, but I still thought it was pretty.

"I came across that today when I was unpacking. I don't know if I ever told you, but my mother gave this to me, before—" She looked down quickly. "Well, before she kicked me out of the house . . ."

" . . . Because you were pregnant with me," I finished. I knew it had been a painful time for her but I didn't want her to be afraid to say it out loud or to keep any secrets from me. I didn't blame her for anything. And it had all turned out just fine, hadn't it?

"Yes. It reminds me of her. But I think it's time you have it now. You never met her, but I'm sure she would have loved you." Her eyes filled with tears, and I felt a lump sticking in my own throat.

"It's so beautiful," I said, holding it up to the light and letting it twirl on its chain. "Thanks, Mom. I'll take good care of it."

"I've also made a decision." My mom grasped my shoulders and met my eyes. "Willa, this will be the last time we move. I promise you."

"Yeah?" My voice caught between a laugh and a sob. She'd never promised me anything like this before, and I was almost afraid to believe it. Staying put for a while might actually mean we could live like normal people did—making friends, having more than a handful of possessions, really being part of a place instead of just adopting a background for a while.

But this place was beyond normal. We were surrounded by beauty, and I could already feel it seeping inside me, a bubbly, dizzying mixture that went straight to my head.

She smiled and the amazing Arizona light gleamed in her eyes. "That sound good to you?"

It sounded awesome. I was ready to give the luxe life a shot.

THREE

CHERISE WAS RIGHT, it turned out. I had a lot to learn. It was only my second day at Valley Prep, or VP, as the locals liked to say, and my head was already spinning. It was like learning another language. The principal was called the headmaster. Grades were called forms. My English and history teachers went by their first names—that would be Julia and Eugene, respectively.

"There are three types of first-name teachers," Cherise explained as we walked together down the hallway after fourth period. "Either they're just out of college or they're into radical politics or they're gonna end up in a hot tub with a student."

"But is it ever all three?" I asked, testing her with a teasing smile.

She seemed to think about this for a moment, folding her arms across her emerald-green tank top. "Not that

I've seen. Doesn't mean it couldn't happen, though."

"And what's down there?" I asked my helpful tour guide—and, I hoped, PF (potential friend)—as I pointed down an adjoining corridor to a glassed-in diorama of a mummy.

"That's the anthro wing. Ethnology, apes, diachronic studies—that sort of thing." She returned my puzzled look with a waving hand. "You know, old cultures. Anyway, the mummy's the real deal."

I gasped. "It is?"

"I mean, I haven't personally peeled back the gauze myself, but so I'm told. You going to the dining hall?"

That was another thing. The school called its cafeteria a "dining hall" and it was clean and white and actually smelled good. In fact, it looked like a place where Martha Stewart and the Barefoot Contessa might conduct secret-recipe swaps. A massive stone wall embedded with a pizza oven curved out from the hallway into the kitchen, so that students could watch their made-to-order creations sliding into the fire. Other kids were lined up by the espresso machine and the sushi bar.

After I'd filled my tray with organic salad greens and fig-balsamic-stuffed pork loin and quinoa—a lunch that would have surely impressed my mom, who was obsessed with goat milk and alternative grains—I got in line for freshly squeezed juice. There was a changing selection of exotic flavors like papaya, açai, and coconut water. Two days in, I could sense a dangerous habit forming. Was there rehab for wheatgrass?

"Do they have orange?" a girl behind me asked. Her curly dark hair was pulled into a high ponytail and she was wearing a denim jacket over a tight black dress.

I stood on my tiptoes, trying to see ahead to the menu. "I think so. Well, I see blood orange."

"Blood orange. It sounds disgusting," she said.

"As long as there's no pulp. Pulp is nasty," the girl next to her said. She also had dark coloring, though she was more curvaceous than the first girl and she wore her hair loose and straight. Then she said something in Spanish. I'd always studied French so I couldn't translate it. Whatever it was, it must have been funny because they were both laughing. I felt paranoid suddenly. Were they making fun of me?

I turned back and gave them a preemptive smile. If I smiled first, they would have to be nice.

That tactic seemed to work. The first girl smiled back at me. "Sorry. Didn't mean to be rude. We're just new here. Everything's a little strange."

"Me too," I said, eager to meet other new people. So far I'd felt like the only one. "And I know what you mean."

The curly-haired girl introduced herself as Mary and she said her friend's name was Sierra.

Mary gestured to her tray. "They call this a Japanese cutlet. I call it a major upgrade from the meat loaf at our old school."

"Don't even remind me," Sierra said with a shudder.

"The food at my old school was gross, too." I was ready to wager they came from a public school, just like I did. "Where'd you guys go before?"

"You wouldn't have heard of it," Sierra said, dismissive. "It's in the city."

"Don't be like that," Mary tsked.

"What?" Sierra said, brow furrowing. "She wouldn't."

"Actually, you're right. I probably wouldn't have because I just moved to town," I explained, wanting to put them at ease. "And if it's any consolation, I'm sort of the professional new girl. I've started a new school every fall, more or less."

"Wow. I guess we can't really complain then." Mary smiled at me—I couldn't tell if it was just politeness, but it seemed genuine. "Well, nice to meet you."

I got my juice and stepped back into the throng. By the time I'd paid for my lunch with the school-issued credit card, I'd lost track of Cherise and Mary and Sierra or anyone else I recognized. I stood pivoting my tray and looking for my next move.

Another thing that was weird about Valley Prep—and more obvious when everyone was in one room—was that there were no scruffy gutter punks, no Goth kids, no superpretty boys, no metalheads, no art nerds. Just about everyone blended together in a smooth, bland swirl of expensive fabrics, which only made people like me and Mary and Sierra stand out more.

That meant they were easy to spot—they were already sitting at their own table at the very back of the room. Another Mexican girl was with them and they were huddled over their food. I felt somehow intrinsically connected to them—it had to be the public-school thing and the new thing. I had an urge to go over and tell them that it wasn't so bad being new—it was going to get easier. But who was *I* to tell *them*? They clearly already had a clique going, whereas I was the one standing there with my tray, trying to figure out where to sit.

Cherise grabbed my sleeve. "And our tour continues . . . please lower your lap bar and keep your arms and legs inside the car. To our left, the condiment bar, an example of twenty-first-century innovation in food service."

Relief washed over me as she led me toward a booth along the back wall. There were larger tables in the center of the room, but the booths sat four people, and most of them were filled up already with various combinations of serious-looking girls and baby-faced guys.

"This is our usual table," Cherise explained. "We always get a booth."

I didn't have time to wonder who "we" was, because as we were setting down our trays, Aidan Murphy passed by. He was wearing a pale blue button-down and his hair was as messy as the first day I'd seen him. I'd like to say I hadn't thought about him since then but it just wasn't the case.

"Hey, Cherise," he said. And to me, "Hey, you."

"Hello," I replied. As I met his eyes, I felt a tingling flash, like my whole body had gone to sleep at once. Or maybe it was just coming awake.

Yep, as good-looking as I remembered.

Cherise glanced at me and raised an eyebrow, as if to say, *There's your boy.* Then she looked back to him. "What's up, Murph?"

"Sitting with the Glitterati, I see. The new girl moves fast."

He hovered for a moment and I wondered if he was going to sit with us, but then he sauntered off, waving a hand behind his head and carrying his lunch straight out of the dining hall. He must have had something better to do, another girl to torment, or another criminal plan to act out. I watched him go, feeling a tiny bit disappointed and wanting to kick myself for it.

"What's this Glitterati business?" I asked Cherise when he was out of hearing range.

"That's what they call our crew. Me and Kellie and Nikki. I don't know who came up with it. It's stupid, I know, but somehow the name has just stuck. There they are now."

I looked up, and it seemed that everyone else did, too. The clanking of trays and din of cross-table chatter seemed to hush. A breeze stirred the room, fluttering the edges of the Valley Prep banner with its lion-flanked motto: "Honor. Respect. Fidelity." From the entrance, two girls approached, walking with long strides, their matching stiletto boot heels hitting the floor in unison like their own personal theme song. They were the girls I'd seen in the parking lot the other day. The glowy pretty girls. Both had long dark hair. Both were slender and effortless in their movement. Both seemed to know that all eyes were on them, and they were wallowing in the moment, working it. It wasn't so much coming into the room as arriving.

The Glitterati. Of course.

I drew in a breath, gathering courage and making some quick calculations. So what if I'd avoided these types of girls in the past? This was a new school, and a new start. There was no reason I couldn't fit in here. I just had to bring my A game.

"Fashionably late, as always," Cherise said, as they found their seats at the table.

"We had a little cream-blush moment in the bathroom," said the girl next to me.

"See?" the other girl said, smiling and touching the apples of her cheeks.

"Lovely," Cherise said. "Guys, this is Willa Fox. She just moved here from Colorado. I met her in homeroom. Well, I guess technically we met in the parking lot."

The girl next to me tossed her thick brown hair and revealed diamond studs the size of dimes. "The girl with the bike, right? I'm Kellie Richardson," she said. The confidence of her voice matched her whitened teeth and flawless skin. Could they be natural? Some people were just lucky like that.

"That's me," I said. "The girl with the bike."

The other girl introduced herself as Nikki Porter. Up close I could see that she was less conventionally pretty than Kellie—her lips and nose were more pronounced, her eyes more hooded, but she had long, slim fingers that were wrapped in multiple platinum rings that I totally coveted.

"Well, now that we made it I guess we may as well get started," Kellie said, reaching into her bag. She produced a few photocopied sheets and handed them around. I saw that the sheets were some kind of checklist. She turned to me. "Sorry, I would've made one for you, but I didn't know you'd be here. Wanna share?"

"Great, thanks," I said, smiling. The fact that Kellie was willing to share anything with the newbie was a pretty good sign. I'd thought there were just certain irrefutable social rules that went across all high schools, and that one of them was that popular girls were always catty, but that didn't seem to be the case at Valley Prep. Maybe in a place with house heads and prefects and independent studies and an honor code everything was bound to be a little nicer.

"First item is VPLs," Nikki said, giggling.

"Anyone get it?" Kellie asked.

"I was so counting on Madame Bruning," Cherise said. "She's usually got serious VPLs going on. But she let me down. She has, like, Spanx on or something today."

"Ew," Nikki said, waving her hand over her eyes. "I'm having a bad visual right now."

"What's VPLs?" I ventured.

"Visible panty lines," Cherise explained. "Sorry. This is just a game we play on the first week of school. Kellie made it up in fifth grade. It's kind of like a scavenger hunt, but it's all about the teachers."

Then again, maybe they were just as catty.

"I got this one," Kellie said.

"Who?" Nikki demanded.

"Ms. McDevitt."

"The Middle School English teacher?" Cherise said. "That doesn't count."

"It counts." Kellie waved her fork carelessly around the room. "We're not limited to Upper School. I made up the rules and nowhere does it say we have to stay with Upper School."

Cherise looked skeptical as she plunged her teeth into her panini.

"Not only that," Kellie continued, "but she was wearing white pants. Hello, Labor Day is over, lady. Major fashion fail."

"I so got the next one," Nikki said. "Check this: Mr. Page saying 'um' fifteen consecutive times." She picked up her phone and played back the recording.

"That's classic," Cherise said. "Anyone catch a bow tie?"

"Over there," I said, jumping in excitedly, pointing to a white-haired teacher by the condiments bar.

"Oh my God, Mr. Sinclair. Good eye! I can't believe you got that right out of the gate," Kellie exclaimed.

I saw, when she fixed her eyes on me, that she had a magnetic draw about her. It wasn't just her prettiness—it was an aura of calm and control. The girl had never had an embarrassing moment in her life, I was sure of it. She'd probably never been new anywhere, either. She was pure legacy.

"An L.L. Bean bag with sailboats," Nikki said.

"Two tables over," I said. "The woman with the short hair. It's by her feet."

"So cliché," Nikki said. "Does she drive a Civic, too?"

My pride swelled. Hell, yeah. I could play this game, and it was fun. I felt myself relaxing into my seat.

"You're on a roll, Willa," Cherise said. "Okay, how about Mr. Wolf's chalk-smeared sweater?"

I scanned the room, but then realized I had no idea who I was looking for.

"He's not in here right now. You'd know it if you saw it. The chalk is kind of overwhelming," Kellie said.

"I'll keep an eye out for it," I said. "I still haven't met that many people yet, to tell you the truth."

"That's not what *we* heard," Nikki said, giving Kellie a look.

I felt stress—or maybe that was just pork—form a tight ball in my stomach.

What had they heard? Were people talking about me?

Kellie leaned in on her slim forearms and I could smell her perfume. It was delicate and floral and probably called Money. "We heard you met Aidan Murphy and he was macking on you in the parking lot."

I smiled inadvertently. "I don't know if it was *macking*. Just talking, really."

I wasn't sure how much I should reveal, and I didn't want them to think that I had a crush on him or something. As far as I could tell, having a crush on Aidan Murphy was like rooting for the Yankees: an obvious and unimaginative choice. And like Cherise had said, he was all about flirting, so I shouldn't feel special.

Kellie looked at me with interest. "Do you have a boyfriend in Colorado or something?"

"No," I said.

"So no guys there?" Nikki asked, tapping her nails on her Coke Zero can.

I felt their sudden interest trained on me. "There were a few cute ones, but I didn't have much time to get to know anyone."

Kellie, who seemed to be the ringleader, pressed on. "Were you in Aspen? My parents have a condo there and the guys are smokin'."

All the girls were looking at me. "No, Castle Pines."

"Never heard of that," Kellie murmured. "What league were you in?"

"League?" I put my fork down. What was she talking about?

"Like, sports?" Cherise said. "Did you play lacrosse or field hockey or anything against other private schools? My cousin goes to Mountain Crest Academy."

"No, I don't play any sports besides biking. I was in the art club. And it was a public school."

They stared at me like I was an unknown, exotic species dredged up from the ocean floor. Had they never met someone from public school? Someone who didn't play sports with a stick or go on ski vacations in a family condo?

Safe to say no.

"But I was only there for a year, really," I added, trying to regain my comfort zone. Maybe I wasn't used to being the center of attention, but they were perfectly nice. Their faces showed nothing but curiosity. I couldn't blame them for that.

"Does your dad get transferred a lot? There was a girl here last year who came from Singapore," Nikki said.

"It's just me and my mom, but yeah," I said, thinking of her easel. "It's sort of like a job transfer."

"Don't worry," Kellie said, her bright smile and cheerful tone setting me at ease. "We'll make sure you meet everyone here. We like to help, right, girls?"

Cherise nodded enthusiastically. I stared at them in amazement. They just might have been the friendliest popular girls I'd ever encountered.

"Can we get back to the game, people?" Nikki pleaded. "We have a whole other page to get through."

But as she was saying it, a tall kid in a plaid shirt and blue skate shoes approached. He was dark-skinned, with close-clipped hair and the kind of body I imagined you got from, I don't know . . . bench-pressing economy cars, maybe? He carried himself like he had his own clock, his own map, his own laws of gravity. Everyone at the table turned to stare.

"Hey, that's Tre Walker," Cherise hissed. "You know, the son of Edwin Walker?"

"Oh my God, I love his movies," Nikki said, clapping her hands together excitedly.

"No, you idiot. He was the star forward of the Detroit Pistons like ten years ago," Cherise said. "My dad told me that they were moving to town. He just became coach for the Suns."

Kellie laughed at the mix-up, a tinkling, charming laugh that was practically a melody unto itself. "I think he's a junior, right? I'm totally gonna invite him to my party next weekend. It's been a while since we had a celebrity around here."

The kid—Tre—was still walking past us and he caught me staring. Our eyes locked for a moment, and he smiled slightly before turning away.

Then there was the sound of Valley Prep's version of a bell, which was a few harp notes projected over the loudspeaker system. No joke. This school managed to be classy in every possible way. We all gathered up our stuff and stood to leave.

"I like your skirt," Kellie said, taking in my outfit with a sweeping gaze. "Supercute. Where'd you get that?"

Nice. Here I'd been worrying about my clothes, but it was totally fine.

"It's vintage," I said.

"It would look good with chunky heels, or those new Prada platform pumps. There's a great store in Scottsdale that sells vintage Gucci and Chanel bags, like, from old ladies? Have you been there yet? I'll take you there one day. You can find some good stuff."

"That would be great!" I could feel my eyes lighting up like an anime character's.

Okay, take it down a notch. Nothing kills the moment like lameocide.

"Oh my God, you guys, did you see the new sweaters at Neiman's?" Nikki said as she dropped her barely touched lunch in the garbage. "They just got the winter collections in."

"We need to go tomorrow afternoon," Kellie said. "Can you guys do it?"

"I can," Nikki said.

"Me too," Cherise said.

"What about you?" Kellie asked me with a hopeful expression on her face. "Are you free tomorrow?"

Of course I was. I was free in perpetuity! Never mind that I was still sweating in the September heat and not really thinking about woolen goods. Shopping would be fun. It was a girl bonding experience.

"Tomorrow," I repeated, like I was thinking about it. Like I hadn't already imagined the cozy warmth of three new, fun friends. Like I didn't know what I would say next. "That would be perfect."

FOUR

"PAIR NUMBER TWO looks pretty hot, if I do say so myself," Kellie called out from behind the door in the Neiman Marcus dressing room.

We were trying on clothes at the Valley Mall, a huge outdoor shopping center with canopies of green plants, burbling fountains, and ponds with koi fish, and, of course, expensive stores up the wazoo. We'd left our cars (well, Cherise's and Kellie's) with a valet driver, since nobody here seemed to park their own. Add the blasts of cool air pumping out of each store and the personal concierge bringing us beverages, and it was truly an oasis in the desert.

"Which ones were those?" I asked.

"The J Brands. I'm trying the Citizens on next."

I sighed with contentment as I surveyed the pile of Kellie-selected clothing in my own dressing room. Life with the Glitterati was turning out to be as sparkly as it sounded. The crowded hallways seemed to open up when we walked by. People I hadn't met already knew my name. Even the teachers seemed to treat us differently. In our Euro history class, Mr. Barnesworth (aka Eugene) had let Kellie slide with the first two weeks of homework. All she had to do was smile and explain that she was consulting with her tutor about the best approach to writing about the defenestration of Prague. He simply nodded and went back to his lecture.

It was like I'd stumbled into an alternate universe where everything was easy and fun and pretty. Heaven, but with better outfits. I was so not going back to Castle Pines.

I pulled on a soft-as-butter Marc Jacobs sleeveless charmeuse top and a pair of dark-rinsed skinnies and stepped into the plush carpeted aisle between our stalls.

Nikki, who was already standing outside, gasped. "Oh. Em. Gee. That is amazing, Willa."

Cherise and Kellie opened their respective doors to see.

"You're smokin'," Cherise said.

"You think?" I said, looking at myself in the full-length at the end of the room and pulling at the shirt. I'd never felt such a high-quality fabric against my skin. Totally dreamy. The tailoring was so precise that everything fell where it was supposed to.

I did look pretty good. A little more polished than usual, a little more pulled together.

"Leave the ruffles off-center," Kellie advised, reaching over to straighten the seams. "That blue is *made* for your eyes. Okay, you need to buy that whole ensemble."

I technically only had just enough money from the safe to cover it—money that was supposed to last me the whole week. But it was a perfect outfit. And when was the last time I bought something new, something designer, off the rack? How about never.

Nikki's phone beeped and she pulled it out of her purse. She glanced at the screen and started laughing almost immediately. "You guys, you have to see what's on ValleyBuzz today. Serious lawls."

She handed Cherise her phone. Cherise waved her hand and passed it directly to me. "You know I don't read that stuff."

An edge of irritation had crept into Cherise's voice. It was the first time I'd ever heard anything but bubbliness between them.

"Oh yeah," Nikki said, rolling her eyes. "I forgot that you're *perfect*."

I looked from Cherise's face to Nikki's, trying to read what was happening. Were they kidding or were they really butting heads? Was I supposed to take sides here? I didn't even know what they were talking about.

But the phone was now in my hand so I looked down at it. On the screen was a website, a photo blog, with the words *ValleyBuzz* in pink letters at the top. It was like a cross between PerezHilton and Go Fug Yourself, but with photos of Valley Prep students instead of celebrities.

Below was a picture of a girl I recognized from my trig class, passed out on a couch with whiskers Magic-Markered on her cheeks.

"That's Molly Hahneman at Shane Welcome's party last week," Nikki said, her eyebrows dancing gleefully. "They do that to someone every year. Hate to be her. That stuff is hard to get off."

I could feel my stomach free-falling as I scrolled down past the top pic. There were blind items about a girl who had gotten liposuction over the summer and another who had apparently slept with two lacrosse players in one night. All of it was so mean, I could hardly believe anyone with half a heart could stand reading it.

"Someone started the site last year," Cherise explained for my benefit. "Everyone reads it, and anyone can post, but it's all anonymous. Which means that people can write whatever nasty shiz comes into their heads."

Farther down on the page, there was an item titled "New Trash." I wanted to hand the phone back but the TMZ-powered part of my brain went into overdrive and I couldn't help but look.

> Anyone else notice the extratrashy crop of scholarship skanks this year? At least three of them are in the sophomore class, bussed in from Maryvale. Let's hope the diseases these new Busteds bring into school aren't contagious!

I recognized immediately who the commenter was referring to: Mary and Sierra and their other friend—I was pretty sure her name was Alicia. I quickly dropped the phone in Nikki's hands like it was dipped in toxic chemicals. I felt a little dirty just from reading it. How could Nikki even be laughing?

"I agree with Cherise," I said firmly. "I don't like that kind of thing, either."

"Oh, c'mon," Nikki said with an irritated sigh. "You guys need to lighten up. Molly thought it was funny. I heard her talking about it today."

"Did it occur to you that she just didn't want to seem like a fool?" Cherise shot back, a scowl twisting her face.

Kellie emerged from the dressing room all smiles, with three pairs of jeans draped over her arm. "Okay, girls, time to recap our purchases!"

At Kellie's command, the air seemed to clear immediately. Nikki and Cherise were no longer facing off and both were now regarding Kellie with expectant smiles.

"What'd you pick?" Nikki asked.

"I can't really decide, so I think I might just go with all of them. You can never have too many jeans, right?"

"Even if you don't wear them," Nikki agreed readily. "They're just awesome to have."

We followed Kellie to the cash register to pay for our own selections. For a moment there in the line, I faltered. I didn't really *need* the shirt and the jeans. Maybe I should save the money, I thought, just in case.

Then Kellie turned to me and squeezed my elbow. "This is so great, Willa. I knew those things would look awesome on you. I'm totally going to be your personal shopper," she said. "And by the way, you have to come to my party next weekend. It's kind of like an annual thing I do every fall when my parents are away on their yacht."

Cherise and Nikki nodded behind her. "It's massive, *the* party of the year," Nikki said.

"Say no more." I grinned widely. "I'm there."

It was my turn at the front. The saleswoman at the register patted the counter, inviting me to put the clothes down. I followed her command, admiring the way the shirt fell in a shimmery puddle on top. Kellie was right. I had to buy it. And I couldn't wait to try it on again when I got home. I handed over the money and the saleswoman wrapped up my purchases in perfumed tissue paper.

I could definitely get used to this, I thought, swinging the bag on my wrist on the way out. *Definitely.*

Cherise drove us back to her place, a charming single-story house on a thirty-acre horse ranch that overlooked the mountains. She parked the Jetta in the driveway and we went inside. A woman I assumed was her mother was hanging out in the kitchen, standing over the island with a cup of coffee.

"I didn't think you'd be home so early," Cherise said, giving her a kiss.

"One of my patients canceled. I'm Cherise's mom,"

she said, holding out a hand to me. She was tall and slim and she had the same sweet smile as Cherise, though she wore her hair much shorter, in a pixie-esque style. "They call me Doctor at work, but you can just call me Gwen."

"Willa," I said. "Nice to meet you. Cherise has been my guardian angel at Valley Prep."

"She does the angelic thing pretty well, doesn't she?" Dr. Jackson said, giving her a sardonic look. "You girls have fun at the mall?"

"Yes, and I didn't even bankrupt you—*today*." Cherise pulled out some Coke Zeros from the fridge. "Come on, Willa."

I followed her to her room, which had lime-green walls and white modern furniture. A decal mural of hot-pink flowers hung over her desk while a bunch of framed vintage album covers were arranged over her turntables. She walked toward them and put on a record.

"You're going to love Jurassic Five," she said. "'Contribution' is my song of the moment."

I sank down in a cushy armchair in the corner, checking out her bookshelves, which were lined with foil-lettered paperbacks.

"I'm kind of obsessed with thrillers," she said, noticing me looking at them. "But I have to hide it from the lit-mag snobs at school. I'll never get anything into *The Camel's Back* if they find out I read Patricia Cornwell."

I smiled. "I'll keep it on the DL, I promise."

"There are no secrets in this town, don't you know? People are blabbermouths."

"Speaking of which . . . that Buzz site was pretty harsh," I said tentatively. I didn't want to bring up a sore subject, but it had been nagging at me ever since the scene in the dressing room and I wanted to know more about what Cherise really thought. "All that stuff about Busteds—they were talking about the Mexican girls, right?"

"I don't know." She slid a record back into its cardboard sleeve. "Like I said, I don't read it. I think it's poison. But one of those girls is in my comp class. Mary Santiago, I think her name is. She seems nice. What'd it say?"

"Something about them being bussed in. About not wanting to catch their diseases."

"Yikes," she said, wincing.

"What's that about?"

"I don't know. Some of these Prep kids have never met anyone beyond their zip code. They really don't know how to handle outsiders. But even for them that's pretty disgusting."

I felt a tightening in my chest. I was an outsider, too. Was there stuff about me on this site? If there was, I didn't want to know.

I thought back to the nasty words and I hoped Mary and Alicia and Sierra never read them, either. I imagined what it would be like for one of them to stumble across that post about them being "bussed in," and I felt queasy all over again. I knew what it was like to be new, and something like that—well, that would make it ten times worse. That was enough to make you want to crawl into a hole and never come back to school.

It was possible that no one had told them about the site. They seemed to be in their own social bubble. But still, if everyone else was reading it, they were going to find out sooner or later what these bullies thought of them. I wished, suddenly, that there was something we could do to intervene.

Cherise sat down on her bed, facing me. "When I first got here, they didn't accept me, either. I mean, c'mon now: I don't really look like most of the kids here." She pointed to her face with both index fingers. "It took me a few years to figure it out, make friends. Learn the rules, the language."

"And now?" I asked, biting my lip nervously as I waited for her answer.

"Things are different. It's much better, I'll tell you that. I would never want to go back to the way it was before. I used to have stuff thrown at me. Names." She sighed, remembering. "I had to give a few girls the smackdown, and Kellie was one of them."

"Really?" I asked, shocked. I had a hard time imagining the friendly, elegant girl I'd been shopping with being mean to Cherise, let alone participating in a schoolyard brawl. "And now everything's cool?"

She nodded. "Well, that was a long time ago. We all

grew up. Some of us more than others, I guess. Not the people posting on that site."

I had an idea. "What if we did something to get it shut down, like report the mean stuff?"

"Someone tried that last year, but as soon as it got shut down by the headmaster, another site just like it popped up. They can't really control this kind of thing. People are going to talk no matter what—this just gives them an easy outlet." Cherise sighed. "Look, Willa, don't worry. That post was just some random loser. Not everyone at Prep is like that."

"I hope not," I said, meeting her eyes. I *really* hoped not. Everything had been going so well. I'd just started to feel at home here. I would hate to think I'd walked right into some kind of lion's den.

"Just ignore it. Everyone really likes you. You're different, you know? In a good way. Kellie invited you to her party, right? She doesn't just give out invitations to everybody."

I smiled, letting the flattery wash over me. Was that true about Kellie, or was Cherise just trying to make me feel better? She wouldn't make it up, would she?

Did it even matter? I had Cherise on my side, and that felt good.

"Now, to a more important question," she said, sashaying around so that her silk cowl-neck tee fluttered. "What are you wearing on Saturday?"

FIVE

"YO!"

It was a guy's voice, deep and commanding. I was hunched over my bike, trying to unlock it from the rack in the parking lot. The afternoon sun was like a laser singeing my back, and I was already feeling a little flustered and a little wilted at the end of a long school day.

When I turned around, I saw that a silver Porsche Boxster had pulled up in front of me. The guy stuck his head out the window and the shag of hair caught my eye first. Then the tanned elbow. My eyes traveled upward again. It was Aidan. With that grin of his.

Oh boy.

Was that my face flushing, or was it just the sun?

"You're flat."

What the . . . ? Now my face definitely burned. Mortifying.

Yeah, my chest was a work in progress, I knew

that—but, wait, what about him, *how dare he*?

"I'm really—" I gasped, pulling my bike out of the rack, about to launch into an attack.

Losing my mind.

Because I suddenly noticed what he was talking about. The front tire was sagging. "Oh man."

"You've gotta take care of that."

Okay, so this had nothing to do with my boobs. That was good. Flat tire, not so much. I chewed on my thumbnail, trying to gather my composure and think. I could probably ride it home, I reasoned. It was only a couple of miles.

He had put his car in park, with the blinkers on, so that now it was clogging up the lane. It was the end of the school day on a Friday, and other cars were forming a line behind him, understandably eager to get out of Valley Prep's parking lot and start their weekends. But Aidan had already hopped out of the driver's seat, leaving his car door open and blocking anyone from going around him. He knelt down beside me on the pavement.

"It's okay. Maybe you should just move the car," I said firmly, but my insides were like mattress springs. For some reason, Aidan had a way of making me extremely nervous, like I was going to spaz out at any moment. "People are waiting. Seriously, I don't need help. I got it."

"But you can't ride this home." He moved closer to

the bike and I involuntarily drew in a breath. Touching my bike was like touching me.

I looked around. A few more cars had pulled up.

He leaned in and hunched over the front wheel, detaching it from the frame. His hands were broad, his fingers skillful and quick. He knew his way around the anatomy. I watched him, at first, with a sense of awe.

But wait a minute . . .

I never let anyone mess with my bike. It was an antique. It was my only means of freedom. And like I said before, it was my most prized possession.

Paging brain control. You're losing it here.

"What the hell are you doing?" I blurted as I snapped out of my reverie.

"I'm giving you a ride home, dummy."

He carried the wheel and the frame toward his car and popped open the trunk. Then he pushed down the backseat to make more room.

"No, thanks," I said, following close behind. "I'd rather ride."

He put the frame in the trunk and set the wheel beside it. "Bike safety one-oh-one. Riding on a flat is no joke. You can permanently damage your rims—or get killed. Nope. Not on my watch."

The girl in the Jeep behind us started honking her horn. Then two more cars beeped, too. Within seconds, a whole orchestra of cars was sounding.

"Well, new girl, it looks like you're about to piss off

the entire student population," he said, and hopped in the driver's seat. He patted the passenger seat. "C'mon, don't make me beg."

I was pretty sure I'd figured this kid out the other day. And Cherise had confirmed my suspicions about him. He was bad news with a dollar sign for an *s*. But now what choice did I have? He was right. I couldn't afford to screw up my bike. I took one more look over my shoulder. The girl in the Jeep was holding her hand down on the horn and simultaneously sticking her head out the window, looking like she might just gun it and mow me down. So I got in next to him, reluctantly.

He turned to me and smiled—not the grin this time, just a standard-issue sweet smile, and I softened. No doubt about it. Aidan had some serious genetic gifts.

"Sorry about that," he said, steering the car out of the lot with the heel of his hand. "My usual car has a bike rack, but it's in the shop right now. I've been having some transmission issues."

"So this is your backup?" I asked, half joking, but also half impressed. The sheer wealth of VP kids was still a source of wonder.

"My dad's," he said, shrugging. "He's got a whole collection but this is the only one he'll let me drive."

"Of cars?" I gave him the side-eye.

"Of Porsches." *Naturally.* "Where to?"

Did I really want him to know where I lived? I thought for a minute of giving him a fake address or letting him drop me off at a mini-mart or something. But then, he seemed pretty harmless. Besides the killer eyes and the public disturbances, of course. A quick risk-to-attractiveness analysis told me to go with it. "I'm on Morning Glory Road."

"Out past the golf club? I think I know where that is." He reached down and turned up the stereo, which was already blaring Queens of the Stone Age, the reissued first album—I knew this because I'd downloaded it myself a few weeks earlier. Then he shifted gears abruptly and the car jerked forward, throwing me back against the leather seat. "That's a funky bike you've got there."

"Thanks. I hope you didn't break it."

"Nah. I know what I'm doing. I worked at Cadence Cycle a couple summers ago."

That surprised me. "You did repairs? Like with your hands?"

"No, I hired a migrant worker to do that part." He looked at me with a smirk. "Of course I did it with my hands. So if you ever need help, you know who to call."

"Thanks," I said, looking down at my own hands and twisting them around in my lap. Nerves I'd never felt before thrummed through them. "But I usually do my own tune-ups and stuff."

"Nice. I like a girl with a good work ethic." He'd put on mirrored aviators so that now he looked like a NASCAR driver, minus the jumpsuit. Forget his mind-blowing hotness—I was having a hard time taking him seriously. Wouldn't anybody? "So, how do you like Valley Prep so far? Just so you know, I've put a halt to my stunts so that you could settle in."

"Gee, thanks," I said, holding back a grin. "VP is okay, I guess."

"Just okay, huh? What, you're too cool for us, Miss Colorado?"

"How'd you know where I'm from?"

"Word gets around," he said, and when our eyes met, I could feel the smile I'd been fighting spreading across my face. He was talking about me? To other people?

"I'm not too cool. I just—" My phone was buzzing. "Hang on. I have a call."

I answered, cupping my hand to my ear to hear over Aidan's music.

"Willa, mmmhereem."

"Who?" I yelled.

"It's mmmerehrm." The voice was tiny and muffled.

"Who?"

"It's me. Your mother?"

"Mom! It's so loud—I couldn't hear." I glared at Aidan, hoping he would turn the music down. When he didn't, I reached over to do it myself. He slapped at my hand. *Jerk!* I had to completely plug my other ear closed with my finger to try to make out what she was saying.

"Where are you?" she asked.

"Oh, nowhere." I didn't know how to explain in a

simple way that I was getting a ride from a guy. "On my way home from school."

"Are you in a car?"

"Yeah. It's a friend's."

"C'mon, Willa," Aidan shouted. "Tell her the truth about us."

I gestured vehemently, slicing my hand across my mouth to tell Aidan to shut up.

"Who's that?" she asked. "Who's with you?"

"No one," I said. "Just some guy."

"Some guy?" Aidan chided. "Come on. Is that all I am to you?"

"Mom, I—"

"What's going on?" she asked.

"This guy's just being stupid," I said. "It's just a stupid joke."

"Who is he?" She sounded worried, her tiny voice straining inside the speaker.

Aidan was making kissy faces at me, and I wanted to punch him. This wasn't cool. Flirting was one thing. But this wasn't flirting . . . it was just douchery.

"Mom, I'll be home in a few minutes."

"Tell her I said bye!" Aidan called out as I was hanging up.

"What do you think you're doing?" I demanded, staring him down.

"I'm entertaining you on the ride home."

"You're freaking out my mom is what you're doing."

"Aw, I gave her a little thrill." He glanced at me, and then back at the windshield. "Besides, is your mom that freak-outable?"

"Maybe she is."

"I doubt it. I can't picture someone like you having a prissy mom."

"What's that supposed to mean?" Was it a compliment or an insult? How exactly did he define "someone like me"? I was afraid to look at him in case the answer was on his face.

"You know, tough chicks. Chicks with attitude. The apple doesn't fall far from the tree. I bet your mom is one of those cool young single moms. Am I right?"

Of course he was right, but I didn't have to let him have the satisfaction of knowing that. "Not at all," I muttered, though my anger was softening. How'd this guy know so much? Was he an armchair clairvoyant, too? "Make a right here."

Aidan braked suddenly and veered onto my street, so quickly I could hear gravel hitting the wheels. He'd almost swerved into a neighbor's agave plant. I yelped.

He pulled the car into the driveway next to my mom's.

"Next time give me a little more warning," he said.

I went eye to eye with him. "Next time don't mess with my mom."

"Next time don't make it so easy for me, and I won't."

"Hate to break it to you, but I don't know if there's

gonna be a next time," I said. "Your driving scares the daylights out of me."

"We'll have to work on that." Then he flashed me another grin.

I leapt out of the front seat and went to pull open the trunk to retrieve my bike. In my mind I had the ending to the scene planned out—I would play it cool, haul out my bike, shut the door, and dash off toward my house, not looking back at him for one second. Let him wonder.

But the perfectly scripted drama in my head had to make way for reality because the stupid trunk was locked. And Aidan was fumbling around inside, looking for the driver's-side button. Which he couldn't find. Because it wasn't his car. So I had to wait for him to finally turn off the engine, unbuckle his seat belt, open the door, and mosey around to where I was standing. He handed me the pieces of my bike, still smiling.

"Do you want me to fix that flat for you? I could probably just take it back to the shop and replace the tire," he asked.

"No, I can patch it myself." I held the bike against my body like a shield. I was all out of sorts now—nervous and confused—and I wanted him to leave before I did something embarrassing.

"Okay, Colorado, I get the message. You're on a DIY kick," he said, holding up his now-empty hands in defense as he walked in reverse back to the driver's side. "You'll let me know when you need my assistance."

"Will do," I said, nodding. My lips were pressed together in what I hoped was a sardonic expression but they were just barely holding my face together. Underneath I was a jumble of jelly. How did that happen?

"You're welcome for the ride," he called out the window.

He sped out of the driveway, the music and his tires squealing in unison—leaving me in front of my new house, watching him go and wondering what he was thinking. Was this all in a day's work for Aidan? Did he go around rescuing girls on bikes all the time? Why was I so flustered?

And why am I still standing out here? I thought. Not only had Aidan left me with a bike in pieces. Somehow, the guy had managed to sneak away with my cool.

SIX

I BURST THROUGH the front door, ready to tell my mom everything. But once inside, I could hear her voice, obviously talking on the phone. I followed the trail across stacks of broken-down cardboard boxes to the kitchen, where she was bent over the counter, dressed in jeans and a flowy white blouse, speaking into her mobile phone in a low tone and writing something on a piece of paper.

"Are you sure? Okay . . . Yes, I've got it . . ." She looked at me quickly and then back to the pad of paper. "Yes, thanks for the information. Thank you. I'll be in touch."

She hung up in a hurry and ran a hand through her hair, frowning—not her usual expression when greeting me. And, I noticed, there were no cookies, no smoothie, no snacks to speak of. She must have been busy in the studio zone.

"Who was that?" I asked.

She folded up the paper into eighths and put it into her pocket. "Oh, just an organization, a local group I was hoping to volunteer with. They give art lessons to poor kids."

"That sounds cool," I said. She had always used her free time to volunteer, wherever we were living. She believed in giving back—that was a big thing she was always going on about, how important it was to participate in the community. "Are you gonna do it?"

"Maybe. Probably. I need to think about it." She straightened herself up and slipped her phone into her pocket. She inhaled, then exhaled a long slow stream of air. "Sorry I don't have any snacks prepared. It's been a busy day. I meant to go to the market but just never got there. I haven't eaten anything myself, now that I think about it. How was school?"

"School was good. Classes are good," I said, swinging my bag over a kitchen chair. I opened the refrigerator, scrounging for something to drink, but we were all out of juice. She handed me a glass and I poured myself some water from the refrigerator door. I flopped down at the table and sighed happily. "It's all pretty much . . . great, actually."

I was as surprised as anyone. Usually my mom had to give me a few pep talks in the beginning of a school year. Reminding me how I'd adapted to Searchlight and Corvallis and Eastsound and Sandpoint just fine. Only now it seemed like she was only half listening as she stared in my direction—or was she looking behind me?

"Great . . ." she echoed. "So who was the guy in the car? Someone from school, right? I hope you weren't just riding with a stranger."

I turned behind me to see what she was looking at, but there was nothing. "Yeah, no. It was just this kid Aidan."

Just this kid. Um, yeah. He was much more than that in my brain already, but once I said it out loud that would make it a thing, a thing I was going to have to get all freaky and obsessive about. No, playing it down was a better idea.

"Is that the guy you were talking about the other day? I believe your word was 'intense.'"

I nodded, picturing him leaning out of his car in the parking lot, picturing him expertly handling my bike. My breath caught in my throat a little. *Okay, Willa. Calm down.* "He's kind of the poster child for arrogant, sexy sons of CEOs."

I told her the story. But by then, a few minutes had gone by and whatever outrage I'd had about my bike, the phone, his cockiness, had dissolved somewhat, so it was not as convincing as I hoped it might be. In fact, it all sounded a little silly, especially because I was smiling the whole time and feeling like I was going to burst.

My mom was standing there with her arms folded, watching me but not smiling at all. "Well, he sounds like a flirt. Just be careful."

This wasn't exactly the reaction I was hoping for. Laughter, yes. Sympathy, maybe. I wrapped my fingers around my glass. "That's his reputation, yeah."

"I just don't want you to get hurt."

She almost looked like she was scolding me. But for what? This was strange. She'd never been that overprotective in the past. She'd always encouraged me to go out and make friends. And this town seemed as safe and crime-free as they came. Then again, maybe the whole guy thing just made her uncomfortable.

"I don't even like this guy, so there's nothing for you to worry about. I just thought it was funny." I picked up my glass and put it in the sink. "Should I go see what's on pay-per-view later?"

"No, don't bother. I actually have to be somewhere tonight." Her eyes darted around the room as if she was looking for a cue card to read from. "There's a meeting for the natural foods co-op. I was thinking about joining."

"But it's movie night," I said with plummeting disappointment. This was the first time she'd ever canceled on our weekly tradition. It was like a sacred thing for us. "I guess I can watch by myself."

"Or we could do it tomorrow," she offered.

"There's a party tomorrow night. I'm supposed to go with this girl Cherise. My new friend."

"Do you need a ride?"

"No, she said she could pick me up. She invited me

to stay over after, too. She's actually really cool. I think you'd like her—"

"That's good," she said vaguely. She looked at her phone again, and then her watch. What was up with her? I would've thought she'd be jumping for joy that I was going to a party, that I'd made friends, but she was acting like an angsty teenager: distracted, moody, and downright weird. Was there some sort of spontaneous *Freaky Friday* effect going on? "I should actually go. I'm running late."

She grabbed her purse from the counter and moved past me toward the door.

I watched it close behind her, and then sat back down in the silent kitchen, feeling all of my excitement about the day fizzle in the sudden stillness.

"Well, have fun, then," I said, my words reverberating through the house.

Kellie's house sat at the top of a winding road on its very own foothill of a mountain, the sky stretched overhead like a shiny violet awning. It was enormous, a low and sprawling neo-medieval-style chateau with stone-faced wings hugging a front courtyard. Tufts of succulents and cacti were planted strategically to make it look natural, like the whole mansion had just sprung up here organically, security gates and all. Cars were lined up the entire length of the driveway, from the porte cochere down to the front call box at the street entrance and across the bridge that spanned the small valley between them.

"This is where she lives? Are you kidding me?" I said, my jaw dropping as I surveyed the majesty of chez Kellie.

"I know, right?" Cherise said as she parked her Jetta, smoothed her eyebrows, and straightened her emerald-green tank top. "It's sick. Her dad has his own fund."

I gave her the eye. "Do you know what *everyone*'s dad does?"

She shrugged. "It's just common knowledge."

I was teasing but I was also preparing for the moment when the subject of my own dad—or lack thereof—came up. It wasn't that I didn't want to talk about it, but it was a complicated situation to explain. Both of Cherise's parents were heart surgeons, I'd recently learned. Married forever. She had a brother who was a freshman at Cornell. They all got along. She had a totally normal setup, in a privileged, Paradise Valley kind of way.

We walked out into the mellowed heat of the evening, Cherise leading us to the arched front door. I was still trying to pick my mandible off the ground. Inside the cool tiled foyer with mosaic flooring and marble columns we were greeted by a five-tiered iron chandelier that hung from the thirty-foot vaulted ceiling, so massive it made me feel like I was in a church. That is, until I saw the empty red plastic cups strewn on the antique front table, and heard the blast of a Killers cover ringing through the house.

The peals of electric guitar were like a siren song. We went in search of the music, which was coming from a five-piece band set up in the living room. Cherise turned back to smile at me as we were sucked into the pulsing crowd that was jumping up and down in place and screaming along with the lead singer.

"Are all these kids from Prep?" I asked Cherise, astonished. I didn't recognize most of them.

"Nah. Some are from other schools, mainly from the league—Perkins Day, Willard Academy. I think she also invited a few guys from UA. Kellie pretty much knows everyone. She's, like, infamous."

"You mean famous," I said.

"No. I mean infamous. You'll see."

I looked over to see if Cherise was being sarcastic, but her face was totally serious. I was immediately intrigued. Kellie was gorgeous and lived in a freaking castle *and* she was a local legend? Her star quality was glowing brighter by the second.

We went through the kitchen, which made our fancy new place on Morning Glory look like a child's play set. My head bounced around on my neck like a bobblehead doll's. A gigantic marble island commanded the room, surrounded by restaurant-sized appliances and a media center with a giant flat screen showing football. A few guys were huddled around watching. On the pure white countertops were bowls of every snack I could think of, plus a bunch of stuff I wouldn't have expected to see at a high-school party, like a cheese platter and raw oysters. A floor-to-ceiling refrigerator was stocked with wine bottles. On the other side of the room was a giant hearth fireplace, the old-fashioned kind people used to cook on. It was big enough to roast a human.

For all I knew, human-roasting was on the agenda. If anybody could make it into a trendy drinking game, Kellie could.

Cherise led me through the French doors onto the back patio. From there, a covered walkway led to a lit-up pool with waterfalls, a built-in bar, a little island with palm trees, and a connecting hot tub. Beyond that were tennis courts, a fenced-off area with grazing horses and stables, and a glowing glassed-in building that looked like an art gallery but was filled with cars. A laser light show projected onto the sky and flared in bright colors.

"People. Actually. Live. Here?" I asked.

"And she's an only child," Cherise said. "There's like twelve bedrooms for three people."

"Can we go in the hot tub?" I bounced on my tiptoes like a little kid.

"Of course," Cherise said. "There's some bathing suits in the cabana, if you didn't bring one. Kellie always buys a few extra ones for guests."

"Hey, guys," Kellie said, rushing over to us. She was wearing a sequined minidress and stiletto heels and carrying something in a martini glass that was dribbling over the edges. She kissed us each on the cheek.

“Oh my God, Kellie, your house is out-of-control amazing,” I gushed.

“Thanks,” she said, waving a hand like it was nothing, the glamorama vibes bouncing off her like the light on her glittery frock.

Standing next to her, I felt noticeably underdressed. I was wearing a new pair of jeans I’d scored at the mall and a repurposed sundress that I’d sewn and belted into a tunic. Cherise had assured me that it was fine, but now, as Kellie was eyeing me, I wondered.

“What happened to the new shirt, Willa?” she asked, frowning, as she reached out to feel the fabric on the sleeve.

“I don’t know—I tried it on again and it was a little too big.”

“We’ll have to exchange it then, won’t we?” Kellie said, linking my arm with hers as the three of us walked across her lawn. “I love returns just as much as shopping. Maybe we can look at the new jackets, too. Next week?”

“Absolutely!” I said. Actually, it was more of a squeal. I wasn’t sure how I could score more money from the safe without my mom noticing, but I’d worry about that later.

Two guys holding cups of beer walked by. One was tall with light brown hair and a rumpled button-down shirt; the other was blond and shorter with a soccer-player build. Both were seriously cute in the preppy private-school way, which was starting to grow on me.

"Hey, Kellie. Hey, Cherise. Hey, Willa."

Did I know them? I never remembered seeing them before. I smiled anyway, not really knowing quite how I got here, how this could actually be a scene from my own life. But it was, and it felt like an amusement park.

"This is Willa's first Richardson throw-down," Cherise said. "We have to make sure she has fun tonight."

Like it would take a lot of effort. This place was a hotbed of awesome.

"Totals," Kellie said. "Feel free to wander around, you guys . . . the hot tub's going. The keg's in the gazebo. We're putting *Superbad* on in the theater. I've gotta check if Donovan's here yet. I'll be back in a minute."

"Who's Donovan?" I asked, after she left.

"Donovan's her new man," Cherise explained, eyebrows lifting suggestively. "He's a senior at Willard. But who knows with her? There might be someone else by the end of the night."

"So that's why she's infamous?" I asked, watching Kellie from a distance as she draped her arms around the blond guy who'd just passed us.

Cherise laughed in a surprised chirp. "Sssh. No. That's not what I meant." Then she looked around to see if anyone else had heard us. "You never know who's gonna blab to the Buzz."

"I haven't looked at it since that day in the mall," I admitted. "Though I *have* heard people talking about it at school."

She rolled her eyes. "Yeah, it's best just to ignore it. That thing is bad karma."

Cherise and I milled around outside between the palm trees. She stopped to talk to a guy she said she knew from her parents' tennis club. I could tell by the way she was tilting her head to the side that he was crush material, so I left her for a moment and continued on to check out the grounds. Who knew what else was out here? A Ferris wheel? A petting zoo?

Outside the lighted windows of the garage I could make out a silhouette of a figure. As I got closer, I recognized him as Tre Walker, the kid Kellie had pointed out in the lunchroom. You couldn't *not* notice him, then or now. He was at least six foot five, wearing a thin windbreaker and jeans that barely seemed to contain his muscular frame. He was holding a red plastic cup between his teeth as he typed into his phone. He put the phone away when he saw me, and his forehead was crunched into a serious expression.

"Sorry, I don't mean to interrupt," I said.

"No, it's cool. I just needed to step away from everything for a minute."

"I'm trying to put my eyes back into my head. This place is reedonkulous."

He smiled, the seriousness melting away to reveal the soft folds of his face. "I hear you. I'm Tre. You're Willa, right?"

Someone else who knew my name. Amazing. "Yeah."

"You should see the cars in there," he said.

I peered into the garage. "What's the one with the orange stripe?"

"That's a Bugatti. It's an Italian company—very rare. They cost about two million. Jay-Z has one, supposedly. Beyoncé bought it for him."

"Jeez," I said. "For two million, I hope it pumps its own gas."

He laughed, a deep infectious laugh. "It flies and sails and makes dinner, too."

"In that case, I'll put it on my Amazon wish list."

"Hey, you never know around here." He pointed to the gatherings of people in the yard around us. "Buddy up with the right ones and you just might get your wish."

I sighed. "A girl can dream. But if not, a girl can bike. So I heard you just moved here."

"You heard right. My dad's coaching the Suns. Big deal, right?"

"I don't know anything about basketball," I confessed. "But it definitely sounds like a big deal. I mean, I'm impressed."

He flicked his head to show his indifference. In the yellow light his long-lashed eyes were even and opaque, but there was a mystery to them, too. They would never give too much away. "I'm not a fan, either, to tell you the truth. It bores me."

"Yeah?"

"But don't tell him I said that—he'd probably cut me

out of the will. If I'm even in it to begin with. He's got like six kids. That we know about." He swigged at his beer, and I wondered if he was a little drunk. He was certainly talking freely.

"So I take it you two aren't tight?"

"I grew up in Detroit with my mom. Lived there all my life. But, you know, they decided it was time for me to get to know my pops. It's your typical *Fresh Prince of Bel-Air* story: boy from the streets gets sent to live with fancy relatives. Fancy relatives try to mold him into a gentleman."

"But then the fancy relatives come away with street smarts they never expected," I said, "and everyone wins."

"Exactly. Well, we're working on the warm and fuzzy part. So far they're still treating me like the pool boy. But I'll let you know what happens."

"Hey, guys." Kellie was loping toward us across the grounds. At first I thought it was just her heels sinking into sandy soil, but as she approached I could tell it was the martini that was throwing her off balance. "Willa, I've been looking all over for you."

"Hey," I said. "You two know each other, right?"

"Yeah, we've met. Hello, Tre," she said sweetly. "Can I talk to you for a minute, Willa?"

"Sure. What's up?"

"But not here, okay?" She gestured me away from the garage with a tilted head.

Figuring it was girl talk, I shrugged in Tre's direction.

"Well, smell ya later." I heard him laughing as we turned away.

Her ankles wobbled and she grasped my arm before she almost bit it right there in her yard. I pulled her straight but I could feel that her body was already gelatinous, saturated in booze.

"Whoa," I said, tightening my grip. I was worried that she'd slip again. "Easy there."

There must have been more than one cocktail in the time since I'd seen her last. I hoped she hadn't overdone it.

"I'm okay. I'm okay. So—" She swallowed, pushing her chin down against her chest. "So I saw you over there—and it's just—I don't think he's such a great person for you to talk to."

I pulled back in surprise. "Why not?"

"I've heard some things," she whispered, but probably not as quietly as she thought she was whispering. "Like, he was sent to one of those boot camps before he came here, Willa. You know, he's got a *record*."

I had to laugh. After what he'd just told me about his past, I could see how a rumor like this could start. Detroit was worlds away from Paradise Valley. Possibly galaxies.

"It's not funny," she insisted. "I'd already invited him here and everything, before I knew, but, like, I don't think we want him glomming on to us."

"I don't know if he's a glommer. He seems pretty

laid-back. Are you sure it's not just a story?"

"I'm sure."

"Who'd you hear it from?"

"I don't know. That doesn't matter," she snapped impatiently.

I recoiled a bit, surprised at her suddenly sharp tone.

"You don't know this place like I do, Willa. People don't take well to shadiness." Her voice strained with impatience and annoyance. It was too dark to see her eyes but I could see her metallic makeup glinting. "Don't you get it? I'm just trying to look out for you."

"Thanks," I said. "I appreciate that, but I don't want to go around judging people—"

She convulsed with a hiccup and her chipper mood from earlier returned. "Don't worry about him, okay? Let's have fun."

"Hey, Kell." A skinny, awkward-looking guy in a brown shirt walked toward us. He had to be in his mid-twenties at least—maybe even thirties, because he was balding.

She gave him a flirty little wave. "Hey, Doug!"

He pointed to a brown manila envelope that was tucked under his arm. "So where do you want me to put the goods?"

"Oh, just throw it on top of the desk in the library. I'll wire you the extra cashola tomorrow," Kellie replied.

My stomach tied into about ten sailor's knots. From where I was standing, this kind of looked like a drug deal.

One of the nicest, cleanest drug deals in the universe, but a drug deal nonetheless. I never wanted to admit that Kellie and Company were too good to be true, but if ever there was a moment of reckoning, this was it.

"It's a pleasure doing business with you, K. As always," Doug said. Then he spun around and disappeared into the crowd.

"What was that all about?" I asked, praying that Kellie wasn't about to invite me to do a few lines with her in the library.

"Oh, Doug is my tutor—my parents pay him to help me maintain my stellar GPA." She leaned in and whispered, "Don't tell anyone but he basically writes my papers for me. It's kind of an agreement we have. I give him extra money to do all the work so I have more time to, you know, hang out with friends and throw parties."

I looked at her and smiled with relief. Cheating was bad, but nowhere near as bad as speedballs.

She linked her arm through mine again. "But seriously, that's top secret. You're the only one I've ever told. Not even Nikki or Cherise knows and they're like my BFFs."

"Lips are sealed," I said, flattered by her confidence, even if the secret was a little incriminating.

"I knew I could trust you, Willa." She let her head drop on my shoulder, and I could smell the booze on her breath.

"Are you okay, Kellie?"

"Just a little . . . dizzy . . ." She trailed off.

I guided her to the door. "Maybe we should go inside."

"Yeah, maybe I should just lie down for a little bit," she slurred. "My room's over here."

We walked down a long hallway past at least ten doors.

The room was, in keeping with the rest of the house, giant and luxurious. The adjoining closet from my view reminded me of a TV show I'd seen on Mariah Carey's house—rows and rows of clothes like a boutique, but color-coordinated. I guided Kellie to the four-poster bed and then helped her unbuckle the straps to her sandal heels. She fell back against the pillows and closed her eyes.

"Just a quick nap," she murmured. "Wake me up when Donovan gets here."

"Okay," I said, though I wasn't sure she was in any shape to see Donovan, or anyone else, at this point.

I shut the door behind me and started back toward the rest of the party. Kellie was going to have to sleep it off, big-time.

After a quick trip to Kellie's bathroom to freshen up, I stepped out of the room to look for Cherise or Nikki to let them know that Kellie was potentially out for the count. I did what I hoped would be an easy walk-through of the wing off the living room. A doorway opened into a family room lined with mahogany shelves, which opened into a game room where a bunch of dudes were playing pool, and another room, which looked like the movie theater, and beyond that, some sort of library. The house just kept going.

"Hey, Willa." Nikki was waving at me. She was sitting with three guys at a table, wearing a lace cami. "We're playing beergammon. Wanna join us?"

"I don't think so," I said, feeling dizzy myself now. Maybe it was the enormity of the place, or just the overstimulation of all the sights and sounds. After surveying the damage with Kellie, the last thing I wanted to do was start playing a drinking game. "I just took Kellie to lie down. She was kind of wasted. Do you think we should kick people out?"

"No way," Nikki said with a rasping laugh. "She'll be up in like an hour."

"If you say so." I shrugged, signaling my ignorance. I didn't know Kellie well enough, either drunk or sober, to suggest otherwise. "Have you seen Cherise?"

"No. Maybe she's hooking up?"

"Your turn, Nikki," one of the guys said.

Nikki waved sloppily. "Let me know if you find her, Willa. Come back and visit me in a little while, okay?"

I nodded and turned to make my way back through the labyrinth. I could have easily gotten lost in the house, never to be seen again.

Through the window in the hallway, I saw Tre sitting alone on one of the stone walls surrounding the property. He was holding his red plastic cup and staring up at the sky. I wondered if Kellie had gone around and told everyone at the party about him. I still didn't know what to think, but if she was taking the time to look out for me, it was probably best to just trust her. These were my people now, and they knew the scene a lot better than I did.

"Willz. Sorry I was MIA," Cherise called. She was standing at the opposite end of the corridor and her voice echoed my way. "I had to use the bathroom, and you know how it is—I ended up running into a million people."

"What happened to tennis-club guy?" I asked, walking to meet her.

"Eh, he has a girlfriend, it turns out."

"Sorry," I said, putting a hand on her shoulder. "Are you okay?"

"Yeah, he's kind of a douche, anyway." She shook her mass of curls. "I'm over it."

"Kellie got really drunk, so I took her back to her room to lay down," I said. "Maybe we should check in on her at some point."

"Yeah, that's probably a good idea. She's been known to ride the regurgitron on a few occasions. Party's crazy, right?"

I nodded enthusiastically.

"Told you it would be hot."

She pointed beyond me to the window. "Hey, look,

there's your best buddy."

At first I thought she was talking about Tre, but then I turned to see Aidan Murphy strutting across the yard. A tingling buzz ran through my extremities. Was I *happy* to see him? This was going to have to stop.

As we watched, I expected to see him zero in on the pack of girls in skimpy dresses standing near the gazebo, but he walked past them and kept on going to where Tre was sitting. He and Tre exchanged some sort of greeting and Aidan sat down with him. These two were friends?

Then, without warning, he turned to look in our direction, as if he sensed us watching him. Cherise waved nonchalantly, and I wanted to hide, but what was I going to do, jump behind Cherise?

He waved back, and he was looking right at me. I smiled through the glass.

"He's got it bad for you," Cherise said.

"Naw," I said, blushing. "He's a player."

Still, when he got up from the wall, and seemed to be headed in our direction, I gripped the window ledge for support. I tried to catch a glimpse of myself in the glass. Did I look okay? He was coming closer.

Before he got to the house, he turned, though, and stopped to talk to someone else, a guy that I'd never seen before.

Oh well. Maybe I scared him away.

I let out a soft sigh that I told myself was relief.

"Must be that time!" Cherise exclaimed, interrupting

my thoughts. “Here comes the ritual chugathon.”

Outside, people were cheering as a kid in a Prep hoodie gulped down a cup of beer and started on another.

“Let’s go dance and then we’ll check on Kellie,” Cherise said.

She took my hand and guided me back toward the living room, where the moving crowd had swelled and was going crazy. I’d always wondered what these kinds of parties were like. This was the first time in my entire history of moving from town to town and school to school that I’d been invited to one. Now here I was in Kellie Richardson’s house, at the epicenter of Valley Prep social life. I let the room and all the sensations in it—the lights, the moving bodies, the music—take over.

Life couldn’t get better than this, could it?

SEVEN

"COULD THIS BE any more painful?" I asked out loud, to no one in particular.

We were running laps around the school track. It was at least one hundred degrees—I could've sworn I saw shimmering mirages of puddles on the asphalt ahead. I was sort of getting used to the dry heat, but it still made me feel like one of those spotted geckos I'd seen tucking in between rocks on the side of the road. Hiding until nightfall wasn't really an option, though, as Ms. Lonergan, our pixie-haired, windbreaker-clad teacher, urged us on periodically with her whistle and cries of, "Keep it moving, people—stillness kills!"

I hadn't participated in much physical education in the past, unless you counted the halfhearted attempts at dodgeball and square dancing my public schools called gym class. Valley Prep, with its walls of trophies, regulation-size golf course, and spalike locker rooms with saunas and Jacuzzis, was on an entirely new level of sportage. I thought I was in good shape from all the biking, but apparently running required a different set of muscles because I was finding it difficult to keep up.

"Tell me about it." Mary Santiago answered my call, panting and clutching at her side. Her dark hair was pulled high in a ponytail elastic, but now some damp ringlets were sticking to her neck, and her smooth cheeks were reddened in blotches. We were about the same height—short—so we fell into step easily next to each other. "I have a serious cramp."

As soon as she said it, I felt a stitch pulling at my right ribs. If it was the power of suggestion, it was an exceptionally painful, exceptionally persuasive suggestion. "Oh no," I said. "Is that what that is?"

"No slacking, ladies!" Ms. Lonergan yelled from the bleachers.

"But we have cramps," Mary said.

Drew Miller, a peripheral member of the Glitterati, snickered as he ran by us, his bristly shaved head pink with the exertion. "Get some Midol. Better yet, get some Vicodin and share it with me."

"Not that kind, idiot," I said.

"Then walk with your hands over your head," Lonergan said. "But keep it moving. I'm looking for an eight-minute mile."

Eight minutes? Had the spandex squeezed too much blood to her head?

Mary and I walked as the others kept jogging. Her friend Sierra passed us, slowing down. "You okay?"

Mary waved her on. "You can keep going. I'm just taking a break."

Sierra gave her a skeptical look but continued on.

"I think I hate running," I said, wiping my face in the crook of my elbow.

"Me too. We should try out for volleyball, because I heard they don't make you run so much. You know, if you play a team sport you don't have to take gym."

This was news to me. "But I don't know how to play volleyball."

"How hard can it be?" She kicked at some gravel on the track, sending it flying across the ground. "People play it in bikinis. I'd give up a body part to never have to do another suicide sprint."

"I'm with ya there," I said.

"Plus my college counselor said it would be good for my record. Colleges like the whole team-sport thing."

"You met with a counselor already? I haven't done that yet." At VP, where everyone was destined for academic greatness, you were supposed to start planning for college from day one, but as far as I knew, the official college conferences started in October.

"I asked if they could see me in the first week. I didn't want to lose any time." She shrugged, looking a little self-conscious, like I would think she was a nerd. Actually, I was impressed. "I came here to work—my school in Phoenix didn't have such a great track record. And if I want to keep my scholarship, I need to do really well. Like three-point-five or better so I can get into college, and then medical school, hopefully."

I nodded, feeling a pang of guilt. Mary seemed so driven about her future and I really hadn't given the matter much thought. My mom, of course, had a grand plan for me involving an East Coast college with a leafy campus and a mountain of turtleneck sweaters. All along, I'd been telling myself that I was so busy just settling in that I wasn't ready to deal with the bigger picture, that I had plenty of time to worry about college or my future. But the real reason was that I couldn't bear to imagine starting over in yet another new place—especially without my mom.

"I mean, if the whole doctor thing didn't work out, I wouldn't mind being a costume designer for TV." She made a couture pose with sucked-in cheeks. "I'm obsessed with *Project Runway*. I wish Tim Gunn was my father."

I cracked up, imagining him working VP's halls. "I don't know if he'd come to your volleyball games."

"Seriously, I love him. I love clothes. These girls here are so lucky. Most of them never wear the same thing twice. I know because I'm watching. Even you. Like that shirt you're wearing today. It's awesome."

"Thanks," I said, my guilt fermenting as I looked into her earnest heart-shaped face. There was no jealousy, no hate, no ickiness in it at all, and somehow that made me feel worse about my sudden reversal of fortune—our fancy house, the tuition to this school, all of my recent purchases. It was the injustice that struck me. So I was lucky and Mary wasn't. Were we both just supposed to accept that?

"Where'd you get it?"

"Neiman Marcus," I said, pulling absentmindedly at my gym shirt, which was the same as hers, a white polo.

She whistled. "Nice if you can afford it."

"It was on sale," I added, which wasn't true. Why was I so uncomfortable all of a sudden? "My friend kind of talked me into it."

"Which one was it? You can say. I know you hang out with those girls Nikki and Cherise and Kellie, right? I heard that girl Kellie has two different cars."

"I don't know," I said, never having heard this myself.

Ms. Lonergan blew her whistle again and everyone dropped back and headed for the locker rooms. We'd completed the mile in a record thirteen minutes—that was a record for lame slugs, maybe. Ms. Lonergan advised us to practice after school.

"Practice? Yeah, right," Mary said, when we'd walked away. "So I guess you were at Kellie's big party last weekend."

"Yeah," I said, relieved the conversation was moving away from clothes. "It was cool. You guys should've gone."

"No, no. Not my scene." She shook her head quickly just as Sierra was joining up with us.

"What are you guys talking about?" Sierra asked, looking at both of us suspiciously through her heavy-lidded eyes.

"Willa's friends. The Glitterati. Willa, you know Sierra, right?" Mary asked.

I'd met her that day in the lunchroom but even if I hadn't, I would've known who she was, as I did most people at Valley Prep. It was almost embarrassing to pretend you didn't. But if Sierra remembered meeting me, she did not seem particularly friendly. In fact, there was some twisted-up sneering action happening on her face.

"Ah, yes, the Glitterati," Sierra said slowly, trilling out the syllables.

My face must have shown my bewilderment because she broke out into a sarcastic expression of shock. "Don't tell me you haven't read the Buzz blog."

"Once or twice," I stammered, feeling her accusing gaze like a laser. So they *did* know about it. Why was she looking at me like that? It's not like I wrote anything on there. It's not like I even followed the thing.

But that didn't matter. If I'd seen that stuff written about me, I'd think everyone was against me. I would be totally humiliated. And that's what I could feel radiating off Sierra now, hot and prickly.

"So you know that your friends have been writing nasty stuff about us since the first day of school." She flung a towel over her shoulder and stared me down, her brown eyes almost daring me. My heart was pumping faster than when I was on the track. "If you took your head out of your ass long enough, you'd see that people laugh at us in the hallway. Or maybe you'd have heard that Alicia was crying the other day in the girls' room after someone called her a Busted to her face and shoved her."

Her words were like a slap. I pulled in a breath. I hadn't heard that about Alicia. Could it be true? Even if it was, it wasn't my friends. There was no way. I'd be the first to admit that Kellie and Nikki made snooty comments sometimes, but they would never go out of their way to torment someone or incite violence. And Cherise had made it plenty clear that she was not a fan of the Buzz. My brain was working quickly trying to process this information and make sense of it. No. It couldn't be.

Meanwhile, Sierra was still glaring at me.

"I'm sorry," I said. "But I think you've got it wrong. I really doubt it was them that wrote any of that . . ."

"No, *you've* got it wrong." Her eyes narrowed and she pointed an accusatory finger at me. "I know it's them. Those girls are raging *bitches*."

Okay, that really, *really* burned. I looked at Mary, hoping she would say something. She seemed more reasonable than Sierra, who clearly had a chip on her shoulder.

"We're pretty sure," Mary said, almost apologetic.

"They act all phony to us in front of other people but I can just tell by the way Kellie looks at me, like I'm something on the bottom of her shoe."

"I don't know, you guys. They're totally nice people."

"That's because you fit in with them," Sierra said. "You're white like they are, and rich."

"I'm not rich," I said, dialing the combination to open my locker. It was too complicated to explain my situation, but I'd never been a rich person, and I still didn't think of myself that way. "And that's ridiculous. I mean, Cherise isn't white."

Sierra smiled ironically. "You can be white without being Caucasian, you know? Anyway, I'm just saying. Maybe you don't know them like you think you do. Maybe it's time you open your eyes." She slammed her locker shut with a metallic clang. "Unless, of course, you don't really want to see."

Sierra huffed off to the shower, leaving Mary and me standing there, facing each other over the center bench of the locker room.

"I'm sorry she's acting like that," Mary said. "She doesn't mean anything."

"But it wasn't me," I said, flopping down on a bench, confused and defeated, battling a swirl of emotions that included sympathy for all they were going through, hurt that Sierra had basically called me a clueless gringa, and a tiny bit of feeling sorry for myself that I was being falsely accused.

"I believe you. It's just—Sierra and Alicia and I have been friends for a long time. I convinced them to come here with me, and Sierra really didn't want to. Her dad's been out of work. They're struggling to get the books she needs. She just looks around and feels out of place, you know?" Mary unwound her hair from her ponytail elastic, so it fell full and fluffy around her face. "And then all this stuff with the blog. She's threatening to transfer. I keep telling her to stick it out, that none of this is gonna matter when we're at college, or ten years from now, when we're living in our own fancy houses in the Valley."

"It won't," I said, but I heard the hypocrisy in my own words. Why should I tell her to suck it up and wait for a better life when I was all about the here and now—parties at Kellie's, giggling lunches in the dining hall, and afternoons at the mall? But I deserved to be happy, too, didn't I? It wasn't my fault they were unlucky, was it?

Mary ran a brush though her hair in even strokes. "I know. We just need to be patient, is all." She smiled at me, but her smile seemed to catch at the edges. "It's just high school, right?"

Friday mornings at Valley Prep began with assembly. It went like this: The headmaster, Mr. Page, got up in front of everyone and said some things. Then the Head of Upper School, Mrs. Fields, got up and said some things. Then the mic was turned over to the student council president to make announcements about upcoming meetings. And then it devolved into general chaos as everyone and their brother with a club or cause jumped in.

As far as I was concerned, assembly was actually a pretty good time. At least it ate up a nice chunk of minutes between first period and lunch.

On this particular Friday I was running late—I'd overslept—so when I rolled into the auditorium, there were only a few seats left. I spotted one next to Tre Walker and sat down. He was wearing an orange hoodie and fiddling with his phone, which was not allowed during assembly or any class at Prep after there had been some cheating episodes a few years back. But I'd seen lots of kids sneaking them anyway. It was a rule that was only rarely enforced, it seemed.

Tre flicked his chin at me in greeting. Then he went back to typing intently, smiling or frowning occasionally to himself. From his profile I could see his jaw muscles rippling as he worked. I peeked over and glimpsed an email with the subject line "Sunday NFL Spread."

Somewhere between Drew Miller's attempt at a rap about the upcoming bonfire and Missy Crosby's ten-minute diatribe on the Ethics Club's latest accomplishments, Ms. Davenport leaned over from the end of our aisle to swat her hand at Tre's Droid.

"I hope you're not doing what I think you're doing," she hissed, holding out her palm for him to hand it over. "Didn't I warn you about texting during assembly last week?"

Tre's face went slack and I immediately felt the weight of the situation. Whatever was on his phone was clearly not for teacherly consumption. Ms. Davenport was ready to throw down some private-school discipline, and unlike Aidan, Tre probably wasn't going to slip under the radar. Word of his criminal past had spread, and he'd already been in detention at least once, I heard, for talking back to a teacher. Now he was about to get busted for running a gambling ring during assembly and I couldn't let that happen.

"It's actually my fault," I interjected. "I was thinking about joining next week's Ethics Club discussion and I didn't understand what Missy was talking about when she referred to 'moral absolutism,' so I asked him to look it up for me."

Ms. Davenport turned to me, hazel eyes set in anger behind her spectacles and her thin lips knitted into a tight line. So far I'd been a model homeroom student, and I'd given her no trouble. Plus, I was Glitterati, and that was a whole other layer of protection. "Well, Willa, as you know, we have a no-phone policy, so you should be looking up words on your own time."

"I forgot. I'm sorry." I looked up at her with a repentant expression, and she settled back into her seat. I wasn't sure if she entirely bought my story, but then another kid was talking loudly behind us and her attention shifted to shushing him. Tre flashed me a look of gratitude and I smiled to myself, relieved that my on-the-spot thinking got him out of a jam.

"You really saved my ass," Tre said, when assembly was over and we were filing out of the auditorium with everyone else. "If she'd caught me, I probably would've been suspended. I owe you big-time."

"No big deal," I murmured shyly.

"It is to me," he said, holding the door open for me. "Which way you going?"

"The library. I have a free period."

"I'm going that way, too." We climbed the stairs together. Two freshman girls in leather jackets and four-hundred-dollar jeans—I knew because Nikki and I had just bought ourselves a pair (my last big purchase, I swore to myself)—squeezed past us on the stairwell, tossing their hair and looking around to see who was watching them.

Tre nudged me. "Think they ever get whiplash?"

I laughed and the girls turned around to glare at us.

"You just don't see that kind of thing in Detroit," he said.

"What's Detroit like?" I asked.

Out loud, it sounded like a lame white-girl question. He gave me a look to see if I was making fun, but then I guess he could tell I was genuinely curious, because he answered it. "I don't know. . . . Just real. I wish I could go back."

"Do you have a lot of friends there?"

"Yeah, and a girl. Don't know if that will last, though."

I looked up at him as we made our way down the hall, our feet squeaking on the freshly waxed floor. I wondered if what Kellie had said about him was true. In a nosy moment, I'd Googled him, but there was nothing online, just a Facebook page that seemed barely used. According to Kellie's "sources," the crimes he'd committed should make him a social leper, but I couldn't imagine what they could possibly be. Maybe it was just the gambling thing that had gotten him into trouble at his old school. My instincts told me that whatever it was, he probably hadn't hurt anyone. Even just standing next to him outside the library I could feel how protective and gentle his body language was—and, I knew, without really knowing why, that I felt safe with him.

"Is this girl giving you trouble, T?" Aidan was behind us, with a hand on each of our shoulders. He flicked his hair out of his eyes so that they blazed, all green intensity. Looking at him this close made me dizzy.

"She's all right," Tre said.

"Because if she is, I can take care of it, man."

I felt my balance falter. *Feet, floor. Floor, feet.* "I should probably get to my locker. I forgot something."

Of course, I hadn't forgotten anything, and Kellie was waiting for me in the library, but I wasn't prepared to deal with Aidan just then. I felt like when I saw him I needed to be prepared, armed with attitude. And a fresh coat of lip gloss.

If he noticed me trying to get away, he didn't seem to take the hint.

"Hey, so I saw you at that party the other night, Colorado." He was close behind me down the hall.

"Kellie's? It was cool," I said. I neglected to ask him why, if he saw me, he didn't come over. Because no way I trusted myself to say something like that in a normal tone of voice. I'd be all warbly.

He caught up to me. "So you've been indoctrinated, huh? You're one of us."

"Am I going to grow extra appendages or something? 'Cause if so, then I might not want to be in this club." I looked at my watch. Time had a way of stopping when I was with him, and I was afraid I might really slip into another dimension or something. Then again, did I actually care that much about being late for a free period?

He took my wrist in his hand and looked at my watch himself.

"Plenty of time," he said, dropping my wrist, which was now burning from his touch. "I'm just glad to see you're getting in the spirit of things. I thought you were going to be salty all year."

"Me? Salty? And that makes you . . ."

". . . That makes me sweet." He had a cute little gap in his teeth that I'd never noticed before.

"Sweet, huh."

"Yeah, together we'd be like a chocolate-covered pretzel or one of those French caramels with fleur de sel."

Together. And his French accent was perfect. *Oh man. I'm a goner.*

"I don't think I've ever had one of those caramels. They sound fancy."

"I'll have to bring you some one of these days. What's this?" he asked, reaching in to touch my necklace.

I could smell his soap—it was musky with a little touch of herbal sweetness, like lavender or rosemary. A natural, clean scent that could potentially drive me crazy.

Don't breathe, I told myself. *Nothing to smell here.*

"It was my mom's. Actually my grandmother's," I managed. "Kind of a good-luck charm."

"Very nice," he said softly, then moved his hand to rest it on my locker. "I was just thinking about going to Scottsdale for First Friday. There's some bands and stuff—it's usually pretty cool. So if you haven't been—"

No, this can't be happening. I can't. I must not. Resist. *Resist.*

I grabbed my locker door to shake his hand off. "I've got plans," I said.

"Yeah, okay," he said, grinning. This guy wouldn't know rejection if it crushed his fingers in the doorjamb. "I see how you're playing. You're new so you're keeping your options open. That's cool, Colorado."

As he walked away, I wiped away the beads of sweat that had collected around my hairline. There was nothing cool about it.

EIGHT

"YOU GUYS, I think the waiter is kind of cute," Nikki whispered conspiratorially, spearing a cherry tomato.

This was a break from our Thursday shopping, an afternoon snack at the Nordstrom Café. We were seated at a booth for six, our shopping bags taking up two of the seats. I'd bought a cute knit dress and a pair of ankle boots that I was thinking of wearing to the bonfire the next night. (So much for swearing off shopping—it was impossible with these girls!)

"Are we talking about the same guy?" Kellie dropped her fork, put her palms on the table, and gave Nikki a *no you didn't* head swivel. "The one with the rabid facial hair crawling over his chin?"

Nikki shrugged. "What? He has nice eyes."

Kellie shook her head in a definitive no, then turned her attention to me. "Is that the shirt you got last week?"

"Yeah," I said, looking down. It was a knit top with ruching. "It's supercomfy."

"*Loves* it. She's really turning into a VP girl, isn't she?" Kellie said to the others, her voice ringing approval.

A VP girl. I beamed with pride, like I was accepting an award. "Thanks, guys. I couldn't have done it without you. The last few weeks have been awesome."

It was true. They'd been so fun and welcoming. Having all of these brand-new clothes that Kellie helped me pick out had changed not just the way I looked but the way I felt. I could walk the halls of VP like I owned the place. And the transformation had been so fast, hadn't it? It was like my whole life had been leading up to this. Maybe all along I'd been a Glitterati girl waiting to happen. It was like it was meant to be, me coming here to Paradise Valley. Destiny, almost.

I sat back, basking in the glow of the compliment. I'd arrived. Kellie said so.

But as I chewed on my wild-mushroom pizza with truffle oil, a vaguely uneasy feeling crept in. This was the sixth time I'd gone shopping with the girls in as many weeks. The pizza alone cost twenty-nine dollars for a measly few slices. None of my friends seemed to be the slightest bit worried about their own expenditures—their black AmEx card bills were always paid, by magic or by little elves or, more likely, by their loaded parents. But I was starting to wonder how long I'd be able to keep it up—at this pace, the safe would be empty by spring break. And by then, a whole new set of trends would be upon us.

Oh well. I'd just have to worry about it when the

time came. Carpe diem and all that. For now, it was about having fun with the girls. Which included a few more stores after this and then a trip to Cherise's to listen to music and model our new stuff.

"So for tomorrow, I think we need to get—oh, hang on." Kellie reached into her pocket for her phone, her eyes widening with delight as she studied the screen.

"Is that Donovan again? Can you tell him you're spending time with your friends, please, and that your friends are going to disown you if he keeps texting you and interrupting?" Cherise said.

"No, no, no. It's the Buzz," she replied with amusement, a smile cratering her face. "Somebody just posted a new pic of that girl Alicia."

"Ooh, let me see." Nikki grabbed the phone out of her hands giddily. "Oh my God, look at her dye job! I'm sorry but Mexicans should not be blond. And what is she wearing? Is that from Forever 21? Another skanky wardrobe choice for the Busteds."

Cherise and I locked eyes across the table, distress and anxiety pinging between us in invisible rays.

The Busteds. They were using the name on the blog, which could only mean that they were still reading the blog. Maybe writing on the blog, too. Possibly they'd even made up the name in the first place.

I wanted to throw up my last bite of pizza.

Nikki typed into the phone, her perfect teeth bared like a wild dog's.

"What are you writing? I'm logged in under my account." Kellie craned over to see. "I want to make sure it's good."

Nikki tossed her glossy amber curtain of hair. "Who cares? It's anonymous."

My stomach turned even more. Anonymous. Well, they'd certainly fooled *me*.

Mary and Sierra had been right, and like an idiot I had defended these people. These people who were supposed to be my friends. How could they? I felt betrayed by them, as if they had deliberately tried to hide this.

But had they? Maybe the fault was mine. They were who they were and I had just refused to see it. Clearly, my character judgment was way off.

I dropped my pizza and grabbed the edge of the table—dizzy suddenly in realizing that nothing was what I thought it was. I had just *thanked* them.

No, I'd gotten it really wrong.

They were bullies, plain and simple.

"Are you okay, Willa?" Kellie asked, frowning at me.

I could barely look at them, I was so angry. What gave them the right to post these things? Who the hell did they think they were?

"She looks like she's having a menstrual moment," Nikki said, laughing loudly at her own joke. "How do you spell 'gonorrhea'?"

I looked at Cherise, pleading. On her side of the booth she seemed like she was gearing up to say something.

Maybe tell them what she really thought. Good. I was ready to back her up.

We made eye contact again before she opened her mouth to speak, and she gave me a look like, *I got this.*

"Nikki, do you really need to do that?" she asked. "I mean, what's the point?"

Nikki sat up straighter on the banquette. "The point is it's hilarious. Why don't you chill out, Cherise?"

"They've had a hard enough time already. I mean, everyone is repeating this stuff in the hallway." Cherise looked back to me for support and I nodded.

"That's not our problem," Kellie said. "We're making *observations*. It's just our opinion. No one has to agree with us."

I had to jump in. "But why the negativity? What did they ever do to you?"

"They bug me," Kellie said plainly, and a chill ran over my skin. I felt like I was seeing a whole new side of her coming out. "Their presence bugs me."

"Maybe you need to ask yourself why that is," Cherise said. Her tone was calm and even, like she'd thought this through.

"Whatever, Cherise," Kellie snapped. "Spare me the condescending new agey lectures."

Cherise shrugged, obviously trying to resist her own anger. "I'm just saying, it's kind of juvenile. I think we're all better than that."

Kellie glared at her venomously. "Then maybe you

shouldn't lump us all in together. Maybe there is no 'we' here."

"What's that supposed to mean?" Cherise asked.

"It means that maybe you and I are just different."

Cherise's face dropped and I could feel her hurt as acutely as my own. This was about more than the other girls for her—this was an old wound that was just ripped open.

The waiter came back to take our plates. "All finished?"

I let him take my pizza. I'd lost my appetite. I was numb with grief as I watched the scene unfold around me. It was all slipping away—I was losing everything I'd been so thrilled to have just a few minutes earlier.

"So we're still going to Armani, right?" Cherise asked, breaking the silence. The question was supposed to be directed at all of us, but Cherise was focused on Kellie, offering a peace branch. "Then back to my house?"

They looked at each other, and I saw something in Kellie's face harden. "Yeah, I don't think so. I should probably get going."

"But what about the records I wanted to play for you?"

"I'm not really in the mood for your music anymore, Cherise. I feel like this shopping trip is suddenly not fun *at all.*"

Kellie was right about the latter, at least. We settled up the bill and split up to go our separate ways. Dread weighed on me with every step as I realized that things were probably never going to be the same—or at least not like they had been. I couldn't unhear what I'd just heard. I couldn't get the image of Kellie's face, twisted up in spite, out of my head.

Cherise and I made our way back outside to the walkway between shops and I squinted at the sudden brightness. It was sunny, as it was every single day in Paradise Valley, but for some reason the light searing through the cloudless sky came as a painful surprise.

A high-pitched grinding sound was the first thing I heard when I opened the front door. My mom was crouched on the floor in her office; her back was to me but I could see she was surrounded by boxes of documents. The paper shredder was going at full blast, shooting sheets into even strips of ribbons. A knee-high pile of them had accumulated on the floor, while several plastic bags filled with paper remnants sat neatly bundled around the room.

"What's going on?" I shouted.

"You scared me!" she practically shrieked, whipping around.

"That's because this machine is so loud. What are you doing?"

"I'm just organizing my files!" she yelled, too loudly this time. She looked harried, her hair all over the place, and she was wearing the same old sweatshirt and cargos

I remembered her wearing the day before.

"It looks like you're destroying your files!" I yelled back. "Can you turn that thing off?"

She turned off the shredder then and stood up, wiping paper dust on her pants. "What's up? You look upset."

I exhaled a despairing sigh as I leaned against her desk for support. "I just found out that some of the people I've been hanging out with are secretly a-holes."

"Your new friends? What'd they do?"

The story came flooding out with a new swell of anger. "They've been writing stuff on this stupid blog about these other girls. Making fun of the way they look, calling them names. They call them The Busteds because they've been 'bussed in' from a poorer neighborhood and they're on scholarships. I just don't get it. The other girls didn't *do* anything to anyone. They're just not rich."

Her phone rang. She scowled at it and stood up to leave the room. "Hang on. I need to take this call, okay, honey?"

"Fine. Whatever." I made sure she could see that I was pissy. This was starting to become a theme; she was always busy lately. And I really needed to talk to her just now. Why couldn't she just let it go to voice mail?

"I'll be right back. I promise."

I wasn't going to wait around. I went into my room and tried to focus on my reading for Comp, but I was all balled up inside with rage and sadness and confusion.

A few minutes later, she knocked on my door. "Can I come in?"

"Sure," I said in exaggerated monotone.

"Don't be mad at me, Willa. I'm sorry we got interrupted. It was—business." She sat down on the edge of my bed and twisted her hands together. Now that I could see her closer I noticed that her sweatshirt was loose. Had she lost weight? And her skin looked dry and dull. Perhaps she was still adjusting to the Arizona climate. "So about these girls. Maybe you're being too sensitive. Maybe it was just a joke?"

"I'm not," I insisted. "And it wasn't."

"Well, maybe you should try to stick up for them, then. Tell the bullies that you won't stand by and watch," she suggested.

"It's so much more complicated than that, Mom. I can't just tell them not to do it." She was trying to help, I got that—but I was frustrated by her simple answers.

"Why not? I saw a thing about this on TV and they said that bullying usually happens because everyone else just stands around and watches. It's the bystanders that have to speak up."

"This isn't some *Dateline* special. Just forget it." She might have been younger and cooler than most other mothers of kids my age, but she still sometimes acted like a clueless middle-aged adult. I was starting to regret that I'd brought it up with her at all. What could she possibly say that would make the situation any easier? Nothing.

Time to change the subject. "Who was on the phone, anyway?" I asked. "Was that your art dealer?"

"Who? Just now? Yeah, he just wanted to touch base about another sale," she said, chewing on her thumbnail.

"So that's good news, huh?"

"Uh-huh," she said absently. Then she picked up the shopping bags I'd dropped in front of my closet. "What's all this? Did you go shopping again today?"

"Yeah," I admitted. Lately I'd been stowing bags away so she couldn't see them, but there was really no point in trying to hide it from her anymore. She'd see me wearing the clothes eventually. And maybe she'd already noticed the emptying safe.

I looked at the bag and thought of the new purchases inside it. The memory of the afternoon came flooding back, a sickening tint shading everything that had originally seemed fun and innocent. So this was what guilt by association felt like.

She looked at me with concern. "It's a little much, Willa, isn't it?"

Yes. It was. I could see that now.

The senior bonfire at Valley Prep was supposedly a tradition that dated from the school's founding in 1952. Valley Prep was full of traditions that harkened back to a time when you could only get into this school if you had a trust fund and your dad's name was Biff. That was before they let people like Sierra and Mary and Alicia in.

It was them I thought of the day after I found out the truth about Nikki and Kellie. I was considering skipping the bonfire altogether. I didn't want to spend another night partying while they were being tormented and laughed at. If that was what the Glitterati were about, I wasn't going to be a part of it.

All afternoon and evening I'd stalled and stalled, taking a shower, painting my toenails, and brooding while looking out the window in my bedroom. But then there was Cherise to think about. She'd texted me multiple times, wanting an ETA on when she could pick me up. I didn't want to punish her. She'd done nothing wrong. In fact, she was the best friend I had here.

I needed to do something to help the Buzz victims, something to try to change things. I grudgingly thought about my mom's suggestion. She was right about bystanders. I'd been too quiet at the mall. I should have spoken up more instead of letting Cherise do all the talking. I could try confronting Kellie and Nikki myself, couldn't I? A small part of me had already started to fantasize that they would actually listen and apologize for their wrongs and then things could go back to the way they were before.

The more rational part of me knew that was probably too much to ask for, that it would never go down like that. But what was the worst that could happen?

I knew the answer to that: It was what had happened to Cherise over the past twenty-four hours. Kellie and Nikki had been giving her the cold shoulder in school—I saw them barely acknowledging her in the hallway before homeroom. Cherise seemed to take it in stride, talking to them anyway like nothing had happened. Maybe she was used to this kind of thing. Maybe it would just blow over.

So I could go and act like I didn't care. I could actually try to make myself not care. I could stay home and keep brooding. I could go and try to tell them how I felt and hope that it would somehow influence them to stop doing what they were doing.

Yes, I had options, but none of them were any good.

By the time Cherise was at my door in her Kellie-approved bonfire outfit of a gingham plaid shirt and denim shorts, I had a burning pit in my stomach.

"Nikki and Kellie just texted me—they're on their way, too," she said as we walked to her car. She seemed upbeat, like nothing was bothering her. How could that be? It was eating me up inside. "Are you going to Nikki's after?"

"I'm not sure," I said.

"What's your deal? You seem really tense."

"I kind of wanted to talk to you about them."

Her face glowed in the light of the dashboard, the slope of her forehead accentuated by the headband holding back her curls. "What's up?"

"The ValleyBuzz stuff. I'm just really bugged by it."

Cherise nodded slowly, but she didn't look completely surprised. "I know. I am, too."

"Did you know they were posting on there before yesterday?"

"No," she said. "Not really. I mean, I wondered. But I was trying to ignore the whole thing."

This bothered me. I personally would've wanted some warning before I got involved with this crew. "Why didn't you tell me?"

"I don't know. I didn't want you to look down on them. I wanted you to hang out with us." She sighed and fiddled with the car's air-conditioning vents. "It's effed up. I know. But they're not that bad."

Not that bad? To who?

We pulled into the parking lot where the tower of wood had been stacked and set aflame. The smell of charred bark wafted through the warm night air, and a crescent moon hung overhead like a burned-out bulb. It was already crowded, students milling everywhere wearing Valley Prep football jerseys with the scorpion mascot. Others had on senior T-shirts: CLASS OF 2012: GAME OVER. One of the class officers, wearing flip-flops and a tie, was shouting into a megaphone.

"Well, what should we do?" I asked Cherise plaintively as we got out of the car. I felt like we needed some kind of plan before we saw everyone.

"*We* should do *nothing*," she argued, almost with

force. “We didn’t do anything wrong.”

“But I thought you were really against this. I talked to Mary and Sierra the other day, and they know it’s Kellie and Nikki. If we don’t do anything and it gets out, people will think we were in on it. I think we should say something.”

She shook her head. “I’m telling you, Willa. I already said something. And you saw what happened. What good would it do?”

We headed toward the marshmallow-and-hot-dog table, where we loaded up on marshmallows on sticks for roasting. We held them over the fire and watched them suddenly puff up, then go brown and soft.

On the other side of the woodpile I could see Mary and Alicia standing at the edge of the fire. They were apart from the crowd as usual, and Sierra was nowhere in sight. Mary had her hands on her hips and she was wearing jeans and a fitted button-down. Alicia, who was tiny, was similarly dressed down, like they were trying not to call attention to themselves. Still, they’d shown up, and good for them. Other people—myself included—might have avoided school functions at this point.

“I’ll be right back,” I said to Cherise, suddenly struck by the urge to clear the air with them, and let them know they had my support.

Before Cherise could say anything, I marched over to where the girls were standing.

“Hey,” I said.

"How's it going, Willa." Mary wasn't smiling like she usually did. Now she regarded me like I was a spy or something. Like I was there to mess with them. Of course she did. All of her experience so far at Valley Prep had taught her to think like that. But my intentions were good. She would see that, right?

"So what are you guys up to?" I tried to sound normal and friendly, but inside my head, the moment felt big and important, like a critical scene in a movie.

"Just roasting marshmallows," Alicia said. Then she added, a bit snarkily, "Like everyone else here."

I chose to ignore her tone. "Are you guys going to the game tomorrow?"

"I don't know," Mary said. "I have to work."

"Probably not," Alicia said, shrugging.

"But you came tonight," I said, smiling encouragingly. "That was good."

"Why *wouldn't* we?" Alicia asked. "We're not hermits."

This was going all wrong. I was trying to be sincere and friendly but instead I was implying they were social mutants. Ugh. The last thing I wanted to do was insult them.

"I don't know. I mean, you just made it sound like you weren't exactly rah-rah Valley Prep," I backtracked.

"We've got nothing against the school. Hell, they're paying for our education," Mary retorted. "But football is stupid."

"I don't even know who they're playing," I admitted.

Could I be any more of an idiot right now? "But it's supposed to be a big game. You should go."

"Hi, guys. Can you excuse us for a moment?" Cherise said as she grabbed my elbow. I should have been thankful for the emergency rescue, because I was bombing, but I hadn't gotten a chance to say what I really wanted to say and I watched them over my shoulder as Cherise dragged me away. "What were you doing over there, Willa?"

"I'm just talking to them."

"That's not cool," she hissed. "Look, the girls are going to be here any minute. You saw how Kellie has been icing me out since yesterday."

"So?"

Cherise confronted me with her hands on her hips. "So, do you want her to do that to you? You just got here. Do you really want to deal with that? And do you really think those girls want to be friends with you, anyway? They know you're not one of them. Believe me, it's better just to let it go. It's not our fault what happened. But it's not our problem, either."

"It is, though," I insisted. "Don't you see that? As long as we hang out with the Glitterati, it's like we're behind it."

"You don't know Kellie like I do." Cherise pulled on her earring nervously. "It's just easier to stay on her good side. I know it's lame, but seriously. Trust me."

What happened to the girl who once gave Kellie the

beat-down, I wondered? Or even the girl I'd glimpsed at the café? What had happened to Cherise over the years to make her so afraid? Whatever it was, it depressed me.

I stared up at the sky, where little trails of smoke seemed to be curling around the stars. I knew Cherise was saying what she thought was the truth, but I wasn't sure I believed her.

"Hey, guys," Nikki said, coming up from behind Cherise, her hair bouncing high in a ponytail. Drew Miller was with her in his lacrosse jacket, his scrawny shoulders not much broader than Nikki's, though he always appeared to take up more room—maybe that was ego.

"Look what we've got. I swiped it from my dad. It's an heirloom." Nikki produced a square silver flask from the pocket of her suede jacket and handed it to Cherise. "Isn't it pretty?"

Cherise took a swig, then passed the flask to me. I hesitated.

"It's vodka," Nikki said to me, her eyes narrowing in suspicion. In them, I glimpsed the gossiping snob I'd seen the other day, and my stomach soured. "Take it. It's good."

"No, thanks. I'm just going to stick with my marshmallow." I turned back to the fire and let it toast over the flame. I was hoping it would sound like a rejection, but it came out silly and prudish.

"Little miss purity over here," Nikki snorted. "S'mores

are like five thousand calories, you know."

"I'm not on a diet," I said.

Kellie emerged next to Nikki, teetering as usual on ridiculously high heels, and draped her arms around Nikki and Cherise. "Hey, byatches."

Look who's talking. Everything she did seemed to be sinister now, especially the way she'd sashayed across the parking lot like she didn't have a care in the world. No, changing her was hopeless. And so was pretending I didn't care, because I was furiously pedaling through my angry thoughts as I stood there and watched her.

I was just going to have to give up the parties, the shopping, and everything else that went along with my Glitterati status. Pretty much exiling myself to social Siberia. But, hey, at least I'd be able to live with myself.

"Hey, Kellie," Cherise responded brightly.

So I guessed everything was okay with them now? Just like that? A forlorn vision of me sitting alone in the dining hall flashed through my head. Would Cherise choose them over me if it came to that? I was afraid to hear the answer to that question.

A flame burst in my peripheral vision. When I turned back, I saw my marshmallow had caught on fire. I tried to extinguish it but it was too late—it had already turned into a lump of coal, so I threw the whole thing into the flames.

"Nasty," Nikki said.

"This place is beat," Kellie said. "I say we go back

to your house, Nik. Who are we still waiting for?" She twirled a lock of hair and frowned as she surveyed the crowd.

"You could ask those Busted girls," Drew Miller said, snickering. "I think I saw them here earlier."

"Did you see what they were wearing? It was like they walked here off the streets. Could they be any more ghetto?" Kellie said.

"Not everybody wears Jimmy Choos to a parking lot. And they're not ghetto," I said, unable to control myself. But it didn't feel good. Because now that the anger had spewed out I feared it was going to engulf me completely.

"I'm sorry. Where do they live, then?" Kellie asked, fake-sweetly.

"I don't know where *they* live. But *they* have names, you know." My indignant rage sounded small and ineffectual out here in the open.

I could feel something pinching my arm hard. I looked sidelong at Cherise, who was giving me the eye, wordlessly warning me to cut it out.

"Oh well, thanks for pointing that out. See, I thought they were just nobody skanks." Kellie turned back to Nikki. "Are we ready or what?"

Nice job. You really made your case.

"Where's Aidan?" Nikki asked. "I thought you invited him."

"He was going to Scottsdale tonight, for some art thing," Kellie said. And I remembered then that he had asked me to go with him to that art thing. *What I wouldn't give right now to be in Scottsdale.*

"Are you guys coming with us? I don't know if Drew can fit all of us in his car . . ." Nikki's voice trailed off.

"We're coming," Cherise said firmly, staring at me.

"If you guys can sit on laps, it'll be fine," Drew said.

We circled around the fire, moving through the crowd. The light was primal and flickering, and it felt like we were on our way to an ancient sacrificial slaughter.

"Maybe you should just drop me off," I whispered to Cherise. My mood was worsening and I saw no point in hanging out. I especially had no interest in snuggling up in Drew's car like besties.

Kellie and Nikki and Drew had skipped ahead of us, passing the flask between them. On the other side of the fire, I could see Mary and Alicia, standing with Tre and holding steaming cups of hot chocolate. Alicia was telling them a story with animated gestures and the rest of them were laughing. It looked fun. I wanted to be over there.

Tre's eyes locked on mine as we passed. They were a few yards away but I could feel his stare like something cold and precise, a thermometer or a bicycle tire gauge, reading me.

I was ashamed to be trotting off to Drew's car with the rest of them, knowing that they probably thought I was going along with everything the Glitterati did, including the mean posts. They probably thought I'd gone over to them earlier on some kind of stupid dare. I felt like a phony. And hadn't I just sworn off hanging out with Kellie and Company a few minutes ago? Already I was copping out. Pathetic.

Cherise's grip on my arm tightened. "C'mon, Willa," she whispered back. "We don't have to stay long."

Drew had already started up his Beamer and was flashing the lights at us to hurry up. I knew what side I wanted to be on, and this wasn't it.

Not knowing what to do, I waved good-bye to Trey, Mary, and Alicia. The girls didn't even seem to see me. Tre gave us a nod, which only made me feel worse as we buckled into Drew's backseat and sped out of the parking lot to the next big party.

NINE

MY MOM WAS out—volunteering at the art center, her note to me said. I flung my bag down, folded up the note, and poured myself a glass of lemonade. I was still in my pajamas, and I sank down into the couch in front of the television with my drink, bleary-eyed from sleep deprivation.

I'd spent the night at Cherise's, where we'd stayed up until four, listening to her records on headphones. Her mom made us pancakes in the morning before Cherise dropped me off at my house.

It would have been a perfectly fine night if we'd just been hanging out there the whole time. But we hadn't.

We'd stayed at Nikki's until one thirty. It was really just a bunch of people playing drinking games. One of Drew Miller's lacrosse thug friends spilled beer all over Mr. Porter's felted casino table and Nikki had a meltdown and locked herself in her bedroom. Kellie spent most of the night on her iPhone, texting with some guy from UA. At the end of the night, Nikki and Drew had hooked up, cringingly, on her living room couch in front of everyone. It was beat. Even Cherise agreed with me that we should've stayed in.

What haunted me most was that scene in the parking lot as we were leaving the bonfire. I felt like I'd made several mistakes. I should have let Mary and Alicia know the truth—that I knew. I should have confronted Nikki and Kellie right there and then and refused to go with them. Why did I care what they thought? Why was I such a wimp?

Well, it was obvious, wasn't it? I'd loved being part of the Glitterati over the past several weeks, and it was hard to shut the door on that and accept that it was over.

Even harder was knowing that by rejecting them, I was also opening myself up to ridicule. Who knew what lay in store for me in the hallways, or what kind of comments would end up on the blog? I wished I could just steel myself against it. I wished I was as tough as Mary and Sierra and Alicia, who, despite it all, seemed to hold their heads high. No, I was as soft as Kellie's weekly manicured hands.

I rubbed my eyes and pulled our old afghan over my legs, letting its warm wool fringe hang over the edge of the cushion. Sometimes, on a weekend, my mom and I would have a pj's-'til-five day. We'd set ourselves up on the couch, each taking an end with our feet crossing in the middle, a bowl of popcorn set strategically between us on the floor.

It was a lot less fun on my own, and this being Saturday, there was nothing much on at all—a few cartoons for kids, some politicians on talk shows, and random sports like cricket and fishing. Robotically, I scrolled through the channels with the remote.

"This will change everything," a short lady with dark hair proclaimed, so confidently that I stopped to see what she was talking about. "You're going to be a different person."

I propped myself up on my elbow and set the controller on my lap. It was one of those cable shows where someone gets secretly nominated by their friends for a makeover and a team of stylists shows up at the person's house to ransack her closet.

The other woman was thin and attractive but dowdily dressed in a college sweatshirt and baggy shorts. She had tears in her eyes and her voice quavered as she said, "I don't know if I'm ready."

"Oh, but you are," the host assured her. "Guys, let's take Melanie on a little shopping expedition."

The show flicked into a montage of scenes: Melanie walking down the streets of a city, which I assumed was New York. Melanie in a trendy store, frowning at a fuchsia-and-orange dotted sweatshirt. Melanie coming out of a dressing room in a slim-fitting navy pencil skirt and matching jacket. Melanie scurrying down the sidewalk to another store. Melanie coming out of a dressing room in slightly flared jeans. Melanie piling up clothes on her arm to carry over to the register. Melanie emerging onto the street again with several bags of purchases.

"Well, let's take a look at Melanie now," the host said. "Melanie, come on out."

Melanie appeared on the stage, wearing a flattering, sexy red dress and nude-colored heels, smiling broadly. Her hair had been trimmed and blown out so that it fell neatly on her shoulders, and her makeup, in strong neutral colors, highlighted her cheekbones and wide eyes.

When the crowd's cheers died down, the host turned to her miracle makeover guest. "So, what do you think?"

"It's just . . . incredible," Melanie said, her face still registering the shock of her transformation. "I never knew I could look this way."

The host nodded approvingly with a somewhat maniacal grin.

"But the best part is that I feel different. . . . I used to feel so bad about the way I looked but now I can look in the mirror and see that I'm letting the best part of myself show through. I've gotten a new job. I'm dating again. It's a fresh start for me, and this new confidence—well, it's really like being reborn."

The show broke to a commercial and I lay back on the couch, thinking about clothes and how having Kellie lavish all that attention on my looks had made me feel special. How it had improved my life in some small but essential way—for a time, at least, I could see so many more possibilities to who I was and who I could be. The new clothes made me feel like I could be a new person here, a popular girl, someone who blended in in all the right ways. And having control over that, in a place like Paradise Valley, where money was everything, was a different kind of power.

Then, the idea hit me all at once: If I could somehow give Mary, Sierra, and Alicia access to some nicer things, maybe they wouldn't get teased as much. Maybe they'd feel more confident and fit in better at Valley Prep, or at least they'd have a choice. I'd be evening out the playing field, and then Nikki and Kellie wouldn't be able to make fun of them anymore. It would be a chance to start over. To set things right.

I could be their fairy godmother, I thought gleefully, and make sure they had everything they'd ever need. Like the host of that show. I'd have to find a way to keep it secret, of course. It would look like charity, and no one would want to accept that from someone they knew, let alone another kid in school.

All it would take was some cash. Which they didn't have—but I did.

I leapt off the couch and dashed into my mom's room. Her gigantic closet was mostly empty—as I said, she herself was not much of a shopper—and the safe was just where it always was, under some shoe boxes on the floor.

I knelt down and tried the combination. I tugged on the door but the lock didn't give. I tried it again, thinking I must have made a mistake. It had worked just a few days earlier. No go. I tried a third time. And a fourth.

"What are you doing in my closet?" my mom asked, her distrusting tone its own kind of alarm.

She'd startled me. My heart was racing, and I scrambled up to my feet. "I was just—what happened to the safe?"

"What do you mean?" She looked panicked, her brow creased and her eyes darting quickly as she came closer. "Is it gone?"

She plunged forward as if diving into a pool and pushed past me to look, so that I was pressed up against her hanging clothes.

"No, it's here." I showed her. "But I just tried it and couldn't get it open."

She surveyed the safe and patted the top of it, as if to prove to herself it hadn't really disappeared. Her face relaxed a little as she turned back to me. "That's because I changed the combination."

"You did? How come?" I demanded.

She shook her head disapprovingly. "You've been abusing the system, Willa. I gave you the combination because I wanted you to have some freedom here, but I didn't mean you could take out hundreds every week to spend on clothes." She ran a hand over her hair. She had dark circles under her eyes, like she'd been up late at a party, too. Her skin was as sallow as it had been the other day. "We need to be conservative about our spending for a while, now that I'm paying for this house and the tuition."

This was no good at all. "But I already spent what I had and I need some for the next few days," I blurted.

"You'll just have to wait. For the time being we're going back on an allowance system." She placed both hands on my shoulders and stared me squarely in the eye. She looked as if she'd aged five years since we'd been here, but maybe I just hadn't been examining her as closely before. "Willa, we're not here to keep up with the Joneses. I told you, we're here for you, for your future. And while I can afford private school, our lives are always going to be a little different than your friends'."

"I knew *that* already," I muttered.

"Look, we're lucky to have this money—God knows where we'd be without it. But it's a finite amount. We really do have to be careful."

"But why?" I asked. And before I could stop myself, I blurted, "Why can't you just get a real job like normal parents?"

I'd never asked her this before, though I'd always wondered it. There was so much about our lives that wasn't normal—things I cherished and things that bugged me. The job thing was one of the latter. Lots of artists also worked regular jobs for money, and though I supported my mom's dreams I sometimes thought it was a little selfish of her to put them ahead of our needs.

"Painting *is* a real job." My mom pulled away from me, looking hurt. "Besides, it's not that simple."

"Why not?"

"Because. I just can't."

"But you can. You could do lots of things. You're young. You have skills besides painting."

"Willa, we're not going to talk about my situation, okay?" she said quietly. "There are certain things you wouldn't understand. But you just have to trust me. I have your best interests at heart. And it's more than a couple of sweaters that you'll hate next year."

"I trust you," I said, though I wasn't entirely sure I did. I wondered what things I wouldn't understand. How was I supposed to understand them if she wouldn't even tell me what they were? We'd always been in sync, but ever since we'd gotten here, it seemed like we were speaking two totally different languages, and hers was increasingly secretive.

"Well, that's a relief." She put her arm around me and squeezed me tight. "I was starting to think you were going to leave me for one of your new friends' families. Wanna watch a movie tonight?"

"Maybe," I said reluctantly. The whole conversation just wasn't sitting right with me. I couldn't just snap back to mom and daughter bonding. "I should try to do some of my English reading first."

Once I was in my room, though, I realized I wasn't really ready to face Thoreau and his lonely cabin in the woods—he would have to wait for Sunday. Instead, I sat down at the computer to check my email.

There was a new message from Nikki, sent to all of us, as she was wont to do. The girl lived for the mass email, whether it was a personal update or angels promising good luck for the next decade.

> *I'm sooo hungover, you guys. But look what I found this morning.*
>
> *XXX, N*

It was a link to the Buzz. Out of boredom or some perverse curiosity, I clicked on it.

The top entry was a photo of Sierra. She was wearing jeans, high-heeled boots, and a tight V-neck T-shirt that revealed a faint blue tattoo on her arm. Someone had used a Photoshop program to draw nipples on her breasts and arrows pointing to where her flesh bulged.

Hey, fatty, is that a homemade tat? the caption read. *Fashion Fail.*

I drew in a breath as utter disgust and anger surged through me.

Other people had logged on and made mean comments below, suggesting that she was a slut, that she'd hooked up with teachers at Valley Prep, that her mom was a prostitute. As I read I felt my whole body knotting up—every last muscle constricted with fury.

I clicked the window closed, feeling as ashamed as I might have if I'd stumbled on a picture of her naked.

I didn't need any more evidence that Kellie and Nikki were behind this—I could practically hear Kellie saying the words out loud. And I didn't need any more signs that my anonymous makeover plan was the right way to go. Now I just needed to figure out how to get the money to pull it off.

TEN

BY MONDAY, I'D turned the dilemma over in my mind countless times and I'd finally come up with a workable solution. It was so obvious, I wondered why it had taken me so long. No access to the safe meant I had little choice: I would have to steal the money I needed and then I would deliver new goods anonymously to Mary, Sierra, and Alicia.

And who better to steal from than the people who had more than enough, the people responsible for all of the teasing? I'd be making things right while getting a little revenge. I'd be kickin' it Robin Hood–style. The idea made me positively giddy.

Since I'd never even shoplifted a lip balm, I knew I was going to need some assistance for the stealing part—preferably from a professional in the criminal arts. I didn't know many people in Paradise Valley, but there was one person who could possibly help me.

I found Tre during a free period, practicing ollies on his skateboard behind the performing arts center. His baseball hat was cocked sideways on his head and he was wearing a red plaid shirt buttoned up over a hoodie. He did an ollie in front of me with ease, rolling by, and I could see that his body was meant for skating, a central core of balance smoothly guiding his long limbs. He waved, then circled back, darting in and out of the pots of blooming succulents someone had thoughtfully cemented here. Above us, a single row of clouds was drifting across the sky like curdled cream.

I wished suddenly that I was coming here under different circumstances, because it wasn't going to be easy to ask what I had to ask him. It's not like we were close, and I had no idea how he would respond.

It was too late now, though, because he'd seen me. *Gulp.*

"What's up, Willa? Are you out here for a smoke or something?" This was where kids went to sneak cigarettes, and probably lots of other things that may or may not have made the pages of ValleyBuzz.

"No," I said. "I'm actually looking for you."

"Oh yeah?" He smiled, almost flirtatiously. "What for?"

I took a deep breath. There was no subtle or polite way to do this. I just had to come out with it. "I guess I'm wondering if you can help me. I need to steal something."

He broke out into a laugh. "You're kidding, right?" He skated past me, looping across the pavement on his board.

I jogged after him, my heart thumping in time with my feet. *Not kidding at all, Tre.* I had to get his attention before I lost my nerve.

"It's kind of important," I called out. "It's for a good cause."

He stopped again and stared at me, his smile collapsing into a deeply creased scowl. He looked offended. "Now why would I be able to help you with that?"

I shrugged, feeling sheepish. "I don't know . . . I just . . . I just heard some things."

"Don't believe everything you hear." He got back on his board, dismissing me.

Stupid. What was I thinking, that I would insinuate he was a criminal and then expect him to want to help me, like he would just be all gung ho?

This whole thing was a bad idea.

Maybe I should just forget about it now, I thought. Go back inside. Actually do something productive during my free period, like read or study. But I thought of the girls I could help, of all the stuff they'd dealt with, and something in me—the stubborn, angry part of me—pressed ahead. I needed to make him understand.

"Tre, seriously. I mean, I wouldn't ask unless I really needed your help. Please. Just listen, at least." I had to shout to be heard above his scraping wheels as he whooshed back and forth.

"I'm not into that," he called back to me. "And even if I was, why would I teach some nosy girl my secrets?"

"Because I'm . . . nice?" I asked feebly.

He just stared at me under raised eyebrows.

His phone buzzed. He stopped to take it out of his pocket and look at the screen. Then he looked back at me as if surprised I was still there. "Sorry, Willa. I can't help you," he said with finality.

I wasn't going to let him brush me off just yet. I saw an opportunity and I seized it quickly.

"That one of your—um—clients?" I asked, thinking of the other day in assembly. "I seem to remember you saying you owed me one."

He sighed wearily and put his phone away. "This wasn't what I meant."

"I just need one little lesson," I pleaded. "Maybe a half hour of your time, tops. Then we'd be even."

"Look, Willa, you don't know what you're getting into." He looked beyond me, as if remembering his past, then his eyes trailed back to where I was standing. "And I'm trying to do things differently here."

"I understand," I said. "But you can trust me. I won't mess it up for you, I promise."

"How do I know that? I barely know you. And no offense, but you don't seem all that slick."

I looked up at him, noticing for the first time that he had a tattoo peeking out of the collar of his shirt, one that he'd always kept hidden. It was a colorless face made with scratchy lines. It looked like Sierra's tattoo—the one the blog had made fun of. I wondered if it was a picture of his girl.

"You can trust me because we both have things to lose," I said. "And because we're both new here, and that makes us more alike than different."

He seemed to think this over for a moment.

"So if we were gonna do this thing—and I'm not saying we will—I don't want to know anything about what you're planning, okay? *Nothing.*"

"Okay," I said, my hopes rising bubbly in my chest. "I won't tell you. Ever."

"And you can't ask me any questions, either. The past is the past. I wouldn't expect anyone around here to understand, anyway."

My eager smile retracted a bit—I felt like he wasn't really giving me enough credit—but I nodded all the same. "Absolutely. I get it. No questions."

"So when, *hypothetically,* did you want to start?"

"As soon as possible."

"And where?"

"Wherever you want. You tell me."

He kicked his board and grabbed the other end to pull it upright. "We couldn't do it here. But there's a park a few miles down the road. You free after school?"

"Today? Yep." The girls were going shopping but I'd already made up an excuse to avoid it, telling Kellie I had a paper to work on.

"Okay, Willa. I'll think about it. If you see me at that park at four, we're good. If not, you'll have your answer." He tipped his board back down, jumped on it, and cruised past me again.

"Okay. See you," I said. "I mean, hopefully."

By then he'd sailed off across the asphalt, so I turned and walked back toward the main building, trying not to look behind me. The whole future of this plan was riding on Tre. And now I'd exposed it—not completely, but enough that it could be ruined if Tre decided to mention it to anyone.

And what if he did? In all my efforts to convince him I was trustworthy I'd forgotten the simple possibility that maybe I couldn't trust him.

I had an urge to go back, make him promise he'd show, make him promise not to say anything to anyone, but I knew my desperation would get me nowhere. I had to play it cool. Wait and see.

Keep walking, nice and slow.

There was a skate ramp at the park, which is where I would've expected to find Tre, but he wasn't there. He wasn't at the volleyball court or basketball court, either. I chained up my bike and looked at my phone. I was still fifteen minutes early. My breath was short and I felt light-headed, but it wasn't from the bike ride, which was completely flat and only a couple miles from school.

Calm down, I told myself. It was like I was already doing something illegal.

I sat down on a bench and waited, surveying the neatly clipped lawn that had to have been shipped in from somewhere else, then irrigated like nobody's business to stay this green. A tiny sparrow hopped into the thick blades and disappeared, probably reveling in the suburban vegetation. I didn't blame him. I was longing for a little lounge action myself.

I reached into my bag to get out *Walden.* The page hung in front of my eyes but its neat rows of text were just patterns to me. Then I pulled out my little cookie-shaped coin purse and walked toward the community center building, looking for a vending machine.

Would he show? I wondered. Or was he sitting on a couch at home, playing *NFL* on his Xbox and laughing at me? He'd made it clear that he wasn't really planning to help me out, that he thought the whole thing was a bad idea.

I carried my soda back to the bench and watched some kids riding their bikes around. This was what parks were for. To help kids do wholesome activities and stay out of trouble.

For some reason I thought of Aidan, and his bike shop. I was sure he hadn't really needed a job, if what everyone said about his family was true. He must have taken it because he loved bikes. Like I did. Which made him . . . kind of cool. My mind drifted back to the last day I'd seen him, in the hallway, when he'd asked me out. Had he gone to Scottsdale by himself or with someone else? The thought of him asking someone else gnawed at me. He'd looked so cute that day, by my locker. . . . But he was a flirt. Everyone said so. *Forget him*, I thought. I had other things on my mind right now.

Like the sinking, uneasy feeling that Tre wasn't coming. It was now five after. I would give him ten more minutes to show up, and then I would head home. The kids on their bikes swooped and swerved, laughing as they did another lap around the fields, tearing up the perfectly manicured turf.

I heard the board before I saw him. He coasted around the corner, his backpack slung over one shoulder, the red flannel shirt rippling against his muscled arms. He jumped the curb and stopped in front of me.

"Wow. You made it," I said. Before I'd realized what I was doing, I'd flung a hug on him, throwing my arms around his back.

He pulled away and gave me a perplexed look. "Against my better judgment."

I immediately regretted the hug. Awkward much?

"Well, I'm glad," I said, toning down my enthusiasm. I was afraid that he might change his mind again. "So? Where do we start?"

"What do you need?" he asked.

"I just need to know some basic techniques, I guess."

He smiled wryly. "Entry-level boost, huh?"

"More like pickpocketing. I don't want to break into houses or anything."

"You never know. One thing always leads to another—that's what they say. Pickpocketing is just a gateway drug. Next thing you know, you're sending bad checks and hiring a bodyguard."

"Not in this case."

"Of course. You're *special,*" he singsonged.

His sarcasm and the suggestion that I was embarking on a life of black-market toasters and pool-hall pals with face tattoos was bugging me. "Can we just get on with it?"

"Fine. Well, I'll tell you what I know, most of which comes from other guys. I never did a lot of this stuff myself, but it seems easy enough."

"Okay."

"First of all, the number-one thing when you're trying to get into someone's pocket, purse, whatever, is to be patient. You choose your mark and then you watch. And wait. You start at a store, maybe, and watch them pay at the cashier, so you can see where they keep the money. Or you notice them patting around, making sure it's still there. Usually with guys, it's a back pocket. Girls usually keep it in a purse, but you never know." He picked up my bag. "May I?"

"Sure," I said, already riveted by his lesson. I knew I'd picked the right guy to help me.

He unzipped the front pocket. "To get into the purse

you have to open it quick, no sound—muffle the snaps if it's got snaps—and dip your hand in and get it in a single motion." He demonstrated the motion with one pinching hand. "Looks easy but it takes practice."

He handed the bag back to me.

"I'm gonna need practice for sure," I said. My skillz were nonexistent.

"Sometimes it's easier to just grab the whole bag, but don't rip it off them. Wait for it to be left on the floor or on a chair. You have to move really fast or hand it off. Never run. Never. And if you get a whole bag, you have to get rid of the phone right away. Are you getting all this?"

I nodded. "Maybe I should take notes." I reached into my bag for a pen.

"No. Don't do that. Stay focused." He pointed two fingers at his eyes and then at mine, commanding me to watch. *He should be a teacher,* I thought. I had a feeling he could make just about any subject interesting.

"All right. No notes."

He tipped his head toward the café building. "Let's go over there where the people are." We walked over and stood outside, looking in through the large window at the brightly lit room. Inside were a counter and some vending machines. A bunch of young moms with strollers were sitting at one of the modern red booths. A teen couple was sitting at a small two-top and a few other older people, two men and a woman, were gathered around cups of coffee.

"See, the best mark is someone who's busy and distracted, like that woman who's trying to cut her muffin into five million pieces," he said, pointing. "People on the phone are good. So are people carrying drinks. That guy there, with the tray of coffees? He'd be easy to get. See how far his hands are from his pockets?"

I stood on my tiptoes to see him. "Yeah. But what if he heard me coming?"

"You just smile at him, all cute. The last thing he's thinking is that you're robbing him. Especially you. You've got that innocent face."

"Thanks—I think." I squinted at him, trying to ignore the blush I felt creeping across my cheeks.

"You can also create the distraction. Like, you spill something on someone's back—you have another guy show up to tell the person and pretend to help them, while you reach in and grab the wallet. Are you planning on working alone?"

"Yeah." It hadn't occurred to me to involve anyone else.

"Cannon-style. Okay. Okay." He seemed to think this over. "So forget that last one."

We walked away from the café and back into the park area with benches where we'd been sitting before.

"What we should really look at then are some simple maneuvers," he said. "But distraction is still important. Say I have my wallet in my back pocket here. I'm going to walk down the street. You come up from behind me, bump my shoulder, and say, 'Excuse me.' Maybe you're listening to loud music on your iPod, or maybe you're flirting with me, but you do something to catch my eye, while your hand slips back and grabs my money."

"Distraction. Okay, I got it."

"Now you have to work on your hands. They gotta be lightning quick. It's all in the claw. Watch me."

I imitated his gesture, joining my thumb to my index and middle fingers in a quick grasping movement, uncertain whether I was doing it right. "Like this?"

It was weird, pretending, but I guess people learned how to do this stuff like they did anything else. With practice.

"But faster." He moved his wallet to his back pocket. "So let's try it."

"Try it?"

"You wanna learn this, right?"

"Yeah. I just wasn't—" The idea of trying to get anything past Tre, who was towering over me, and already knew exactly what I was doing, was daunting. It was also a little bit intimate, dipping into his pocket—and I felt afraid, for some reason, of crossing a line.

He looked annoyed, like I was a child. "Let's not mess around, Willa. If you're gonna do this and not get caught, you need to practice." He patted his butt. "Come and get it."

I snickered into my hand at the suggestion, then took a breath to regain my composure. He threw me shade.

"Are you ready or what?"

He started walking and I sped up to catch up with him. As I walked by, I bumped him and started to reach back.

"No. It's gotta be more subtle. It can't be your bony hip slicing into me. Plus, I could see you and it looked like you were trying to hit me with a line-dance move. To the left. To the left," he sang, mimicking my movement. "Now try it again."

This time I came up using my shoulder, brushing against him as I passed. He turned to give me the eye. "Excuse me," I said, and batted my eyelashes. He smiled and I reached back. He slapped my hand.

"Your smile looks fake. And I see you coming at me. Try it again."

I cracked up the third time, just as he turned to look at me. It was probably just nerves. And I was feeling pretty silly.

"This isn't a game," he said, shaking his head. "Again."

After I came up with a reasonably good approach to the back pocket, we worked on side pockets, backpacks, and jackets. Each maneuver had its own set of challenges and each one seemed to require a ninja's stealth. I had a newfound respect for professionals.

By six o'clock, the sun was setting, slipping behind the distant mountains and leaving a blurry halo of pink, but Tre was still going strong, trying to show me how to lift a watch off of someone's hand—a move I considered well out of my beginner's grasp.

By now, my mom was probably waiting for me. I was hungry and tired and feeling a little uncertain about the whole future of this project.

"It's getting dark," I said. "Maybe we should call it a day?"

He held out his palms. "Hey, you tell me. This whole thing was your idea."

"I didn't know you were going to be such a drill sergeant." I nudged his arm jokingly.

He smiled. "Anything you want to be good at takes discipline," he said. "That's something I learned from my dad. Besides, we're just getting started here. I've got a lot more I can teach you."

"You do?" His energy surprised me.

He shrugged. "This is kind of fun, actually. I never thought I'd get to show anyone this stuff."

"Well, maybe we can keep going? Like once a week or something? I definitely feel like I could use more help. I mean, I don't know if I'm ready to do anything just yet after one day."

"I could do that," he said. "Not much going on right now, really. I mean, I haven't joined any clubs at VP or anything."

"Me neither." I unlocked my bike. "This could be our own little club, I guess."

"Larceners Anonymous." He laughed, then gathered his things to go. "I'll see you."

"See you," I said, meeting his eyes to signal my appreciation. Maybe we would even become friends. I hoped we would. "And thanks."

He walked away a few steps, then paused. "Hey, Willa."

I threw my lock over my shoulder and turned around.

He opened his hand. My cookie coin purse rested on his palm.

He broke into a huge grin before tossing it back to me. "Gotcha."

ELEVEN

"*ALORS, ÉTUDIANTS. MAINTENANT on va discuter les devoirs*. Mademoiselle Greene?"

Madame Bruning stood in front of our French class on Friday morning, dipping forward on her open-toe pumps. She was one of our youngest teachers, with thick red hair, huge blue eyes, and impeccably applied makeup, and consequently she was also one of the most crushed on. Our chairs were arranged in a horseshoe shape around the smart board, which she was using to go over some discussion questions on the reading, Camus's *L'Étranger.*

I was feeling pretty strange, all right.

"Oui, madame?" Cassidy Greene sat up straighter in her chair, her blond head practically bouncing off of its skinny stem of a neck as she opened her book to show off pink-highlighted text. If there was such a thing as a nerd at Valley Prep, Cassidy Greene was it. In a school of superhigh achievers with superhigh-pressure parents, the difference between nerd and normal was only by degrees of enthusiasm.

Madame Bruning was asking her about the themes of the story—or at least that's what I thought she was talking about. My French from freshman year at Castle Pines High had not exactly prepared me for full-on discussions of existential novels, and Madame Bruning prohibited us from speaking in English during class. That left me stranded on Non-Comprendre Island. Even when I tried to focus, my brain coasted in and out on waves of indecipherable words.

But truthfully, I had my mind on other things, anyway—like Nikki Porter's silver python leather purse, which was inches away from my feet on the floor. Left unzipped, it gaped open, its metallic Dolce & Gabbana logo plate gleaming tauntingly.

For my first hit, Nikki was the easiest and the most obvious target, for three key reasons: She carried around tons of cash. She was just flighty enough to leave her bag unzipped. And she was personally responsible for much, if not most of, the damage to Mary et al.

I'd set my sights on her during break earlier that morning at the coffee bar. I watched carefully as she pulled out her matching wallet and peeled off a hundred-dollar bill to pay for a three-dollar latte, all the while complaining to the woman behind the counter that she wanted almond milk and that last time she'd gotten soy, which made her break out.

Yes, technically, Nikki was supposed to be my friend, and I was supposed to be hers, but this wasn't about me and her. It was about what was fair. It was about what was right. It was about justice for the underdogs. Besides, I was pretty sure after that s'mores comment that Nikki could benefit from a little karmic kick in the butt.

In the meantime, if all went well, Nikki wouldn't even know what was happening. My role was the invisible but just force, evening things out. Sort of like the wind in the forest or one of those ionic hair dryers.

I was thinking simple swipe. In my last session with Tre, he'd shown me how to cherry-pick cash out of a handbag but leave everything else behind. The name was kind of a misnomer—it was not really so simple. Your hand could get stuck. You could come away with nothing, and if you missed the first time you wouldn't get a second chance.

But given where we were positioned, in the middle of class, it was my best shot right now at getting anything. The only question was whether I had the guts to go through with it.

"*'Aujourd'hui, maman est morte.' Quelle est l'importance de cette déclaration*? Monsieur Simon?"

"Meursault n'est pas heureux, mais il n'est pas très malheureux," David Simon replied.

"Il est malheureux," Nikki piped up next to me. "I mean, his mom just died, come on."

Madame Bruning shook a finger in her direction. "Mademoiselle Porter, *en français*."

"Fine." Nikki rolled her eyes. Then she wrote the word *byatch* on her copy of the novel.

Madame Bruning turned off the lights and flicked a remote. The smart board lit up with a scene from a film based on the book. Like Valley Prep girls at a Burberry sale, everyone was immediately sucked in. It was hard to deny the power of the smart board.

This was it. The perfect moment. I pictured Mary in the locker room the other day. The faraway look on her face when she told me how they were struggling to stay here, like she'd stopped expecting anything good to happen. She deserved better than that. *Now or never.*

I dropped my notebook on the floor by Nikki's purse and crawled under the table, pretending to retrieve it. Her oxblood stiletto boots dangled dangerously by my head as I plunged my hand into her bag. Using the notebook to shield my movement, I felt around until my fingers brushed against the scaly crocodile texture of the wallet.

Under the table, my sense of time got all funny. I closed my eyes so tightly that I was seeing stars on the insides of my eyelids. It was silly, I knew, but it helped me feel like I was less likely to be seen. Besides, I was too faint with fear to keep my eyes open. By the time I'd pinched the roll of bills with two fingers like Tre had showed me, it felt like twenty minutes had elapsed.

If that was the case, it had to be obvious to everyone around me. I was probably going to get busted right then and there. But it was too late to stuff it back. I had to keep going.

I shoved the money between the pages of my notebook, lifted my head, and sat up, not daring to look around, trying to keep my breathing even.

Be ice, Tre had said. You had to have a martial-arts Zen kind of attitude to pull this stuff off. This was hard to do when one's heart felt like a monkey on a poo-flinging rampage.

I tried to watch the video. All I could feel was the blood rushing around in my head and chest. It felt like I was drowning in my own body.

The toe of Nikki's boot struck my calf. She was kicking me to get my attention. I turned to her. Her face was twisted into a frown.

She saw. She knows. Oh my God, what do I do?

What she said came out in slow motion, like the scene in a movie where a boxer is hit and going down—all the sounds and movements warped by my addled brain.

"This class blows," she whispered.

"Yeah, totally," I practically shouted in relief.

"Mademoiselles, *attention*!" Bruning hissed.

I heaved a quiet sigh, trying to release my shakiness by the lungful. Then I sat back in my seat so I could pay attention—or at least fake it for the rest of the period.

• • •

All day I was hyperaware of the notebook in my bag, but I waited until after school, when I'd safely made it to the Mountainside Galleria, to look at it again. In the first ladies' room I could find, I dove behind a closed stall door and pulled out the bills to count them. Four hundred bucks. I stared at them in disbelief. That was a lot of latte money to be carrying around. I folded the bills into my cookie purse and stuffed it into the backpack.

I came out in front of the sink and splashed some water on my face. Then I reapplied my lip gloss, taking my time. I wanted to do this right. I didn't want to rush. A beautiful woman in a camel trench coat came into the bathroom with her toddler daughter, who was grasping a Mylar balloon. I turned around to smile at them and then looked back at myself in the mirror and thought, *I definitely don't look like a thief right now. Thieves don't smile at strangers. Thieves don't wear Tickle Me Pink lip stain.*

I wasn't just a thief, I reminded myself. I was an equalizer, and I was about to make some things right.

I swung the backpack over my arms and stepped out into the mall. I'd picked a different one than the one I usually went to, so as not to risk running into Kellie and Nikki. This mall was twelve miles away and all indoors, lined with marble tile, the whole atrium cool and caged in glass. The splashing of fountains mingled with the hushed voices of shoppers and new agey flute music. The air smelled like new clothes and rosebuds, though the occasional palm tree was there to remind you of the desert outside.

I circled around past Tiffany, and L'Occitane, and a fancy jeans boutique, following the mall walkway until it opened up into the mouth of Saks Fifth Avenue. This was my destination. As I neared the glowing entrance, I imagined Mary and Sierra and Alicia were with me, and I felt as high as if I'd sucked down five bags of Skittles.

I practically skipped in, brushing past displays of resortwear bikinis and maternity clothes. A saleswoman adjusting a display of scarves smiled at me. I was headed for the "Contemporary" department, when one of the faceless alabaster mannequins caught my eye. It was draped in a gold shirred minidress with a deep neckline and a matching belt. It looked like something either a disco goddess or an alien princess would wear, wild and luxurious, and very bold.

I found it on the rack in my size and draped it over my arm, along with a strapless purple dress with a tulle skirt and a few tops. A saleswoman with brassy yellow hair and multiple strands of pearls guided me into the dressing room.

"Let me know if you need any help, dear," she said, hanging up the items before leaving me alone.

I wriggled out of my jacket and dress and tried on the tops and the purple dress first. They were okay, perfectly fine for any other occasion, but they wouldn't wow you, even if they did come in a mysterious packet from a stranger. You'd be like, *Nice shirt. But why is this on my doorstep?* I needed something hot enough that the person getting it wouldn't care where it came from.

That would be the gold dress. It was a knockout—sexy and chic and stunning all at once. I ran my hands over the fine fabric, feeling its weight.

"Fabulous," the saleslady said.

I nodded into the mirror. It *was* fabulous. It would look perfect on Mary. She'd probably never had a dress like this before. To Nikki it would have been just another piece of fabric hanging in her closet, but to Mary it would be something to treasure, a life-changer of an outfit.

Two dressing rooms down, a door opened. Behind it was Morgan Whitney, a girl from Valley Prep who was rumored to have been the heir to the founder of a large oil corporation, at least according to Cherise. With her sharply angled face and large ears, she was not particularly beautiful, but she made skinny-and-rich work for her. She was trying on a pair of jeans, and she pulled the waistband away from her tiny waist, below which her hipbones were jutting out.

"Too big," she pouted.

A petite middle-aged woman carrying a Birkin bag—by all appearances her mother—said, "I'll go back and get you the zero."

"Make the lady get it, Mom," Morgan commanded. "That's what she's *paid* for, isn't it?"

She must have caught me staring because she looked

in my direction. Out of instinct more than anything else, I smiled at her. She was a senior and part of the older branch of the Glitterati—she had been at Nikki's party the other night, and I'd talked to her briefly in the kitchen, though she'd been pretty drunk.

She squinted at me. "Do I *know* you?"

"No," I said, smiling, and slipped back inside my dressing room to change back into my own clothes. A few months ago it might have bothered me that Morgan Whitney didn't recognize me. Now it was proof that I was doing the right thing.

Some of the streetlights were just flicking on as I pulled my bike into Mary's apartment complex in Maryvale. In class, my Comp teacher had been trying to explain the "gloaming," and I was pretty sure this was it, the time of day before dusk decides it's really night. The palm trees rustled together in the slight Arizona evening breeze. Outside, on some of the balconies, laundry swayed like flags. This was technically the bad side of town, and I'd noticed more graffiti creeping up the buildings, more litter on the street as I rode in.

I looked around to see if anyone had seen me but there were no cars going by, and nobody on foot. Just me, and the crazy thing I was about to do. My hands shook as I leaned my bike against the back wall of the building. There wasn't time to lock it properly—I had to move quick to escape detection.

I may as well have been carrying a bomb in my schoolbag. But it was just a neat little package with the tissue paper the saleslady had used to wrap up my purchases: the dress, and a matching gold necklace with a delicate tassel. I'd learned from Kellie that a shiny piece like the dress only needed a tiny bit of embellishment, otherwise I risked overaccessorizing. For that little bit of wisdom, at least, I could've thanked her.

I'd included a note I pasted from cutout magazine letters. Slightly psycho, I admit, but I had to play it safe. It said simply, "A gift for you."

According to Whitepages.com, I was looking for 48C. I scanned the numbers, looking for any visible signs of Mary. The apartment was the fifth one down on the left-hand side, just one unit from the end, where there was a covered staircase leading to the upper level.

One, two, three. I pounced lightly, trying to be quiet on my feet, and quickly set the package down on the front mat. I took a breath. I could hear a TV blaring from inside the apartment, and the smell of dinner wafted out, onions and meat and pepper.

Insides churning, I rang the doorbell, then made a mad dash for the staircase, pressing myself against the adobe wall so that I was cloaked in the shadows. I breathed hard, and it occurred to me that I'd done something like this before: the ding-dong ditch game the kids played in Searchlight. We were in third grade and our objective was to mess with the cranky old lady who lived on our block. She'd step out onto her stoop and yell at us down the street. This version would have a much nicer ending, I hoped.

C'mon, c'mon. I looked at my watch and wondered if I was going to have to go back and ring the doorbell again. Maybe the TV was on too loudly and they hadn't heard. Maybe the doorbell was broken.

But then the door opened, and I saw Mary poke her head out. She looked around before her eyes dipped down and noticed the package. She stuck out her bottom lip, eyeing it, then picked it up and went back inside.

Score.

I wanted to wait longer and see if I could hear or see something more, like her reaction, maybe. But it was too risky now and I needed to get home. The package was in her hands. That was the important thing.

On the ride back, I practically hugged myself with excitement. What was Mary going to think? I could *not* wait to see what happened at school!

By the time I pulled into the driveway, it was nearing seven o'clock, and some of the lights were on inside my house, so I assumed my mom was home.

Act natural, I thought, as I dismounted the bike in the garage and walked in through the laundry room. I was not a very good liar. In fact, every time I'd ever tried to lie to my mom, whether it was about a failed quiz or a lost scarf, she could see right through me. One time

I'd tried to cover up the fact that I'd broken a zipper on a jacket I borrowed, but I couldn't get it past her. "Give it up, Willa," she'd said, and I'd relented, showing her the damage. She always knew. That's why it had been so hard to hide all the clothes I'd been buying.

Lying, she liked to say, *is poison in a relationship.*

This was different, though. I knew instinctually that she wasn't going to get what I was doing, but I couldn't let that stop me.

That's why I had an excuse prepared in case she asked where I'd been—I was hanging out with Cherise. I was hoping it wouldn't come to this, though. For one thing, my alibi could not be corroborated: Cherise had left school early to visit her brother at Cornell. For another, I felt a goofy nervous smile coming on, lurking just beneath the surface. In my delirious, postthieving state, I was in no shape to be lying. How did real criminals pull this shiz off?

"Mom?" I called out tentatively.

Nothing. Maybe I was lucky and she was out, though it was odd for her to leave the lights on—ordinarily she was an eco-fascist about that sort of stuff. No note, either, I saw as I traipsed into the kitchen. I had to assume she'd stepped out for a minute and would be back soon.

I got myself dinner out of the freezer, microwaved a few tamales, and sat down to eat. Then I went to my room and did some homework, like it was any other night, trying to stay focused on the task at hand, even though my mind was racing.

By eleven she still wasn't home, so I went to bed. I stared up at the ceiling and replayed the last several hours carefully in my mind. Had anyone seen me doing anything weird? Had the lady at the store looked at me funny? No and no. Nothing at all had given me a reason to pause. In fact, the whole thing had gone so smoothly, so easily, it was like this was exactly what I was supposed to be doing. Maybe this was my true calling.

My body pulsed with restless energy and I didn't think I was going to be able to fall asleep, but I must have drifted off at some point.

Sometime in the middle of the night, I thought I heard the sound of my door opening. In the cone of light swept in from the hall, I could see that my mom was standing over me, wearing her denim jacket and carrying her purse.

"Mom? What are you doing?" I asked, half-asleep.

"Nothing," she said. She had a faint smile on her face, but it was a sad, regretful sort of expression, like she was dreaming herself. She touched my forehead gently with two fingers, tracing a line across my eyebrows. "I just wanted to check in on you. Go back to sleep."

I watched as she stepped out into the hallway, melting into the shadows, and I heard the whisper of the door dragging over the carpet.

I thought I must have dreamt it, because it was so

strange to see her like that, and because I was so swept up in other dreams—wonderful, undulating, colorful dreams that pulled me back down with them into the mattress and the dark.

TWELVE

THE BREADSTICK ON my plastic tray seemed to form a finger of blame, and it was pointing in my direction. Or maybe that was just my state of mind as I stared down at it.

I hadn't seen Nikki all day but I knew I was going to have to face her sooner or later, and this lunch period was a very probable "sooner." Surely by now she'd noticed something, and I'd have to confess. I just didn't think I could flat-out lie like that—not to her face, not in the middle of the dining hall.

Somehow, the high I'd felt after my Friday escapade had dissolved into serious misgivings over the weekend. And now I was convinced it had all been a terrible mistake. I'd spent Saturday and Sunday at home, ignoring my phone, and feeling increasingly freaked out as a mixture of doubt and guilt set in. It was like the ectoplasm in a horror movie, oozing under the door and coating my shoes to trap me. I knew I would never get away with what I'd done, and even if I got away with it this one time, I couldn't pull it off again. So what was the point? One dress could hardly save the world.

Of course I couldn't tell Cherise any of the things that were on my mind, so I sat there listening distractedly as she talked about her weekend.

"Oh my God, can I just tell you that the guys at my brother's school were total hotness?" Cherise smiled dazzlingly as she sliced into the sashimi on her plate. "You *have* to come with me next time, Willa. Maybe winter break."

"Sounds fun." And it did. Or it would have, if I wasn't fairly sure I'd be suspended from school by then.

I poked at my salad with my fork and watched Nikki emerge from the cashier line with her lunch. Dread boiled up inside me like a carbonated cocktail of poison.

But she was walking toward us jauntily in her patterned tights and tweed skirt.

And was she . . . smiling?

"S'up, ladies?" She sat down next to Cherise, and I noticed she was carrying a new purse, which she set down beside her on the floor, careless as ever. "Cherise, are you actually eating that yellowtail? It looked weird to me."

"You need to get over this mercury obsession," Cherise said. "Where's K?"

"She's still in line with Aidan and Drew. I think they

were coming from gym or something. And it's not an obsession. I just don't want to pollute my body." Nikki shivered at the thought of it.

"You can't see it, though." Cherise held up a piece of fish on her fork. "This looks perfectly fine."

"So you're basically killing yourself and you don't even know it."

Cherise popped the piece into her mouth. "But it's yum."

Nikki turned to me. "Willa, where were you this weekend? I tried calling you."

"Nowhere," I said, looking up and making eye contact with her for the first time. The whole time they'd been chatting I'd been focusing on my tray. "I mean, I was just home."

"I felt like you were avoiding me and I really needed to talk to you . . ."

I swallowed hard, a piece of tomato going down my esophagus like a marble. *Please don't say what I think you're going to say right now.*

". . . about the French homework. Did you do it?"

Was that it? It couldn't be, could it?

"Yeah," I said, trying to mask my disbelief with casual detachment. "It took a while."

"I hate that book. I'm so over Camus. I really needed your help."

Stop staring at her like you're waiting for her to jam her fork into your neck.

"I'm sorry, Nikki. I wasn't trying to blow you off," I said, though that was exactly what I had been doing.

She started forking lettuce into her mouth and I studied her face for any sign of recognition. But there was none. If she'd had any clue whatsoever that she'd lost four hundred dollars—or that I had taken it out of her bag—she didn't show it.

As I saw it, there were four possible scenarios: (a) She knew but she was a brilliant actress; (b) She was completely oblivious; (c) She was so loaded her wallet had refreshed itself; or (d) Some combination of B and C.

When I looked at her again, Nikki was picking the lobster chunks out of her salad and flicking them onto the floor.

D. It was definitely D.

Kellie approached with her tray, Drew and Aidan close behind her.

"I saved you a seat," Nikki said, patting the chair next to her.

"Yay. This is the best side of the table for people-watching," Kellie said. She planted her tray. "And outfit-rating."

Once I would have found this Kellieism cute, but now I knew what she was really up to. Looking for ways to humiliate people. Pathetic.

Drew sat down across from her. "Is there room for both of us?"

"Sure," I said generously. I was relieved that more

people were here because more people made me feel less crazy—even if one of them was Aidan, who I was sure was about to make me feel crazy in some other, completely different way. I scooted over, making room for him while smiling broadly in his direction. Like I was truly happy to see him. Which I was. It had been about six days since I'd seen him last. Not that I was really counting. See? Crazy.

"How's it going?"

He scowled at me, clearly not trusting my welcoming greeting. "What's up with you, Colorado? You drink the friendly juice today?"

"I did," I said, sipping on my freshly squeezed grapefruit. "It sure tastes good."

"Take it easy there. It's potent stuff."

He plopped himself down and started attacking his burger aggressively. His hair had fallen in front of his eyes and he was wearing a plaid button-down with short sleeves. I relaxed a little. The presence of boys took the heat off me, as all conversation was now focused on them.

I went back to my lunch, too, and our elbows brushed against each other in the business of eating. I glanced over and noticed that Aidan's biceps were more defined than I might have expected. My eyes traced the wiry ligaments that ran down his arms to his wide wrists. Had he always been cut like that? My own muscles went whoosh.

"Aidan, you *never* sit here. What did we do to deserve this?" Kellie cooed.

Ugh, gimme a break.

He shrugged. "I wanted to watch you rate outfits."

"Shut up." She giggled.

"That, and I needed a change of scenery." His eyes darted in my direction.

"We're like a drive through the countryside over here on this side of the dining hall," I said.

Hold on—am I flirting? Yes, I think I am. Imagine that.

Aidan chuckled. "More like a road off a mountain cliff."

"But you seem to like the altitude."

Wow. Still flirting.

"When it doesn't make me sick."

"I didn't know you had such a weak constitution. I'll have to find you a Dramamine."

I looked up and saw that Kellie was staring at us with a pinched face. "Are you guys gonna do this routine all day?"

"I'm actually running out of material," Aidan said. "How about you?"

I smiled, not knowing where this confidence was coming from and not really caring, either. "I was just getting started."

"Whoa, you guys. Look at *that*," Cherise said, gesturing with her head.

I turned to look behind me. Mary was standing with

Alicia Gomez at the condiments bar, wearing the gold dress.

"It's amazing," Cherise said. "She looks like a different person."

I drew in a breath and craned my neck to get a better look. This was the moment of truth. As exposed as I felt in front of everyone, I couldn't wait to see how she looked. And Cherise was right. She glowed from across the room.

I wanted to stand up and applaud. She was killing it.

"That necklace is fab," Nikki whispered.

"What happened?" Kellie whispered back. "Where'd she get that stuff? That's a heritage Halston. I saw it at Neiman Marcus the other day."

"I don't know," Nikki said. "She must have bought it at Neiman's."

"There's no way." Kellie choked out a laugh. "Are you kidding me? She must have stolen it. I mean, the girl has always looked so trashy."

Stolen it? Wait wait wait. Worry rang through me. This was supposed to be about raising Mary's profile, not setting her up for my crime. Why couldn't Kellie just give her some credit?

"Maybe she just had a style revelation," Nikki said. "I had one of those. In eighth grade, remember? I woke up after that terrible nightmare about shopping and decided I was no longer going to buy anything from Banana Republic or J. Crew."

"Why do you just assume she stole it, Kellie? Someone else could have bought it for her," Cherise said, and though she was trying to sound carefree, I recognized her pointed tone from that day at the mall.

Bingo, I thought. *That's more like it.* Then I noticed she was looking at me, waiting for a reaction.

"It doesn't matter how she got it. She looks really good," I said out loud, hoping my voice wouldn't falter or otherwise give me away.

"She looks hot," Drew said. "I'd hit it."

Nikki poked him with a bony, manicured finger. "You're so rude."

"What? I didn't say I would date her." He snorted to himself.

"And why's that?" Aidan said, raising an eyebrow. "She too smart for you? The girl is number one in the form right now. I think she'd make you look dumb, dude. Especially to your Harvard dad."

Aidan was standing up for her? I wanted to hug him. Long and hard.

Nikki and Kellie laughed as Drew's face darkened. Apparently Drew's dad was really domineering and Drew was forever trying to live up to his father's expectations. "Shut the hell up, man. All I was saying is she's not my type."

"And all *I'm* saying is money doesn't make you classy," Aidan shot back. "Class does."

"I think she looks great," Cherise said dreamily. "And

she knows it. You can tell. Don't you think, Willa?"

"Yeah," I said, trying not to burst with pride. "It's really flattering, like it was just made for her, you know?"

"Well, as much as I love scoping out new outfits, I think I'm going back for a soda," Aidan announced, standing up. "Does anyone want one?"

"I'll take one, dude." Drew, apparently already forgiving Aidan, reached into the front pocket of his backpack and pulled out a fat black wallet. I watched him slip out a twenty-dollar bill. I caught Aidan looking at me. Our eyes locked for a moment and I was mesmerized. Then I realized he probably thought I was staring at him the whole time so I pretended to be busy dissecting my salad, cutting up ribbons of romaine.

So. Not. Cool.

"I just can't believe it," Kellie said. "This is so not what I was expecting. Up is down. Black is white. Next thing you know Sierra will be wearing Stella McCartney. I feel like the world is coming to an end."

"Get a grip, girl," Cherise said.

I felt a huge smile tugging at the corners of my mouth, but I bent over my lunch so no one would see. Kellie was on the defensive, which meant that things were changing already. I could feel the social order of Valley Prep tilting ever so slightly.

Everything was going exactly to plan, down to the appalled look on Kellie's face. So much so that all of my reservations had evaporated like steam from the hot-entrée line. So much so that I was ready to try it again. And I had a pretty good idea of who would be my next mark.

It was President's Challenge day in PE, where we had to be tested in sit-ups, pull-ups, sit-and-reach, and of course, my nemesis, running. Mary was already rifling through her gym bag by the time I got to the locker room. Since the night at the bonfire, we hadn't spoken much, and I knew I wasn't high on her list, but all day I'd seen her twirling around and looking confident from afar and I guess I just wanted to see how she was doing up close.

"Are you ready for this?" I asked.

"As ready as I'm gonna be," she said, stuffing her gym bag in her locker. She'd worn her hair down today, and it was falling around her heart-shaped face in dark puffs. "Torture."

"I love your dress, by the way," I said.

"Thanks," she said, blushing. "You would not believe how many compliments I've gotten on this thing today. I'm almost afraid to take it off."

A delicious warmth spread over me, like melting Nutella on a banana sandwich. She was so happy, and I was kind of proud to be the reason behind it.

"She thinks she's all that," Sierra said, ribbing her. She was speaking in third person, but more to Mary than to me. She still largely ignored me, but I ignored her ignoring. One of these days, she would see that I wasn't as bad as she thought.

Mary gave her a friendly shove. "You're just jealous, *muchacha*."

"About that dress? That skimpy thing wouldn't look good on me."

Mary rolled her eyes in my direction, and I could see that they were sparkling and light. "Whatever."

We changed into our gym clothes, so that we all looked the same, and headed out for the track, our feet crunching on the dry gravel walkway as we strolled out to the farthest edges of school property. The sun followed us overhead like a metallic eye. Never mind that we were about to be publicly humiliated in the name of fitness standards—everything was just fine, as far as I was concerned. I felt a little bounce slip into my step.

At home, I got online and Googled Sierra. For one thing, I needed her address. But I was looking for other information, too: She was still a mystery to me, and I wanted to know more about her, especially if I was going to go picking out clothes for her. Skimpy was out, apparently.

I found her Facebook page and clicked on it. There were some photos of her with Mary and Alicia, arms around one another, flashing peace signs; and some of what looked like her family, a sister and a brother, maybe. I guess she was religious because she'd posted a quote by St. Francis of Assisi: "For it is in giving that we receive." Under "interests" she had "St. Mary's Mission for Homeless lunch truck, Habitat for Humanity, and the Mesa Children's Shelter volunteer corps."

So her dad was out of work, she could barely afford VP, and she was spending her free time volunteering at three different organizations? Unbelievable. I felt like a total chump. If she was at all grouchy, it was no wonder. The girl was so busy taking care of the planet that she probably wasn't getting any sleep.

Well, one good turn deserves another, I thought as I clicked out of the screen. I opened up Excel and started making a spreadsheet with rows and columns for possible marks and possible gives. There was more work to be done, and I started by making a column for Sierra.

THIRTEEN

IN THE HALLWAY I could hear the faint sounds of piano music drifting out from the auditorium. It was a special assembly, presented by the VP Nightingales, who were previewing songs from their fall concert. Out here I was singing a completely different tune, and it sounded like breaking into Drew Miller's locker.

The job demanded the right tool, and I just so happened to be carrying it in my pocket. Tre had shown me how to pop off a soda-can top and cut and fold it into the right shape to make a shim. I'd practiced a few times with Typhoon Dew and Diet Coke cans we took out of the park's recycling receptacles.

"I feel guilty about this," I'd said to him, as we pilfered more aluminum from the green bins. I was thinking about my mom and her strict recycle-everything policy.

"Why?" he'd said, shrugging. "This is recycling."

Now I just needed to slide the shim into the

combination lock, like so . . . and get the right angle on it . . . not like that, no. It just had to . . .

Click . . .

And voilà.

The lock sprang apart in my hand. Even I was surprised at how easy it was as I pulled the door open. I had to move fast: I guessed I had about a forty-second window, give or take. Drew's North Face backpack was in here, but when I felt around in the front pocket, the wallet—the fat wallet I'd eyed up for three days—was not. *No matter,* I thought, feeling sweat break out all over my body. There had to be something in here. A phone, maybe? I wasn't going to risk locker breaking and entering without some kind of payoff.

Seconds were ticking by. I felt my body temperature rising with each one. Ten left, at most, to find something.

C'mon, Willa. Make it happen.

I hurriedly rifled through the other pockets in the bag and brought up some pens, a lighter, a pack of Trident. And then . . . what was this? Cool metal, heavy links.

No way. He'd left a watch in there.

I reeled it in and saw it was gold and Burberry.

Really, Drew? A Burberry? In your locker? It's like he was just waiting to get ripped off. I would've felt sorry for him, almost, if he hadn't said that vile stuff about Mary the other day.

I pocketed the item, closed the locker, and practically skipped back into the auditorium to listen to Cassidy Greene and her fellow a capellians singing "Ride Like the Wind," like all the other good boys and girls.

The lack of wallet in Drew's locker meant I had to make one quick stop on my way to the mall after school. Finer Things Pawnshop was technically in Scottsdale, on a barren little street in an area with a lot of warehouses and water towers and other things that were probably necessary but best left forgotten. The neon signs flared CASH, EASY TRADE, and WE ACCEPT GOLD from the street. The heat was even less forgiving in this area, with only asphalt road and low concrete buildings to radiate it back. There were palm trees here, as with everywhere else, but they looked ratty and neglected, like they might shower brown fronds on an innocent passerby.

I locked up my bike, taking care to give it an extra few lengths of cable. I was a long way from Paradise Valley, and the last thing I needed was to come out and find my bike wheelless.

Inside the shop a row of electric guitars hung from the ceiling over glass cases of jewelry and coins. Buzzing fluorescent tubes illuminated shelves of TVs, stereos, gaming consoles, and computers, and racks of guns and fur coats stretching for days.

I approached the window in the back of the store, which was like a ticket booth but with bars. An elderly woman with a bright red wig, clashing coral lipstick, and a powdery veneer of foundation stared at me over her bifocals.

"What you got?" she asked in a smoker's rasp. "Be descriptive. I'm almost blind, even with these damn things."

"It's a watch." I slid it into the slot under the window.

She frowned, turning it over in her small, wrinkled hands. "Man's watch. Daddy's? No, don't answer, sweetie. I don't want to know. I don't want to hear any more sob stories. Are you pawning or selling?"

"What's the difference?"

"You pawn you have ninety days to change your mind and buy it back. I need to take ID and your fingerprints. You sell it's mine."

Fingerprints and ID would not do, not at all. "Selling, then."

"Well, I can give you five hundred. The watch is worth a lot more, but this is a pawnshop. We're not exactly known for our fair deals."

"I'll take it," I said, relieved. Five hundred was fine by me—more than enough to get something substantial on my shopping trip.

She winked at me, then pulled off her glasses, exposing watery blue eyes.

"Five hundred it is. Here's a little secret. Next time, you can try to bargain. Can't promise I'll budge, but you should at least try." She opened her cash register and pulled out the bills and tucked them into an envelope, which she slid back to me under the window. "Here you go, kid. Merry Christmas."

It was going to be a very merry Christmas for someone, no doubt.

Inspired by Kellie, I had been tempted to buy Sierra a Stella McCartney top at Saks, but I knew it might give me away, especially since we'd been surrounded by other people when she'd made that remark. Instead, I selected a filmy Catherine Malandrino number. It had a generous fit, a chicly angled neckline, and the softest silk I'd ever brushed my fingers on.

Afterward, I stopped to congratulate myself with a cappuccino at the Plaza Coffee Company, a pagoda-shaped stand in the middle of the mall. Not that I needed it, exactly. My hands were already shaking from the natural adrenaline rush of my day's conquest. And as soon as I refueled I was going to do some more major spending, care of my good buddy Drew Miller.

"I got these shirts two for one at Ann Taylor," the pudgy, fiftysomething woman in front of me said to her bag-mule shopping companion. "It was a *steal*."

You don't know the half of it, I was thinking.

Just then a pair of hands covered my eyes. "Guess who?"

It was a guy's voice. My suddenly blackened vision disoriented me. I had no idea who it could be, and this wasn't exactly the best time for surprises.

"I don't know," I snapped, on edge. "Who is it?"

"Well, that was quick," he said, removing his hands. It was Aidan. I went a little weak at the sight of his face, so close to mine. I could practically count his eyelashes. "You really sucked the excitement out of that game."

"I'm not here to excite you," I said, still flustered.

He wagged a finger at me. "See, that's where you're wrong. I think that's precisely your job."

A very long, loaded second elapsed as I stared into his eyes, speechless.

". . . Because I just so happen to be stuck here, waiting for my car to be serviced. It's the beauty of owning a Mercedes—the concierge will drive you anywhere you want to go."

"Sounds great." I smiled. "But I'm kind of busy. Maybe the Mercedes people can liven things up. Call and see if they can send out a few mimes or a guy in a Barney suit."

He patted me on the arm condescendingly. "Ha. I do love your quick wit. You happen to be very cute when you snark out like that."

I rolled my eyes in order to distract him from the twitching that was happening inside. It felt like my facial features were all going on strike at once.

"The eye-rolling, not so much. That just pushes it over the cuteness edge, you know?" He put a hand on my back and peered over my shoulder. "What have you got there in the bag?"

"Nothing." I felt my face getting warmer. "It's just a shirt."

"Can I see?" He reached for it with a quick hand.

"No!" I practically shouted.

Aidan backed up a couple steps. "Fine. Hold on to your bag, then. I wasn't going to steal it or anything."

I tried to soften my tone. "I mean, it's just a girl's shirt."

But it was too late. He was still staring at me like I was nuts. "What is it with you, Willa?"

"What about me?"

"Why're you so cagey?"

"I'm not cagey." I sighed. This was getting into weird territory. "Like I said: I'm busy."

"Why do you hate me so much?"

Because I have to, I thought. *Because if I didn't, I might actually really like you. And then I'd be in trouble.* I turned toward him, trying to scowl, and he was giving me a fake pathetic look.

"Why do I hate you? Hmm. Let me think about that. There are numerous reasons, really."

"What?" His face puckered up into a frown. "You don't know anything about me."

"Okay, then." I relented. "Tell me something about you."

"Well, I'm a math prodigy, for one thing. I finished Calculus One and Two by freshman year. And I'm pretty great with computers."

"That's just nerdy."

"I had the chicken pox in sixth grade."

"Yawn."

"I've been to five of the seven continents," he bragged.

"Is that it? 'Cause that doesn't really make me hate you any less."

"How about this? I'm leaving Valley Prep."

What did he say? I whipped around quickly, like I was ducking a blunt object. "Why's that?"

Aidan ran his hand through his perfectly tousled hair. "Because I hate that place. I'm just sick of it. And because my dad thinks I'm his little future CEO robot. The guy needs a serious wake-up call."

"So you're transferring?" I tried to picture VP without him and it was like looking at a picture that was Photoshopped into black-and-white. He was a major part of that place, at least for me. He belonged there. I couldn't imagine going to school and never seeing him in the hallways, or in the courtyard, or in the dining hall—who would get on my nerves in the special way Aidan had? For all my trying not to care, I knew then that I would be sad to see him go. Like really sad. Like *was that a lump in my throat?* sad.

"No. I'm trying to get myself kicked out. Like I told you before, it's unbelievably hard to get expelled from that place. I've pulled all kinds of stunts over the years—setting off fireworks in the gym, tagging my biology teacher's black Roadster with hot-pink spray paint. I don't think I've gotten anything more than detention for a week." He closed in on me and stuck his face close to mine. "What's wrong? Are you going to miss me?"

My expression had fallen, I could feel it. He could see it for sure.

I forced a smile. The last thing I wanted was for him to think that I would miss him. "I guess the fire alarm didn't work, then?"

"Nope. Which is part of the reason I've been laying low. I need to act when everyone least expects it. And I need to think big, like a giant, flagrant violation of VP's code of conduct."

"I see. So what's next?" I asked, trying to resume the pace of our earlier conversation. "Growing pot plants in the greenhouse? Or how about bringing livestock to class? That might do the trick."

It was my turn at the coffee bar, and I was relieved that I could turn away from his penetrating gaze for a moment. I couldn't bear for him to see inside me like that. My feelings had swelled up and I could scarcely breathe, let alone make sense of them. I just needed a hot cup in my hands to bring me back to the moment. I placed my order and paid for it.

"Weren't you just here?" the girl behind the counter asked Aidan. She looked like she was eighteen or so, but I didn't recognize her from Prep.

"Yes, I was." He lifted up a bag of chocolate-covered espresso beans and shook it like a maraca. "I'm just waiting for this beautiful young lady here."

Beautiful?

"Well, please step aside, so I can help the next customer."

I took my coffee to the milk-and-sugar area. Aidan watched as I set my bag down and dumped a few sugar packets into my drink and stirred.

"The thing is, Willa . . ."

I looked up from my coffee.

". . . I'm dying. Did I mention I'm dying?"

I had to smile then. He always knew how to make me look.

"Dying?"

"So yeah, now that you know my darkest secrets, and you know that my days here are numbered . . . maybe we can hang out some time."

"Aidan, did you ever stop to think that maybe I have a boyfriend?"

"You don't," he said plainly.

"How do you know that?"

"I have my sources. And who said I was asking you out?"

"You weren't?"

"Well, I was. But you jumped to that conclusion pretty quickly. Which leads me to believe you have sex on the brain. I don't really blame you, though." He stared off into the distance, as if contemplating his own irresistible charms.

"Thank goodness." I closed up my coffee and threw out my trash.

"Don't you know, Willa? With that cute little face, I'd forgive you for anything. Well, nearly anything."

I turned to face him. My heart was ricocheting like a Super Ball on a linoleum floor. Was he serious? Or was this more of his playing around? My senses were all out of whack. I no longer trusted myself.

Oh God.

It was fight-or-flight time and my head was telling me flight. I couldn't let Aidan Murphy distract me anymore.

"Well, I'd love to chat, but I should get going. I have a lot of stuff to do." *Like fixing the social order of our school.* "Good luck with your Mercedes."

I set off, sipping as I walked. I needed to let the caffeine sink in. I needed to process. Maybe turning him down was the wrong thing to do. He was leaving. Who knew how many chances I would get? But all the lights and buzzing and people in the mall—not to mention my nerves—were crowding in on me. I couldn't think straight.

"Wait!" he yelled as he ran up behind me.

Would he ever give up?

Did I really want him to?

I stopped and stared down at my feet, thinking. What was I fighting against? Maybe now was the time I should just turn around and give him my number, make a time to hang out, and finally find out if Aidan Murphy was just messing with me or if he really meant business. Yes, that's what I would do. I drew in my courage with a deep breath and looked up to meet him head-on.

But then he dangled my shopping bag in front of my face.

"Your shirt?"

"Oh, right." I took it back, feeling my sudden bravado collapse like an inflatable lawn snowman midway through the holiday season. "Thanks."

"You got it."

I paused. Something in his face had slackened—some of the toughness had fallen away, like he wasn't expecting anyone to look at him, like he didn't have a line prepared. I felt my own lips part, my tongue pressing against my teeth. I wanted to say something, but my mind went blank as I stared into his eyes. I don't know how long we were stuck there, but it felt like forever.

"Thanks for sticking up for Mary the other day," I said finally. "That was really sweet of you."

"In the dining hall? Yeah, well, I can't just sit there and listen to that guy say stupid stuff like that. It makes me embarrassed to be part of his tribe, you know?" he said, already turning away. "Well, happy shopping, Colorado."

I nodded and spun around, nearly running into a lady carrying a tray of toothpick-speared cheese cubes. There was nothing to do but hurry onward as I clutched the bag and hoped that he hadn't looked inside.

Instead of hitting more stores as I'd planned, I decided to head straight for Sierra's. She lived in the same part of town as Mary, just a few streets over in a small house on a street where identical white boxes were lined up close together like teeth. The air had cooled some, with the sun having gone down. A tiny sliver of moon was just emerging in the sky, though it was less visible amid all the lights in this area. Dogs barked from somewhere nearby, and a car cruised past, bass-heavy music blaring and rattling its windows.

On the bike ride, I tried to push all thoughts of Aidan out of my mind. I'd felt so silly when he handed me the bag, it was mortifying to think of it now. He had thrown me off with his antics, but I had to focus on the matter at hand. This was about Sierra and returning the favors she'd done for so many others.

I set the bag down, tucked my note inside, and rang the doorbell. Then I ran across the street and positioned myself, panting, behind a giant agave plant. I reached into my bag for a pair of bird-watching binoculars I'd swiped from my mom. I felt like a perv but it was the only way I could think of to really take in the scene from afar. Besides, I told myself, people only came to the door in their underwear in late-night cable movies.

As I watched through the double lenses, a heavyset

bearded man walked to the front of the house and opened the door wide so that a shaft of light fell onto the doorstep. I could see a dog, too, a white terrier nipping at his heels. He turned away for a moment, walking out of the round frames of my view. And then Sierra was at the door, too, dressed in a University of Arizona sweatshirt and jeans. I wondered if she had just come home from one of her many volunteer gigs. She scooped up the dog and held it in her arms as she and the man exchanged a few words. I couldn't read what they were saying, but he handed her the package and then they shut the door.

I waited some more, trying to peer into the windows upstairs, but there were heavy shades blocking my view.

Just as well. No need to get totally creepy.

I imagined the major cringe factor if Sierra caught me peeping outside her house. I put the binoculars away then.

As I headed back to my bike, I heard a squeal of delight, so loud it was audible outside the house and echoed across the street. I'd never heard Sierra make a sound like that.

Another happy customer. I gave myself a high five. Oh yeah, baby. I was two for two. Not bad for an amateur crook.

FOURTEEN

I WOKE UP to a rare rainy day on Thursday—rare for Paradise Valley, anyway. At first, the water prattled slowly on my windows and made lazy silvery trails on the glass. In the hour it took me to shower and drink my tea, the sprinkles had escalated to buckets. This would be a serious test for my hair.

As I was brushing my teeth, there was a knock on the door. Tied up with my toothbrush, I called out to my mom to answer it. She must not have heard me because the person kept knocking and then the doorbell rang a couple of times. I spit out a mouthful of minty froth and scurried out to find Cherise on my doorstep in a bright yellow slicker, hood drawn and tied around her chin.

"I've been out here for like ten minutes," she said, looking peeved, and by now, more than a little damp. "I thought you might want a ride today."

"Sorry," I said. "I thought my mom would get it. She's

usually up by now. But yes, totally. Ride. Love it."

"Good thing I came dressed for it," she said, shaking her head. "Otherwise I'd leave you in the puddles, lady."

I led her into the house through the front entrance hall so I could gather up my things for school. I looked down at my jeans and flats and decided to adapt my footwear for the weather. I was going to need something stronger, like my boots and some socks.

Cherise watched me change, looking impatient. Then I slipped on my army-green rain parka and went to knock on my mom's door to say good-bye. "Mom? I'm leaving now," I yelled. "Cherise is driving me."

I heard her feet padding to the door. She opened it a crack. "Okay. Don't yell. I can hear you."

I leaned in to see her face, which was partially cast in shadow. "Why are you hiding?"

"I'm not. I'm just in my nightgown. Cherise doesn't need to see me like this."

"Hi, Mrs. Fox," Cherise said from behind me.

"You slept so late." I peered behind her into the room, which was completely dark. She had the shades down. The sheets on her bed were all twisted up. On closer inspection, my mom's face looked puffy and red. "Are you okay?"

"I'm fine. Just not feeling well," she gasped. Her voice cracked and I knew then that she'd been crying. As if noticing that I noticed, she brought up her sleeve to wipe her face. Then she forced a smile. "Nothing major.

Sinuses. But I'm gonna go back to bed for a bit."

"We gotta go, Willz," Cherise said. "We're running late."

I looked at her and then back to my mom. Something was wrong. But there wasn't time now to get into it. And not with Cherise here, anyway.

"I'm coming," I said, leaning in to kiss my mother. "Mom, I'll call you during break and check in on you."

"I have to go out to the co-op and then to the art center for a four o'clock meeting, so I'll just see you when you get home, okay? Don't worry about me. I'm fine. Really."

Then she shut the door, closing herself inside.

Even in the rain, it was still oddly sunny and bright out, and the cloying smell of creosote rose up from the ground. We dashed through the raindrops to get into Cherise's car.

"What was up with your mom?" Cherise asked.

"I don't know," I said, my unease deepening with her observation. If she'd noticed it, too, then it must have been obvious. "It seemed like she'd been crying, right?"

Cherise reversed out of the driveway. "But she said she wasn't feeling well. Maybe she was hungover?"

"She doesn't drink, really. I guess she could be sick," I said, thinking of her appearance lately. "But I also think she was upset about something."

Cherise raised her eyebrows. "Like man problems?"

"Maybe," I said, doubtful. My mom hadn't dated

anyone in years, at least not to my knowledge. And maybe not at all since the man whose DNA I carry left us.

"Has she mentioned anyone?"

"No. She *has* been really busy, though, running out a lot to different meetings and things. On the phone with people. Out at night. Now that I think about it, she's been acting weird for a while."

"Maybe it's a secret boyfriend," Cherise said, signaling for the turn out of my neighborhood.

"But why would she keep that secret?" I zipped and unzipped my jacket nervously.

"Lots of reasons. I can think of several off the bat."

"Why are we just assuming this is about a guy, though?"

She adjusted her windshield wipers to catch the intensifying downpour. "Think about it. What would make *you* cry and lie around in a dark room?"

I thought about it. She had a point. "Wouldn't she want my support, though?" The thought of my mom alone and heartbroken caused my own chest to tighten.

Cherise guided us into the school parking lot. "She probably doesn't want to upset you."

"I don't know." I frowned as I unclicked my seat belt. "Something is weird about the whole thing."

"I got it," Cherise said, turning to me with widened eyes. "Why don't we find out for ourselves? Do a little investigation?"

I shook my head. I didn't want to turn my mom's off day into a federal case. Besides, if she didn't want *me* to know what was going on, then she definitely didn't want Cherise to know, whatever it was. "I don't think that's a great idea."

"Don't you want to figure this out? She's your mom, and you're not ten years old. You're practically an adult, Willa. I think, whatever it is, you should at least get a real explanation and know the truth."

Cherise's words hung in the air. My mom and I had always had a fairly laid-back approach to each other's personal lives. I never wanted to meddle too much—not that there'd been too much to meddle in. I wouldn't want her nosing around in my life, either—especially not right now. I had my own secrets, after all. So it wasn't exactly fair for me to expect her to tell me everything.

Still, though, I couldn't shake the sense of disquiet that had been trailing me all morning.

I flashed back to her half-shadowed face in the doorway. She'd said not to worry, right?

Okay, but what were the chances I would be able to do *that*? She was my mom. I couldn't stand to see her so upset. If she was crying in a dark room, I wanted to know why.

And then I thought again of how she'd been acting, all the coming and going, the phone calls. The other night when she'd been standing over my bed. I'd thought it was a dream, but now I really couldn't be sure. *Something* was definitely going on.

"Okay," I said finally. "So what do you suggest?"

"I suggest we do it the old-fashioned way. We follow her."

After school, we called a cab service. We'd thought about just taking Cherise's car, but she'd been to our house enough times that I felt sure my mom would recognize the Jetta.

It had stopped raining by then, though the air still hung heavy with a sickly sweet smell, the sky was still gray, and the road was pocked with glittery puddles. As we waited by the street entrance, I started to feel apprehensive about the whole thing all over again. Were we really going through with this?

Following your mom was pretty weird, as far as after-school activities went. Though technically it was no weirder than some of the other stuff I'd been doing. And Cherise assured me that she'd read enough airport paperbacks that she knew what to do.

The car pulled up in front of us, white with turquoise bands down the middle—not exactly the most discreet vehicle to tail someone in, but it was going to have to suffice. We told the driver to go to my neighborhood first, and had him pull into a driveway at the end of the street.

"Um. Excuse me. Are you ladies going anywhere? This house is for sale," the driver said, turning around.

He was skinny, with a graying beard and a voice like tires skidding on the pavement.

"We need you to follow someone," Cherise said.

He shook his head. "I don't do that kind of thing."

Cherise pulled a fifty out of her lime-green Comme des Garçons zip-around wallet. "Not even for a big tip?"

He cocked his head and blinked slowly. "Okay, girls, if you put it that way. But only for an hour, and that's it. I don't have all day to dillydally."

"We don't want to dillydally, either," I promised him. My mom would be leaving any moment to go to the "art center," or wherever she was really going. "We just need to wait for a Subaru to drive by. Follow it at a distance."

"All right, whatever. Just don't get me in trouble with any sort of illegal activity."

"Us?" Cherise asked, putting her hand on her heart. "Do we look like criminals?"

I had to smile to myself. *Well, one of us does, maybe.*

He harrumphed. "It takes all kinds."

From the corner of my eye, I spotted my mom's car coming down the street. "That's it," I said.

The driver watched her roll to a stop at the end of the street and signal her turn before he reversed out of the driveway. The car hissed against the wet road and puddles splashed against the windshield. He let another car go ahead and then turned out himself.

We rode along past the ginormous houses, some ranches, and a country club, the denim-blue zigzag of mountains ever-present behind them. A few smoky clouds left over from the rain hung around, like they hadn't gotten the memo that the storm was over. As the road opened up into the brown reaches of desert, I gnawed at my thumbnail.

"It's cool," Cherise said, instinctively sensing my anxiety. She was good like that.

But what if it wasn't? The back of my mom's head seemed so small from this distance. I had a fleeting thought that we were going down a bad path. What if we saw something we weren't supposed to see? Did I really want to see her with some guy?

"She's turning left," Cherise announced.

The cab turned left onto one of the main thoroughfares, the area of town where the houses started getting closer together. Palm trees swayed over the street, heavier now from the rain. The road was metallic and slick, and the driver's wipers creaked in an irregular rhythm. We passed the community college, an office park, and some hotels, all in matching pink adobe.

"What if she's going to some kind of hotel?" Cherise asked, pinching me.

"That would be very creepy," I said, making a face. "If she's having an affair I'd at least hope that the person had their own place they could go to. Plus, I feel like they only do that in the movies."

"No," the cabdriver piped up. "It happens in real life, too."

I cringed. "Thanks for the input."

The Subaru turned onto an entrance ramp to the highway.

"She must be leaving town," Cherise said.

"That's weird." I frowned.

"One hour," the driver said, following. "I'm not going to California."

"It looks like we're headed south." I rolled up my window as we picked up speed. The heat was stifling, and my anxiety was deepening. Where was she going? "Can you put the air on back here?"

A few minutes later, she signaled again. She was exiting at Scottsdale. What was she doing in Scottsdale? We'd never been to Scottsdale together.

"My aunt lives around here," Cherise said.

We drove through an intersection with shopping plazas on either side, stacked signs listing dozens of stores. When she turned left, a huge expanse of parking lot and a familiar red-and-white bull's-eye came into view.

"I don't know what kind of game you girls are playing, but it just looks like this lady is running errands," the driver said.

"I don't get it." Cherise tapped on the window with her finger. "There's a much closer Target in Paradise Valley. Why would she come to this one?"

"Maybe they're having a special sale here or something?" I suggested.

"But they have everyday low, low prices," she recited.

"No, wait, that's Walmart."

"Are you done now?" the driver asked.

"Keep going," I said. I just wanted to make sure, and I had an instinct we would see more if we waited. "By my count, we have twenty-five minutes left on our clock."

The driver sighed and pulled into the parking lot behind her.

"Don't park really close. Maybe behind that truck," I said, pointing.

It was hard to see from where we were, but my mom seemed to be leaning over, possibly looking into her purse. Was she looking for coupons? Did she have something to return? A prescription to fill? It was possible she didn't know there was a closer Target. We were still new in town, after all.

Then she got out of the car, clutching her purse. We watched her walk a few spots over to a silver Nissan with California plates. A man in a suit climbed out of the driver's side.

"Just what I thought. That's why she's coming to this Target. *Hell*-looo. The booty's on special."

I punched Cherise's arm. "Shh."

My mom and the man were huddled together talking. I couldn't get a good look at him—we were too far away—but he appeared to be of medium build, a good head or so taller than her, with brown hair that was graying at the temples. He put his hand on her back, as if guiding her, and she got into his car on the passenger side.

Okay, that was it. I needed to get a better look and I wasn't going to see squat from here. I opened the car door.

"Where are you going?" Cherise hissed.

"Wait here for a minute," I said, tense with momentum, like a predatory animal about to strike. Only I was not at all graceful and I had no clue what I was doing.

I danced between parked cars, trying to hide myself as I moved closer. I settled behind a Ford Focus parked next to the man's car, and I crouched down by the wheels. I peered up through the Focus's windows and saw my mom nodding as the man talked. Their interaction looked familiar, as if they'd known each other for a while.

He was attractive in a bland sort of way. Dark eyes. Long thin nose. Not what I would have thought was my mom's type, but then, if she was having an affair, I clearly didn't know as much about her as I thought.

My breath was short and shallow, ripping through my lungs as I tried to listen over it. I wanted some kind of sign, some more information—anything.

Their conversation was getting louder then. I couldn't make out words but I could hear the tone, which was strained and then angry. Were they fighting? Their voices collided and I could hear hers getting higher, as it did when she yelled at me.

Then, my mom opened the car door abruptly and stood up. She slammed the door, a sound that echoed across the parking lot.

She was leaving. And heading my way.

I needed to do something, quick, or she would see me. There was no time to think of anything clever. I had to just move and hope I didn't catch her eye. I danced back around the cars as quickly as I could.

The cab pulled around and met me halfway. I jumped in.

"Go," I ordered. "Go!"

The driver put the car in gear and steered us back onto the road.

"That was a close call," Cherise said, patting me on the leg.

I put a hand on my chest to slow down my accelerated heartbeat. "Did she see me?"

"I don't think so. She looked like she was deep in thought, like she had a destination. She barely looked up at all. So what happened?"

"She's definitely got something going on with this guy, whoever he is." I settled back into the vinyl seat, trying to put together this new information. There was someone in her life that I didn't know, someone she was close enough to that she was fighting with him.

I started to rethink everything. Had she been lying to me this whole time? Was there even an art center or a co-op? Was there a volunteer job at all? Probably not.

It's not like I never expected my mom to date again, but this was such a strange way of going about it. It would have been different if my parents were divorced and I was close to my dad and she didn't want me to feel bad. But I never even knew the guy. So why the secrecy?

"But why do you think they were meeting here?" Cherise asked, as deeply entrenched in the mystery as I was. "And why was she leaving?"

I didn't have an easy answer. Nothing was making sense. "Maybe she just needed to see him briefly. Like this was the only time they could fit each other in."

Cherise slid up to the edge of her seat with urgency. "Willa, I just thought of something. You think that's why she moved you here? Because of this guy?"

Whoa. The thought was a sock in the gut.

"I don't know." Could she have known him before somehow? It seemed more logical than the idea that she moved here and met someone right away. "If that was the case, I just don't know why she didn't tell me before."

"Maybe she thought you wouldn't understand."

"But I would have."

Cherise cocked her head to the side. "Would you have, though? You had to leave your life so she could have hers? It seems pretty unfair to me."

It *was* unfair when Cherise put it that way. Somehow, though, I felt like I could forgive my mom, especially if she was in love with this guy. It had been a long time since she'd met anyone. She deserved to be happy, didn't she?

But that brought up another question. Was she actually happy? It didn't seem like it, at least not from what

I'd seen the past couple of weeks.

"Maybe the guy's married," Cherise said. "And maybe she didn't know if it was going to work out. He could go back to his wife."

I shuddered. "That's gross."

"It happens all the time," Cherise said matter-of-factly.

"It does," the cabbie said.

"Okay, whatever." I could do without the commentary. It disturbed me to think of my mom as some guy's midlife crisis. "I just wish she would tell me the truth."

"You should ask her point-blank."

I looked at her head-on. "I'm going to have to, aren't I?"

So much for our "investigation." I was leaving with more questions than answers. My head hurt from all the guessing, all the theories, all the competing feelings swooping around like dive-bombing birds. I didn't know whether to be angry at my mom for keeping something from me, or sorry that she was alone in dealing with it. She needed me, didn't she? All I knew was that this thing, this secret, was making her miserable.

That had to stop.

FIFTEEN

I WAS IN the bathroom after second period when the harp sounded for morning break. From inside the stall I could hear the door open, and then two girls talking, their voices low and conspiratorial.

"So what are we doing this weekend?" Voice One said.

"The usual," Voice Two answered. "Why?"

"Shane Welcome just asked us to his party. And I think we should go."

As they talked, they definitely sounded familiar but it wasn't Kellie or anyone Glitterati-related. I could tell by their tentative tone and nervous giggles.

I opened the stall door and Sierra and Alicia turned around, apparently startled by the sound. I almost jumped out of my shoes myself.

"Hey, guys," I said, flustered.

They were standing in front of the mirrors, lipsticks in hand. Sierra was wearing the new shirt, and the silvery color brought out the shine in her eyes. I took a moment to commend myself on the choice.

"Hey," Sierra said, and she actually sounded friendly for once. She even smiled at me. Then she did her usual thing of pretending I didn't exist and turned back to Alicia. "So do you think you can make it?"

"Ugh. I have to work."

I went to wash my hands and looked at my own reflection. *Yeah yeah yeah. Blond hair blah blah blah.* I was more interested in the other girls—my eyes kept wandering over to Sierra, taking in the new look.

"Get out of it," Sierra commanded.

"Sierra, you know I can't do that." Alicia flicked at her hairline, studying herself in the mirror at different angles. "I need the hours. Maybe Mary can go with you."

They snapped their purses closed and angled for the door.

"But I want all of us to go. It's all of us or nothing." Sierra was still giving Alicia the full-court press as I followed them out of the bathroom and back into the hallway. Then she tried a lighter, teasing approach. "Jed Sampson will be there."

"I can't. Don't try to tempt me. Besides, I have nothing to wear," Alicia said. They broke into Spanish then, and it was the last thing I could hear before they turned right to head for the courtyard for break.

So they were invited to a party. Nice one. I cracked my knuckles with satisfaction.

Kellie and Morgan Whitney were standing by their lockers around the corner and as soon as I was in grabbable proximity, Kellie pulled my arm. "Do you *see* that?" She gestured toward Sierra and Alicia. "Something crazy is going on around here."

"What is she wearing?" Morgan spat through her thin lips. "I mean, I almost bought that shirt myself."

"They're, like, going to the courtyard now," Kellie said, affronted by the mere possibility. "They *never* hang out in the courtyard for break."

The courtyard was exactly what it sounded like, a pretty shaded place where people held court, usually the most popular kids who sat on the six-foot adobe walls and dangled their expensive shoes over the people walking by. It was the territory of the Glitterati and all of its social equivalents in other grades.

I shrugged at their outraged faces and smiled as sweetly as I could muster, though I felt a much less innocent smile threatening to pop through. "I don't know, Kellie. Maybe they just felt like a change."

It was like clockwork. For the third morning in a row, I watched Morgan Whitney get out of her BMW, beep it locked, and drop the key in the side pocket of her leather jacket.

That was something you learned right away as a thief. Everyone had their patterns, their rituals. Take Cassidy Greene, for instance. Right now she was hopping out of her mom's Saab. Every day she took fourteen steps to the front door. Every day she smoothed the front of her blazer before going into the building. (She was the odd Prep student who opted to wear what looked like a school uniform even though we didn't have one.) And every day she seemed to mumble something to herself—a chant or an affirmation of some kind, I couldn't be sure.

Even Aidan had his routine. I couldn't help but notice that he always had a cup of coffee in his hand as he came out of the driver's side, and he chugged the last of it standing by his car. Then he crumpled up the cup and shot it into a trash can on the edge of the parking lot. When he made it, he cheered for himself, which I found kind of cute.

Okay, it was absolutely, straight-up adorbs.

When Morgan was far enough away, I made my way toward her car and peered in. She'd left her aviators on the passenger seat, along with her iPod touch. A bunch of change and singles were stuffed into the cup holder between the front seats. And there was still a Gucci double-G scarf wedged between the front passenger seat and the door. She must have tossed it off her neck at some point, and it dangled tantalizingly. Somehow, for three whole days it had gone unnoticed, leading me to conclude that she probably didn't really need it after all.

I was three weeks into my equalizing mission, but this would be my first official car break-in. In preparation,

I'd consulted with Tre at the park earlier in the week.

"I need to go deeper," I told him. "I need to get into a car."

He put his hands on his knees and shook his head. "You're getting crazier by the day, Willa."

"Seriously, I need to know," I pleaded. I had to help Alicia and I needed more tricks to do it.

Tre's advice was to do it the old-fashioned way. "I can show you how to shimmy the lock with a coat hanger, but that's for a 1990 Hyundai parked on the street. If you're going for a more expensive car, there's no way you can get around the alarm," he'd said. "You're gonna have to pick the key out of a pocket. It'll take more observation on your part, but trust me, it's the best way."

Nabbing Morgan's key would be fairly easy for me at this point. She walked around with her chest so prominently pitched forward that she seemed to leave her pockets behind. Plus, I'd had some pickpocket experience with Nikki, and that had gone swimmingly. And I had one very significant tactical advantage: As a sophomore and a new kid, I was relatively invisible to Morgan. She talked to Kellie but she still had yet to truly acknowledge my presence.

On my way into the building, I saw Aidan pulling up in his Mercedes, head-banging to the strains of doom metal blaring through the windows. Sure enough, when the engine was cut, he got out, stood up, and gulped down his coffee. I eyed up his G550 longingly—I knew he had to have some good stuff in there. Cherise told me he drove around with at least six computers in his car, in varying stages of functionality. And it was obvious he had tons of cash.

Tempting, but no. He was too close. I could never pull it off—not with the way my body reacted every time I got a whiff of his soap. I was bound to screw it up somehow. Besides, I remembered what he'd said about Mary. He might have been Glitterati by birthright, but he was on the right side of things when it counted. I smiled a little to myself as I watched him from afar—he had no idea, but he was off the hook.

At lunchtime, I prepared to make my move. Morgan never ate, and maybe that was why she was so pissy all of the time. I followed from a distance and watched her enter the library with Caitlin Jordan, a model-like waif with a light-brown shag haircut. They usually sat there and pretended to do work, paging through fashion magazines tucked in their notebooks. Morgan took off her jacket and hung it on the back of her chair. I made my own way inside, sat down at a nearby carrel, and waited. They were whispering and giggling to each other.

C'mon, I thought. *I don't have all day to watch you guys gossip. One of you needs to get up. Bathroom. Water. Anything.*

But whatever they were laughing about, it was so entertaining that neither of them was making a move.

Morgan was leaning in, her auburn hair tucked behind her ear. She gestured with her hands, making some bulbous shape in the air. I imagined it had to do with another girl's butt.

All right, wenches. I can outwait you.

I pretended to read myself, watching them in glimpses. Besides the anorexics and the hardest of the hard-core students, the library was pretty empty during lunchtime. Even the librarians had pulled away from their front desk to the office behind it, where they were eating sandwiches.

Sandwiches. My stomach grumbled. It was Vietnamese day in the dining hall and they were serving the noodle soup I loved. If there was one thing I loved about Prep, it was the food. But there wasn't time for eating today. *Note to self: Next time pack lunch when planning midday surveillance.*

And the way things were going, it seemed like I wasn't going to get my shot at Morgan's stuff today. In which case I was going to have to hold out at least a week because I couldn't risk it again tomorrow.

It wasn't the worst thing, I told myself. Justice had no deadline. Morgan was still going to be spoiled and horrible tomorrow. And Alicia would still be happy to get something on her doorstep. *But the party*—if she was going to go to that party, she needed something sooner.

No, I couldn't give up yet. I was so close now. I could

almost feel an ache in my limbs. I was practically craving it.

Caitlin reached into her pocketbook for a piece of gum and slid one across the table to Morgan.

No, ladies. A stick of Orbit *does not have enough nutritional value to sustain you through a school day.*

Then the harp rang. I had to get to trig within ten minutes or I was going to be marked late, and there was a quiz. Never mind that I was dabbling in crime—I still had a scholarly reputation to maintain. Morgan and Caitlin would probably be leaving soon, too. *Oh well,* I thought. *You win some and you waste some lunch periods.*

But then, a break.

They both got up to go to the front desk. I heard the ding of the bell as they called the librarians forth from their office caves. Were they actually returning books? I peeked around the carrel wall to see that both their table and the jacket were left unattended.

My body prickled with energy and fear, the anticipation of a risk about to be taken. *Now.*

I picked up my notebook and sauntered toward their table like I was heading for the door. My heart lurched. I briefly glanced over my shoulder in their direction. They were still talking to the librarian, and Caitlin was handing her an ID card.

Morgan's jacket was finally within my grasp. I dropped my hand. The leather was smooth and butter soft—it felt like the cows had been worked over by a hundred massage therapists. Beyond that was the satiny interior of the pocket. My fingers quickly found and closed around the square plastic casing of the auto-lock fob. I snatched it up and kept walking on out of the library, like it was my job.

Which, in a way, it was.

Alicia was going to that party; there was no question now.

I'd planned Morgan's jacking for this particular day because my last class was a free period. I circled around the rows of cars. There were several BMWs in the lot, but only one had that particular constellation of loot on the front seat and only one had a Swarovski-crystal-studded license-plate holder that said PRINCESS. I looked around again to make sure no one was watching, and clicked the Unlock button. The lights flashed twice and I heard the door release.

I opened the passenger-side door and went straight for the scarf and sunglasses. Tom Ford, very nice.

And what's this?

In the beverage holder was a pair of diamond stud earrings. I snatched those up and slipped them into my pocket.

I briefly considered grabbing the iPod and some of the loose money in the passenger-side door, but I didn't want to be too greedy. Morgan had kindly provided me with more than enough already, hadn't she? I shut the door, stuffing the scarf and sunglasses into my backpack.

Woo-hoo. Somebody needs to be taping this, because this is some graceful thievery right here.

I walked around the driver's side and bent down to set the key on the ground next to the door. After discussing it with Tre, I'd settled on this strategy, which seemed a hell of a lot easier than trying to return a key to someone's pocket without them noticing. This way, it would look like she had dropped it herself, and she—or someone else—would find it eventually.

"Hey!" someone yelled.

I turned around and a teacher I recognized from the science department was behind me.

I swallowed hard, wishing desperately that I could push down the terror that had flared up inside me like acid.

"What are you doing?" he asked. He had longish hair pulled behind his ears. He was wearing large glasses and his eyes looked buggy and bloodshot behind the lenses.

Think fast. . . . Now smile. Good. "I was walking by here and I happened to see this key on the ground. I'm not sure who it belongs to, but I thought I should pick it up."

His face, which had been pinched into teacherly suspicion, relaxed a bit. "Aren't you supposed to be in class?"

"I have a free period," I said. "And actually I wasn't feeling that well so I thought I'd come outside for a little bit of air."

"I see. Well, maybe you should visit the infirmary. In the meantime, I'll take that for you. Somebody will definitely be looking for it."

In a way, I reminded myself, I could've been grateful that he was finishing the job for me, returning the key to Morgan. I handed it over and walked back toward the school building.

I would go to the infirmary to escape suspicion. It was true in any case that I didn't feel well. My head was spinning, my chest tight. My body was giving me away. Maybe the nurse could give me something. But what I really needed was *Yoga Breathing for Kleptos*.

SIXTEEN

LESS THAN A week had gone by when I found myself hanging out in the parking lot again. Only this time it was a Wednesday morning, and I was meeting Cherise. We were running late for homeroom, so that by now most of the morning bustle had died down, leaving just us, the luxury cars, and VP's version of derelicts, which were shorthaired lacrosse players with slightly negative attitudes. Compared to my other schools, this place was seriously lacking in the degenerate department. It occurred to me, with some satisfaction, that I was probably setting a new standard for VP shade.

Cherise was leaning against the bike rack, her bag slung over one shoulder, and her car keys in the other hand. She was jiggling them impatiently. "Any day now," she said. "We don't want to miss the character lecture. What is it this week, persistence?"

"Integrity," I said, looking up from my crouch.

"Whatevs. Not like we need help in that department." She handed me a piece of gum without me asking. A true friend, if you ask me. "Are you going to Nikki's today?"

"I'm not sure," I said, sliding the cable around the down tube and winding it through the wheel rim.

"I feel like you've been MIA lately. You haven't come shopping with us in a while."

I stiffened. For weeks I'd been maintaining the guise that I was still part of the Glitterati without actually spending much time with them. I had been worried these sorts of questions would start popping up. Now Cherise was looking at me intently and I knew I owed her an explanation. "I've been busy with stuff. It's nothing against you, at all . . ."

"I know," she said, but by the look in her eye I could tell that she was still taking it personally. "But I miss having you around."

"I'll come by today," I promised. I stood up and rearranged my striped boatneck, which had gotten twisted from the crouching, and popped the piece of gum in my mouth.

As much as I wanted to avoid hanging out with the Glitterati, I didn't want to avoid Cherise or offend her in any way. She was my best friend at VP and I wanted to keep it that way. If that meant a little time at Nikki's house, then so be it.

As we crossed the courtyard we saw Alicia Gomez sitting on the wall, high heels clicking together. Our eyes traveled up in synchronized wonder. She was wearing a pencil skirt and a sexy Proenza Schouler wrap top that accentuated her curvy figure, care of *moi*. Two guys from our homeroom were sitting on either side of her, clinging to her every word, bug-eyed and entranced. Even Cassidy Greene, who was standing nearby with one of her peppy, high-achieving friends, seemed to be staring.

Cherise gave me a sidelong grin. "Looks like the fashion bug is catching. Kellie's not going to like this."

"No," I said, trying to suppress my giggles. "She's really not going to like it at all."

"Excuse me, ladies." A voice boomed behind us, followed by a boxy-shaped man in a navy-blue police uniform. He brushed past us into the building. "PD coming through."

I stopped in my tracks and clutched at the straps of my backpack, making an *x* in front of my chest with my arms.

Oh my God. Police. What do I do?

"What's that all about?" Cherise asked, her eyes lighting up. Her paperback brain was probably already trying to solve a mystery.

My pulse was doing loop-de-loops, but I shrugged like I had no idea. I was pretty sure they were here for me, whether or not they knew it yet.

But maybe I was wrong. Maybe Aidan had finally pulled that big-time stunt of his. But if he had, wouldn't the entire school population be talking about it already? Word traveled fast around here, especially because everyone had a smartphone practically glued to their hand. I had to calm down. I had to think. I had to stop acting like a freak.

Cherise was still waiting for me, holding the door open.

I couldn't just walk in the building, not right now. I had to figure out a strategy. Or at least get myself together.

"Hey, Cherise," I said. "I just realized I need to ask Cassidy something about French."

She gave me a puzzled look. "Now? We're already late."

"I know, but it's kind of important. You can go on ahead." I smiled, and simultaneously prayed that she was buying it. "Meet you inside?"

"Fine," she said a little huffily.

At any other time, that would've bugged me, but I had bigger issues to worry about right now.

There were many other things I would've preferred to be doing after school, like trying to figure out exactly what the police were doing in the halls of VP that day, but I'd promised Cherise I would go to Nikki's, and I liked to follow through on my promises. It was also a pretty good cover—as in, why would I hang out with the girls I was stealing from? Why, indeed?

So there I was in what I had come to consider enemy territory, Nikki's Mediterranean villa with its vaulted ceilings, oriental rugs, and cheesy gilt-framed artwork that probably cost millions. We were camped out in the TV room on her body-swallowing leather couches facing a wall of four flat-screen televisions, which were tuned to *Family Guy,* a fashion show, MTV, and an Ashton Kutcher movie, respectively.

"This show is so juvenile," Kellie said, aiming the remote toward the *Family Guy* screen. "The fart jokes are, like, funny the first three times, but then it gets old."

She scrolled past the local news on channel eight. A reporter in a shiny blouse with a neat scoop of bangs stood in front of a parking lot.

"That's our school!" Cherise gasped. "Wait. Go back."

Kellie changed the channel back and turned up the volume.

"Authorities here at Valley Prep say they still have no leads in the recent rash of robberies, the total of which has reached five and includes pickpocketing, locker ransacking, and car break-ins. But today, new information has them reeling."

"That's right. We saw the cops today, didn't we, Willz?" Cherise said as she nudged me in the shoulder.

Yes we did. My palms were sweating uncontrollably.

"Finally," Nikki said. "I only reported that I was robbed three weeks ago."

The soda I had been drinking threatened to heave out of my stomach. So she knew after all. This was worse than enemy territory now. I was in the belly of the beast! Coming here had definitely been a bad idea.

I quickly glanced at the other girls but they were riveted to the TV.

The reporter turned to Mr. Page, who'd materialized next to her in his usual argyle vest, wearing a face of official concern. She thrust a microphone at him.

"One student has come forward to tell us that they've been receiving anonymous packages on their doorstep, with expensive clothes and accessories. The packages included an unsigned note that said 'a gift for you.' We definitely think there's a connection," he said.

So one of the girls getting my packages *had also* told. I felt like a piano had dropped on me.

This was insane. This was devastating.

This was game over.

Even if they didn't know it was me yet, I had to stop doing this thing—it had gotten out of hand now, and I was going to have to quit while I was ahead.

That is, if I was even ahead. The police could know more than they were saying. I could be a dead girl walking. Maybe I was even under surveillance right now. . . .

I scanned the room. Nothing looked especially suspicious, but how was I supposed to know? They didn't send you a note when they decided to start watching you.

The camera cut to a shot of Cassidy Greene, her blond hair tightly wound in barrettes and her hands clasped together in front of her blazer. She appeared extremely excited to be in front of a camera. "I'm kind of disappointed, frankly, that this sort of thing is going on here. This school has a fine reputation, and I hate to see it ruined by the work of hooligans."

Cherise snorted. "Hooligans? Could she be any more of a lamecakes?"

"It's not funny, Cherise," Nikki shot back at her. "I lost four hundred bucks."

"I'm not making fun of *you*. Besides, how do you know for a fact it was stolen? Are you sure you didn't just spend it?" Cherise asked with a teasing smile.

Nikki narrowed her eyes at Cherise. "I'm *sure*. Why would I make something like that up?"

"You guys, shut your faces," Kellie said, annoyed. "I'm trying to hear this."

The reporter took over again, addressing the camera. "While officials say they don't know whether the crimes are the work of an individual or a group, they say they're concerned about copycat crimes, particularly now that the media has gotten hold of the story."

Oh God, I thought. *This is so much worse than I thought.*

The camera panned to the courtyard, where a small crowd of students stood capturing a day in the life at VP. Then it cut to a shot of Aidan. I gulped in some air.

He was wearing a military-style jacket and smiling at the camera, completely relaxed. Looking totally seks. It was as if he had spent his whole life on TV. "I'm not surprised this is happening, to be frank with you," he said. Beneath him in white lettering flashed the words *Aidan Murphy, Valley Prep student*.

The reporter nodded and prompted Aidan to keep talking. "We have a situation here where they're throwing in scholarship students with students who have a dozen servants and guaranteed trust funds for their unborn children. Naturally, there's going to be some tension. And if the school can't address these issues in an honest way, they're going to come out somehow." I pulled my arms tighter around my chest, feeling Aidan's words encircle me. He totally got it. I felt like he was staring straight into my eyes as he continued talking into the camera. "I think this person stealing—whoever they are—is just trying to exact some justice."

"God, he's such an attention whore," Nikki said.

"Sssshhh!" Kellie hissed for what felt like the fifth time.

"This may be just what the school's officials fear as a worst-case scenario," the reporter was saying. "That a few pranksters will start glorifying this behavior, and excuse what, in the eyes of the law, is still a serious crime. Bob? Back to you."

"What's wrong, Willa?" Cherise asked, turning to me. "You look spaced-out."

"I—I guess I'm just shocked that this is happening." I didn't specify what I meant by "this."

"I'm so pissed," Nikki said, chucking a tasseled pillow at the TV. "I feel, like, violated."

"Those Busteds can't get away with it," Kellie said, standing up suddenly and blowing up a sigh to her bangs. "Look what they've done to Nikki. And who's next? They marched into our school like they owned it, and now they're stealing our stuff. I say we take matters into our own hands."

I stared up at the ceiling, trying to ground myself. I felt the situation—the room—spinning out of my control. I had to speak up now, even if it gave me away. "How do you know it's the Busteds?" I asked, practically choking on the last two words. They were so ugly.

"Who else would it be, Willa? The tooth fairy?" Kellie marched over to her bag and pulled out her laptop. At the same time, Nikki pulled out her phone.

"What are you doing?" Cherise asked, looking over Kellie's shoulder as she tapped on the keyboard.

"I'm posting something, idiot."

"Wait a minute," Cherise said, squinting at the screen. "Did you just log in as admin? The Buzz is *your* blog?"

Kellie whipped around. "Are you *spying* on me?" She let out a strangled sound that was either a laugh or a cluck of disgust. "Good work. You figured it out, Sherlock. I can't believe it took you this long."

I blinked rapidly. So Kellie was not only posting on

this thing—*she was running the entire show.* ValleyBuzz, the source of all evil in our school, was coming directly from her. But why was I even surprised at this point?

"Can you imagine, you guys? One of those girls going through your stuff?" Kellie said, clicking on her mouse and staring into the screen. "Like, think about them rifling through your bag or your car. No amount of dry cleaning would remove the scum. Actually, that's good, isn't it? That's what I'm going to write. I just need to get a photo of Alicia . . ."

"I think there's one on Facebook we can steal," Nikki said, leaning in to look over her shoulder.

Cherise stood up and put on her jacket. "I'm not going to sit here and watch you guys blog. I'm out of here."

"Oh, c'mon, Cherise. You're going to take a stand?" Kellie stared her down. "Against what? *The truth?* That's real mature."

"I'm taking a stand against your obnoxious site. And we don't know what the truth is, do we, Kellie?"

"I'll say we have pretty good evidence. How about those new clothes? Where else would they get the money for them? Don't tell me you believe that lame anonymous-package story?"

"You don't know what evidence is. This is all conjecture. Just because you have it out for these girls for some bizarre reason. Maybe Aidan was right, that someone is trying to even things out." I'd been watching them volley words this whole time, but at the sound of Aidan's name and the mention of his theory, I had to look away from Cherise. "Did you ever think that maybe you started this whole thing with your nasty blog?"

"Me? *I* didn't start *anything.* It's not my fault they don't fit in," Kellie spat.

"You're right, Kellie. Because nothing is ever your fault, is it? There's always someone to take the blame for you," Cherise said, storming out of the room and leaving a wake of angry silence.

I was angry, too. My hands had involuntarily closed into fists. All the screens in the room, the TVs and Kellie's computer and Nikki's phone, were blinding-bright patches of light. Somehow, though, my mind was reading everything with perfect clarity.

I couldn't give up now, could I? I was going to have to do one more hit. Send a message. Set the record straight. There was no way I was going to let Mary and Sierra and Alicia take the blame for what I'd done.

"Are you coming with me, Willa?" Cherise called to me from the other room.

"Yeah," I said, grabbing my bag.

"See, the beauty of having this blog is that I can post about whoever I want," Kellie said quietly, looking at me as I stood up to leave. "When someone bothers me, I just need to write a few words. It doesn't even have to be true—once it's in print it may as well be."

She smiled with eerie calm and I felt her icy tone chill me to the bone.

"But I do have to be careful, because it's easy to ruin people's lives. Too easy, you know?"

I broke away from her fixed stare and headed for the door, the words reverberating in my head. It was a classic Kellie threat, because Kellie was all about getting whatever she wanted.

And that, I thought, *is exactly why you're next on my list.*

SEVENTEEN

JUDGMENT DAY WAS coming. For weeks, there had been anxious whispers in the hallways about end-of-quarter grades. Sure enough, on Thursday my transcript was waiting for me when I got home from school, sitting on the kitchen table in an innocent white envelope. I quickly pulled it out of the mail pile, ripped open the flap, and yanked out the VP-stamped paper inside.

Somehow, in between stealing money and pilfering goods from students, I'd managed to do pretty well in my first quarter of classes. Really well. I traipsed through the house to find my mom on a ladder in her office, changing one of the recessed lightbulbs. I left the transcript on her desk without comment and went into my room. Approximately forty-five seconds later, the squealing began.

"Oh my God, Willa! A three-point-eight? You rocked it!" She appeared in my doorway, a huge smile broadening her face.

We hugged and I felt just how tiny her bones were in her oversized shirt. She was still claiming that she hadn't been feeling well, and that was why she'd dropped a few pounds. I'd asked her repeatedly to go to the doctor and she'd blown me off. I just didn't know what to think.

I sat back down on my bed. "I'm pretty psyched," I said. "Though I guess technically I could have done a little better in trig."

"I'm so proud of you. We need to celebrate."

"Yeah?"

"Put your shoes back on. I was going to make us a salad, but forget that. I'm taking you out to dinner tonight." She went to get changed.

Within an hour we were in the car driving into Phoenix, where there was a Mediterranean restaurant my mom had heard about. It was called Victor's and it was at the foot of the mountains in The Beekman, a fancy resort hotel. Outside, the building was covered in stucco like a Southwestern version of an Italian villa, with flowering vines cascading down the front. Inside, a maître d' in a vest and tie greeted us, leading us across a cavernous room with beamed ceilings and candlelit tables. A Vivaldi concerto played in the sound system overhead.

I frowned at her as we entered. "Are you sure you want to eat here?"

"Why not?"

"It's kind of . . . romantic." As I said it, my mind flashed to Aidan. Ridiculous, right?

Once I'd batted that thought away, I wondered, briefly, whether she'd been here before with someone else.

Like Mr. Tar-Szhay.

She put her arm around me. "Well, it got amazing reviews in the paper and I wanted to treat my main girl."

I beamed at her, happy I could make her so happy. I hadn't exactly been a model citizen lately—not that she knew anything about that, but still, it felt good to be doing something she could be proud of.

We sat down on plush upholstered chairs and the maître d' handed us menus.

"So get whatever you want, okay? Foie gras. Lobster. Steak. Well, maybe we should see what the market price is on the lobster first."

It was great to be out with my mom—it felt like it had been a long time since we'd had a fun night together. We'd both been so busy lately, rushing around and barely having time to talk. But now she looked so relaxed, her face soft and unlined with worry, her eyes shining at me. Was that just about my grades, or was it the look of love—boy-girl love—I saw?

I scanned the menu, which was as heavy as an encyclopedia and as big as the back of my chair, though it only featured a few different choices. I savored each description, trying to drag out the moment. Being here was the perfect distraction from the media circus at school, the scene yesterday at Nikki's, my impending fear that I was about to be busted. All of it seemed far away in this beautiful place.

A server appeared at our table and told us about the specials, which included heirloom vegetables, local beef, and small-batch cheese. Everything had a home and a name, it seemed. My mom nodded approvingly.

"Ladies, can I get you something to drink?"

"A glass of champagne for me," she said. "She'll have a sparkling water."

Our drinks came and we toasted, clinking our glasses. "To our new start," my mom said.

"To our new start," I repeated, feeling a warm rush of excitement. I reached up to touch my necklace, the little bird reminding me of our early days here. It seemed so long ago, really. We were practically two different people now.

The server brought our salads. I dug into mine, which had tiny gems of roasted beets, toasted walnuts, and shaved red onion. The music was soothing and the candlelight set off our table in a butterscotch glow.

"So I want to hear more about what's going on at school. Besides academic domination, what else have you been up to?"

I stiffened. *Oh, you know. Lying. Thieving. Preparing secret packages. Also, following you.*

"Nothing much," I said, uncomfortable, not just because I was leaving out the truth but because we were talking like semistrangers, like she only had part-time custody of me—that was how little we'd seen of each other recently. Weird.

"What happened with those friends of yours? The ones you said were a-holes?"

"We worked it out," I said quickly. "It turned out to be a misunderstanding."

"That's great news. So what have you been doing after school then?"

I felt my easy, contented mood starting to curl at the edges. It didn't feel good to keep so much from her. I'd never had secrets like this in the past. Here she was, so proud of me, and yet she had no idea what had been happening lately. It made even the true things, the good grades and my hard work, feel like a lie.

"Just hanging out, mostly. Studying at the library."

"Mmm," she said, chewing on her salad. "This is so delicious. Did you want to try mine?"

I leaned in to take a forkful, spearing rich duck breast, dried cherries, and a pale frilly lettuce. The textures and flavors mingled perfectly.

My mom took another sip of her champagne. "Usually I think fine dining can be kind of pretentious, but when you come to a place like this, you understand what it's all about. It's just a shame that not everyone can experience it, you know?"

I nodded. I did know. I recalled what Aidan had said on TV. It was impossible lately not to think about this stuff all of the time, not to think about how lucky I was.

I was almost tempted to say something, to tell her what was going on.

But that was no good. I tried to tamp down the urge by gnawing on some more bread.

As if reading my mind, she put down her fork. "You know, I read something in the paper, about some thefts going on in your school. Have you heard anything about that?"

I nearly choked.

Oh no. Not now. Not her.

"Yeah, I heard something. Someone stealing from rich kids and giving things to poor kids." My voice sounded nonchalant but I felt like I was practically heaving out the words, they were so weighted.

My mother raised a curious eyebrow. "It sounds like they've come closer to finding the culprit. I guess one of the items turned up at a local pawnshop."

They were on to me. My left eye started to twitch uncontrollably. The delicious taste of food in my mouth went bitter and sour.

"Oh, did they?" I looked around the room, desperate for an escape. "I think maybe I'll run to the ladies' room now, before our main course comes."

I needed to splash some water on my face. I needed to regroup. I needed to switch lives with someone.

Inside the bathroom, I stood over the marble sink and let the tap run. I looked up and the blond-haired girl in the mirror was sallow, eyes bloodshot, mouth straight and tight. Fear was all over my face.

Okay, get it together.

The water was cool and calming as it touched my skin. Maybe it wasn't as bad as it sounded. I would just stop now, like I'd said before. Forget hitting Kellie. I'd act normal, be extra-careful to cover my tracks, and I'd move on with my life.

I turned away from the sink to wipe my hands, and a fluffy towel was thrust in front of me. "Thank you," I said to the bathroom attendant.

I glanced up, expecting to see an older woman, but it was a girl my age, someone who looked vaguely familiar to me.

"You go to Valley Prep, don't you?" she said. She was chubby and her hair was pulled back into a braid. She was wearing some sort of uniform, a white button-down shirt with a vest. My eyes traveled down to her feet and I saw that she was wearing black sneakers that gapped at the soles.

"Yeah," I said. "Do you?"

"I'm in your history class? My name's Jocelyn. And you're Willa, right?"

"That's right," I said, still trying to place her. Whoever she was, she'd blended into the background. "Nice to meet you."

Actually, there was nothing nice about it. The bathroom was the last place I wanted to be meeting someone—especially someone I was supposed to know already, someone who worked in the worst possible job ever while I was outside chowing down on duck confit.

"So . . . you work here?" I asked, not knowing what else to say.

"Six days a week."

"It's a nice place," I said.

"I'm sure it must be," she replied, and I felt the burn.

"So today was grades day, huh?" It was stupid but I was struggling for something.

Her face twisted up. "Yeah. More like doomsday for me. I think I need a tutor if I want to stay at Prep . . ." she said. Her voice trailed off, and I got the implication: She couldn't afford one.

I thought of Kellie, and what she'd told me at her party. People like her would always succeed because they had the money to cheat their way through. Whereas Jocelyn couldn't afford the help she really needed. It made me sick.

"I'm sorry," I said, patting my hands dry. "It's definitely tough."

She stared down at her pile of towels. "That's life, I guess."

As I stood there I remembered how Mary had once said, "It's just high school." But how, also, in gym class that very morning, she'd mentioned that she'd gotten asked to the senior winter formal. She said she wasn't sure if she would go. I'd made a mental note to send her some extra cash, just in case it was the limo fee or some other cost that was holding her back.

"I'm afraid to say who it is, because maybe it's a big joke or something," she'd whispered in the locker room. But she was bursting to confess. "Okay. It's Bradley Poole."

Bradley Poole was a dark-haired, Polo-sweatered valedictorian who was president of the debate society and the drama club. His parents had started the Poole Foundation, which gave money to the arts and built schools in developing countries. He was as close to a dreamboat as you could get at VP.

Mary, of course, had never mentioned anything about the secret packages she'd been getting. And I was relieved—I wasn't sure if I'd be able to keep a straight face. As it was, it was hard not to smile too much when I saw her excitement. I knew it wasn't the clothes that Bradley liked—Mary was a pretty, sweet, smart girl—but they might have made him notice her.

"Well, you better get back to your dinner," Jocelyn said, snapping me back to reality.

"I guess I should." But the idea of going back to the table and pretending to enjoy my meal was unappealing now. I stood lingering there for a moment, eyeing Jocelyn's tip basket. Was I supposed to give her a tip? I had no money on me. I didn't want her to think I was cheap. I felt a sudden urge to explain myself, that we didn't usually come to fancy places like this, that I'd never really had much money before now—but what good would that have done?

"I'm sorry but I didn't bring any ca—"

"It's okay," she said, cutting me off. She looked as embarrassed as I felt. "See you in history."

One more, I was thinking on my way back to the table. If I moved quickly, I could try to pull off one more. If they were going to catch me anyway, it would be worth it.

When I sat back down at the table, my mom was smiling at me. "How was the bathroom? Did they have nice soap?"

"There's a girl from VP in there," I said. "Working."

"A friend?"

"No, I just met her."

"Well, that's unusual. I wouldn't think . . . " Her voice dropped. What she was going to say was this: "I wouldn't think anyone at VP would be working in a bathroom."

The server set our entrées in front of us: filet for her; fish for me. My mom was cutting into her steak when I saw her eyes widen. She reached forward like she was getting up, but her hands flailed and she knocked over her champagne. The glass exploded into glittering bits on the floor.

I twisted around and saw a man in a dark suit moving toward us. He was wearing an old-fashioned hat with a brim and his strides were long and purposeful. The server was already at my mom's feet, sweeping up the glass.

"Not now," my mom hissed. At first I thought she was

talking to the server, but the man was coming closer. I knew right away he was the man I'd seen in the parking lot.

"This will just take a second," he said quietly but firmly.

"I'm having dinner with my daughter and we don't want to be interrupted," my mom hissed.

He removed his hat and smiled at me, making eye contact for the first time. I couldn't tell what color his eyes were but there was something pleading and insistent in his expression. Then he tipped the hat to her. "Fine. We'll talk later."

When he walked away, my mom exhaled heavily and clutched at her shoulders.

"Who was that?" I asked.

"No one," she said quickly. "How's the bass?"

She was trying to front, but I wasn't having it. "Why did you look so freaked out, then?"

"Just someone I know from the art center, is all."

This was my chance. She'd given me an opening. "Is he someone you've been hanging out with?" I ventured. "Like dating?"

She pulled back. "Me? Willa, I don't really date. You know that."

"But it would be cool if you did. I mean, it would be fine with me," I said.

"Well, I appreciate that. But you know, the time just isn't right. There's a lot going on. I'm not really looking.

No, he's just a guy."

Her voice had a nervous edge to it. I studied her face to see if she was lying to me, but then she took a drink of water and her glass clouded her expression.

She put the glass down. "Why are you asking me about my love life all of a sudden, anyway?"

"I don't know. You've been out a lot lately, and then this guy just shows up and I figured—"

"There's nothing going on, Willa," she snapped. "I would tell you if there were. I hardly know that man. I think he wanted to sell us something."

The mood had changed then. She seemed to retreat. We finished eating without talking, but I didn't have much appetite anymore. Why was she so resistant to telling me anything? Did she think I was stupid? But I knew that I couldn't press her any further. After all, I had secrets of my own to protect. We were safer in our respective silences.

"Another drink, miss?" the server prompted.

"No, thanks," my mom said. Then she asked for the check.

On our way out of the restaurant, I could sense her tensing up again. The man in the suit was standing by the door. Up close I could see he had dark stubble and he was wearing a silver tie.

"Excuse me," she said to him brusquely. The man just nodded and moved out of the way to let us by.

• • •

At home, in my room, I paced back and forth. Who the hell was that guy? Why was he at the restaurant and why was my mom pretending like she barely knew him?

Then, something occurred to me: Could the man be my father?

No, it couldn't be. Could it? But why was he coming over to our table and why was she shooing him away, like she didn't want me to see him?

I sunk down on the mattress, grasping around me for some support. The very thought of it was overwhelming.

All these years, we'd never heard from him. So long as I never expected to meet him, it was like he didn't exist. But what if he was real? What if he lived around here? What if they were in touch somehow?

But why? Why now?

I dropped my head into my hands, rubbed my temples with my thumbs, and stared down into the carpet fibers. I wasn't ready for this.

Then my phone buzzed. A text from Cherise.

Call me ASAP. Big news.

I hit the call button, hands shaking, but as soon as the phone started ringing, I regretted it. I wasn't sure I could take any more news today.

"Cherise, what's up?"

"It's Aidan," she said, breathless. "He got kicked out of Prep."

My whole body went numb, and I was motionless, frozen in shock.

"Willz? Are you there? Did you hear me?"

"I heard you," I said. "I'm just . . . surprised."

But was I, though? I knew this was coming. He'd told me himself. He was *trying* to get kicked out. Well, now he'd finally gotten his wish. And now I'd probably never see him again.

I fell back against my pillows as the weight of the news hit me a second time, and with this wave came a more powerful blow of despair. No, this was way too much.

"That's the crazy thing. Nobody knows what happened. But it had to have been something serious. His family is like *royalty* in this town."

"So he's kicked out for good? Not just suspended or anything?" It all seemed so final.

"Yeah," she said, her tone growing concerned. "You sound upset. I thought you'd be happy. I thought he got on your nerves."

"It's been a long day," I said, huffing out a heavy sigh. I wanted to tell her about the man in the restaurant, but then I thought better of it. I wasn't ready to share with her the possibility that it could be my dad. I needed more time to think through everything. My emotions were springing all over the place. "Cherise, do you know a girl named Jocelyn at Prep?"

"Jocelyn? I don't think so. Are you okay? You really sound weird."

"I'm fine," I said. "But I should probably go. I have some research to do."

I hung up the phone and sat down in front of the computer, my head full of noise. Focus. I needed focus. As I scrolled through the VP student directory and Google search results, clicking here and there to read more, I started to feel a little calmer. I started to lose myself in this work, which was the only escape I knew.

Maybe I couldn't do anything about my mom, or Aidan, or any of the crazy thoughts in my brain, but this was one small thing I could do, and for now, that felt like enough.

EIGHTEEN

"YOU UNDERSTAND I'VE never actually done this myself, right?"

I did. All of Tre's lessons came with this warning, which I took to be like one of those legal disclaimers on commercials ("Please drink responsibly," or "See your doctor if your erection lasts more than six hours"). At this point, it didn't have to be said but I guess he felt the need to let me know he was protecting himself and possibly me. And he definitely didn't want me to know why he had been in a boot camp.

When we first started meeting, I'd wondered about it constantly. I couldn't help it. We'd be practicing some technique, like the Ronaldinho—a Spanish pickpocketing method named for a soccer star, which involved a hug—and my mind would wander. How did he know all this stuff? My money was on some kind of thievery, given all of his expertise in the area. Had he worked with an apprentice? Had he researched it all on the internet? Or was it kind of a mind-meld situation, where, once you were locked up with a bunch of other delinquents, you absorbed all of their tricks?

For a while I'd tried to ask him what I hoped were subtle but leading questions, like, "Wouldn't it be hard to pull off a razor slice in broad daylight?" Or, "Does the hugging really work with total strangers?"

He'd just give me a frown and say, "I wouldn't know. Stop snooping, Willa."

So I had to give it up, because he was never going to tell me, and I no longer cared.

Okay, fine. I was still an eensy bit curious.

Now we were sitting in Tre's car after school in front of the gated community where he lived. It was called Magnificent Estates—the founders clearly hadn't wanted to leave too much to the imagination. I could see through the front gate to a central landscaped garden with a fountain and a shallow pool. A stone-paved street circled around, leading to some houses—there couldn't have been more than five in the whole development—and beyond them, a golf course. Why people around here insisted on building golf courses in the desert and standing around playing in one-hundred-degree weather was beyond me, but there was a golf course everywhere you went, practically. It was a rich-people thing.

"My dad loves to play," he said, shrugging his enormous shoulders inside his polo shirt. "He says it's very meditative. I guess he's been playing with Aidan's dad at some club."

The very mention of his name—like some magic code—made my insides ripple. Ever since Cherise told me he'd been kicked out, I'd been wondering what happened to him and now I couldn't resist pumping Tre for information.

"So do you know the story with that?"

He shook his head. "He's gone—that's all I know."

"But where is he?" I pressed. "Is he at some other school?"

"Haven't heard from him. Why?"

I looked out the window to hide my face. "I don't know. I'm just curious."

"You sound like you've got a thing for him."

"Me?" My voice rose to an incredulous pitch. "No."

He nudged me with his elbow and grinned. "Naw, of course not. Do you want me to ask my dad to ask his dad?"

Major blushing. "No. No. Forget it."

He rolled down his window and we looked at the little metal keypad that gave entry to the gate. Tre got into lesson mode.

"Now, see, if I were trying to get through a gate like this one, I wouldn't bother guessing the code. You'd be here all day. And that's no good."

"So what would you do?" I asked.

He smiled, revealing long laugh lines. "Easy. I'd

program my own code in. For this one, you hit star and then the default, which is two-three-seven-five. Then it lets you put in a new one. But the defaults are gonna be different, depending on the system. You have to do your research and learn the defaults."

Tre punched in the code. The gate swung open. We drove through, arcing around the curving street to turn onto Happy Valley Road. Tre's house sat at the end of a cul-de-sac, behind a few orange trees.

From the outside it was hard to see how big it was—it had been built in the Southwestern style I'd seen so often around these parts: boxy, with white stucco walls studded here and there with wooden beams. Like everyone else in Paradise Valley, he had a pool in the back, surrounded by a cactus garden.

I wondered if he swam in it, or if he just used the concrete deck for skateboarding. It was fascinating to see where he lived, as he'd never talked too much about home. I'm not sure what I was expecting, but that was just it. He was so private I'd never imagined much of anything. And the more time I spent with Tre, the more mysterious he became to me. In a way, that was one of the things I liked most about him. While everyone at VP was busy plastering their intimate secrets all over the internet, he kept to himself.

He parked his Audi in the driveway and we got out.

"Not enough room in there?" I ribbed, waving toward the four-car garage. "Any Bugattis?"

"Nope," he said, giving me a look, like *Don't start*.

"No one's around?" I asked.

"Nah. My dad's at work. Okay, let's take a closer look at what we've got here."

We circled his house on foot.

He showed me the different sensitive points around the building: the motion sensors by the doors and windows; the mounted security cameras by the back entrance; the access control panels. From where we stood I noticed a scooter, leaned up against the back of the house. Tre must have had a sibling living here. It was cute to think of him as someone's older brother. I could picture him being teasing but protective.

"See here, if this was night, that light would go on if I twitched." He pointed. "I was trying to convince my parents to go with the laser system they have at banks but it was a little too expensive."

"Do you worry about break-ins?"

"Nah, not really. My dad's famous, but he's not like Kobe Bryant or anything. He has a bodyguard when he travels anywhere, though. I think it's stupid. No one's coming after him. He's all paranoid."

"Why the lasers, then?"

He grinned. "Ever see *Ocean's Twelve*? That was dope."

I laughed, shaking my head. "Boys and their gadgets."

We went around to the front of the house and crouched in the pebbled plantings, peering up to the roof at the cameras there. Tre pointed out more motion sensors by the entrance.

"Once you know what to look for, it helps you figure out how to get in and out. You can cover a camera up with Vaseline; you can avoid a light sensor. But when an alarm goes off, you can't silence it unless you know the code. So that's when you have to run like hell."

I nodded. "Alarm equals run like hell."

"You usually don't want to bother with the front. It's too visible—unless you have a key. The main thing to remember is to always go out the same way you come in."

"Out the same way you come in," I repeated.

He turned to me, face serious. "Look, Willa, I'm just showing you this stuff because you asked me. I don't recommend you actually doing this. House break-ins are really dangerous. People have dogs, guns, Tasers. You can get seriously hurt. And I'll be honest with you. I don't know if you're on that level."

I drew up my arms in front of me defensively. "That's for me to decide, isn't it?"

"I'm just saying, for your own good. This isn't for amateurs. And it's only a matter of time, with all the news reports—"

He looked up to see if I was still listening—probably waiting for me to protest—but I was too busy looking behind him at the cop car that was driving around the cul-de-sac—slowly. He followed my gaze and turned around.

"That's weird," Tre said, straightening up to take a look. "The county guys usually can't get in here and just cruise around. We've got our own rent-a-cops."

The car went to the end of the street and circled back before parking in front of Tre's house. Tre looked at me. My palms went sweaty and I felt a throbbing urge in my legs to run.

They'd found me. They'd finally figured out who I was.

Tre must have sensed that I was getting ready to bolt because he grabbed my elbow roughly. "Stay cool. We're not doing anything wrong," he said through gritted teeth. "You run now and you'll screw us both, Willa."

The officer approached in his blue uniform with its stripe, shiny like a car. He was wearing mirrored sunglasses and I could see our reflection, the two of us looking small and warped, in the lens.

"Hello," he said. "Mind if I ask what you two are doing back here?"

"This is my house," Tre said pointedly.

"It is, huh? Well, we got a call from some neighbors about suspicious activity with strangers on the street. Can you show me your ID please?"

Tre reached into his pocket for his wallet. The officer barked, "Slowly, please."

Tre, looking extremely annoyed, pulled out his driver's license with exaggerated sloth. I was amazed at his cool. My own insides were threatening to explode all over the landscaped lawn.

The policeman looked down and up at him, squinting to take in the information. "Tre Walker. You're not—"

"—the son of Edwin Walker? Yes, that would be me."

The cop shook his head, looking flustered. "I'm sorry, Mr. Walker. I didn't mean to bother you guys. I just had to follow up on a call. There's been a lot of crime in the area recently . . . you understand."

Tre didn't say anything, but the cop was already retreating out of the driveway and getting back into his car.

"Have a nice day, guys." He waved to us and drove off, engine gunning like he was off to another crime scene—a real one this time, I hoped.

"Jesus," I said when he left, feeling my held breath flow out of me in tremors. I'd started to picture my own mug shot, and it wasn't cute like Lindsay Lohan's.

But Tre wasn't listening. His back was to me, and he was using a key to open his front door. He let it swing open behind him. I didn't know if he wanted me to follow or not, but not knowing what else to do, I went inside, too, trailing him through an atrium with a soaring ceiling.

Tre dropped his keys on the hall table and continued on into the living room, where he sat down on the sofa and immediately turned on the television, staring stonily ahead.

"I thought you said your dad wasn't a celebrity," I

joked. "You could've fooled me. That guy was ready to ask for your autograph."

I tentatively sat down next to him, but he didn't look at me, and he didn't acknowledge what I had said. His body was tensed and coiled on his part of the couch and I could hear him breathing in short puffs through his nose. He was angry. Really angry.

"Tre, I—"

"Forget it," he snapped.

"No, I want to tell you that I'm really sorry. This was my fault."

We didn't say anything for a while. We just sat watching a cartoon about a little kid turning into different aliens with amazing powers. The kid was going around trying to solve crimes, popping up whenever the police needed him on a case to destroy the enemy, or using his disguises to annoy his sister.

During a commercial, Tre started talking, still staring ahead, still without looking at me.

"Sometimes it feels like it doesn't matter. I go to this lame private school, I live in this place. I mean, my dad just signed a three-year, twenty-one-million-dollar contract. But it's still like they expect me to steal their cars and go joyriding, like that's all I can do, you know? Like I'll never change."

On the TV, the little boy morphed himself into a four-armed alien with sharp teeth. I didn't know what to say, because how could I possibly make Tre feel better about things that were totally out of our control, things I didn't know enough about to explain? I wanted to believe it wasn't true, that people weren't like that, but I knew, from the pained tone of his voice, that it was, and they were. So we stayed like that for a while longer and I waited for him to continue. When he did, his tone had changed. It was softer, more personal.

"I didn't want you to know about that joyriding stuff, because it's stupid. It was a long time ago. But you see, once you get a mark like that on your record, it doesn't go away."

I reached out for his forearm and squeezed it gently. "Knowing that doesn't make me think differently of you."

He gave me a slight smile. "That's good. But I'm talking about *you* now. I didn't want to know what your little project was, either—I was trying to stay out of it. It's really none of my business what you do."

That stung a little. I realized then that maybe I wanted him to *want* it to be his business. I wanted him to care, at least. All these days practicing—it had felt like we were in this together, that he wasn't just helping me out because he owed me a favor.

"But I think you need to stop now, Willa. It's all over the news. If you're not careful they're gonna find you."

So he knew. I didn't want to say anything out loud. I had never confessed it to anyone before. I let him finish without saying anything.

"It's only making things worse. I talked to Mary today and she said she's been getting harassing phone calls every night. The other girls, too. People think it's them."

My mouth dropped open in horror. "That's disgusting. These people are so ignorant."

He looked at me intently, his brown eyes vast and serious. "Yeah, but I don't think you can change that."

"But what if I can?" I asked.

"You know, this kind of stuff will always come back to bite you in the ass. Believe me when I say that it's just not worth it. You'd get kicked out of Prep. I'm sure your parents would never forgive you."

The word *parents* pierced me like a dart. As far as I knew, I still just had the one, but that could change at any moment.

Tre was waiting for a response. I just stared at him, zombielike. I knew what he wanted me to say, but I couldn't make any promises at this point. I still had one more job on my list. The fact that they were on my case almost made me want to do it more—I had to get it in while there was still time.

He sighed, shaking his head at me like I was a little kid. "Well, I'm not going back to boot camp. I don't care what happens, Willa. I just can't. So you're going to have to do your thing without me from now on, okay?"

The message was clear: I'd taken advantage of his generosity.

"I understand," I said quietly. I looked into his eyes

with the sudden certainty that this was a good-bye of sorts. I was really going to miss this time with Tre. "You've been superhelpful, and I don't want you to get into trouble. I should probably just get going."

I stood up and got my bag. My bike was back in the school parking lot, but I could walk from here.

On my way out, I turned back to Tre. I figured I had nothing left to lose by asking. "So, joyriding, huh? What was it like?"

His eyes lit up. "Amazing. Total rush, man. It's addictive, too."

"Yeah?"

"But see, if I were you, that's what I'd ask myself. Am I still doing this to help other people? Or am I doing this because it makes *me* feel good? There's a big difference, you know."

I let his question roll around in my head all the way home. As I stared down at the glinting pavement beneath me, the truth of Tre's words hit hard. He was right, of course: I was nobody's saint, and I was certainly not a medieval archer with a heart of gold.

I just wasn't sure I could stop now. This thing had gone too far.

It had been a while since I'd been in my mom's studio. When I got home, she was out, so I took the opportunity to look around. I didn't know what I was looking for—some kind of clue, I guess. Anything, really, that could explain what was happening.

The door was open a crack and I pushed it wider. Her easel was set up by the window, a half-finished desert landscape propped on it, the white of the canvas peeking through in big swatches. It was the same painting she'd started on my first day of school. Now that I thought of it, I couldn't remember the last time I'd seen her working on it.

The bags of shredded documents had long been removed, though I could still see a shred or two under the file cabinet. I pulled on the handle but it was locked. I briefly considered picking the lock, but my attention was pulled toward the closet on the back wall of the room. It was another long walk-in, and my mom had used it to store all of her paintings. I started looking through them, paging through as if skimming a book. Were there any of people in here? Were there any landscapes I didn't recognize? It was possible that the paintings would hold some secrets.

I'd gone through about twenty of them—all of them familiar—when I started to wonder. How come there were so many of them in here? I thought she'd sold dozens of them by now, to her sales agent in New York. There were all those auctions . . . and if she hadn't sold these, what paintings had she sold, then? I held up a small canvas, about five by five, to the light. It had never been signed, and like the painting on the easel, it looked only halfway finished.

The front door opened, and then there were footsteps. My mom was home. Time to look busy. I quickly put the painting down and scurried out to sit at her desk in front of the computer.

"What are you up to in here?" my mom asked, appearing in the doorway. She seemed rushed, like she'd raced home. She was sweaty and she wasn't wearing any makeup. She looked horrible, if I'm going to be honest.

I tried to keep my breath even as I turned to face her. "I was just going to borrow your computer for a sec, if you don't mind. Mine is acting funny."

"Funny?" She stared at me like I was speaking in another language, like her brain couldn't quite receive the message I was transmitting.

Don't ask for details, I thought. "Just, off."

I didn't need to worry, though, because her eyes were hardly registering what was going on. Her mind was somewhere else. It had to be that guy again.

"What's wrong with it?"

I shrugged and smiled a little. "I don't know. It's a mystery."

"Maybe you should get that looked at," she murmured, and wandered absently out into the hall.

"Yes," I said. "I probably should."

NINETEEN

WITH NO MORE lessons from Tre and nowhere to go after school, I decided, the following afternoon, to take a long bike ride and try to clear my head. It was deep autumn, and the air was cooling off some, or at least releasing its searing grip of death. I pedaled down the school driveway and out onto the road. This late in the day, the sun was disappearing behind the mountains, leaving long shadows between me and the pavement.

At this point, I had some known knowns. (1) My mom was lying to me about the man in the suit, and maybe about other things as well; (2) The police were getting closer and they were probably only a few steps away from catching me; (3) Tre was no longer going to help me.

Then there were the known unknowns. (1) What exactly was going on with my mom?; (2) Had I done enough, really, to help the less fortunate kids at Prep?;

(3) If not, could I pull off one last job?

I probably should have been worrying about whether I could survive much longer at Prep myself, but my other concerns seemed more immediate.

I'd gone about four miles when I saw some people in orange jackets gathered on the side of the road. As I neared I recognized one figure in the pack. Aidan Murphy. He was holding a trash bag and picking up old cans and potato-chip bags. Yep, there was the mop of hair, the chiseled face.

Holy Hotness.

I braked in front of him, practically flinging myself off my bike with the sudden movement.

"Fancy running into you here," I said, though the only thing that was fancy about it was the way my heart was threatening to jump out of my mouth.

He smiled, but only partially. "What's up, Colorado?" The orange was a strange look for him, but from the neck up he seemed very much the same, with an extra layer of tan that made him glow even more gorgeously.

"What are you doing here? I mean—"

He interrupted me, holding up an open palm. "It's exactly what it looks like. I'm doing my community service."

So it was big, his transgression that got him kicked out of school. He was being lumped in with criminals. Feeling a pang of worry, I took a step toward him. "Are you okay? Is everything okay?"

He nodded, closing his eyes for a moment. Like he was mentally calculating something, or maybe just blocking out the sun. "Yeah. I'm out of there, finally. I did what I had to do."

I couldn't imagine all that he had been through, but it seemed to be serious. At least his face was telling me that it was. And for Aidan, that was weird.

"Did it have to be so drastic?"

He looked at the ground, then back to me, with a brief flick of the head.

"You're not going to tell me, are you?" I asked, clasping my hands in front of me.

"I can't. You know that."

As he spoke his voice was quiet and his eyes were apprehensive, no longer staring at me squarely as they had in the past.

I used to find that stare unnerving; now it was strange to see him without it. I remembered him that day at the mall, bragging and being adorably pompous. I was looking at a different person now. Whatever had happened between then and now had changed something for him, I felt certain of that. He looked more vulnerable here on the open road.

"How long have you been out here?" I asked.

"Today? About four hours. Only a hundred and ninety-six left to complete."

He smiled weakly at his own joke and then he wiped the sweat off his brow.

I felt sorry for him, that he was dealing with this on his own. I didn't know much about his family, but from what he'd told me it didn't sound like they were the cheerful, supportive type. I had the sudden urge to do something for him, to take care of him. "So you'll be here for a little while then?"

He nodded. "Until five."

"Be right back," I said. "Don't go anywhere!" The last was a joke but he only gave me that faint smile in response.

I got back on my saddle and rode on to the nearest convenience store, where I bought an extra-large iced coffee. Then I biked back to him, just a few yards farther down the road from where he'd been earlier, and handed the coffee to him. His eyes lit up instantly as he took a big gulp, downing half of it.

"You didn't have to do this," he said, shaking his head.

"I wanted to."

"I mean it. I'm really—" He looked around to see if anyone was watching us, and stepped closer. I could barely look at him, he was that close. He took my chin between his thumb and forefinger. Everything else seemed to slip away—the street, the other guys in orange jackets, even the omnipresent Arizona sun. Then he leaned in and brushed my cheek with his lips. They were soft and smooth against my skin. A sensation like an electric shock ran through me to my nerve endings.

"—thankful?" I squeaked.

"Yeah. That."

We stood looking at each other for a moment. An older man behind him blew a whistle. He turned to look, then shrugged a little reluctantly. "I think you should probably go. I'm not supposed to have visitors here."

"Okay," I said, standing up straighter. I realized that I'd been digging my fingernails into my palms the whole time, probably leaving permanent indentations. "See you . . . soon?"

"Yeah," he said, but he didn't say when or how. He was probably in no position to make any plans at this point, I told myself. So really, I thought, as I rode away past the rest of the line of guys in orange jackets, my body still reeling from his touch, I had no way of knowing.

Later that night, one of Nikki's mass emails was waiting for me in my in-box. Subject line: *Have u seen this?*

Below was a link to the Buzz, and photos of Alicia, Sierra, and Mary. I recognized them from Sierra's Facebook page. They'd looked so cute and happy there. But the faces were Photoshopped onto obese naked bodies, with rolls of flesh hanging out everywhere. Scrawled across their faces were the words *dirty thieves*. Below it, the text of the post said:

> We all know who's responsible for the VP crimes. Just look around at the Busteds' new wardrobes. If you want to see these lowlifes punished, tell Mr. Page

you've seen them in the act. Anyone else have any evidence? Leave your comments below.

There were already around thirty comments of people claiming to have seen them stealing firsthand. I scanned the page quickly: A few said they'd seen locker break-ins, while another poster said they saw Alicia stealing a handbag in the dining hall. *Liars,* I thought. Talk about dirty. I couldn't believe anyone would just make this stuff up.

I sucked in a breath. I was racing against the clock. If these people were already forming a virtual vigilante mob, I had to hit Kellie's house so that everyone knew the truth. And I needed to do it before it was too late.

TWENTY

"I'M SO GLAD you called," Kellie said as she adjusted the straps of her silver bikini top. "I was dying of boredom today here by myself. Nikki's working on a history paper and Drew has some family thing. Everyone else was watching football."

Thank you, Kellie. As always, you have made me feel so lucky to be here. Glad to know that I was your first choice, that it was me you really wanted to hang out with and not just any person to fill your hot tub and make you seem like less of a loser.

Now, where was I?

5-8-2-6-1, 5-8-2-6-1, 5-8-2-6-1.

It was only five numbers to remember. It would be easy enough if I kept repeating them in my mind like a little mantra. I sank deeper into the hot tub and let the bubbles ripple over my back and shoulders. The hot water and steam felt great against the cooling air. It was finally a manageable temperature in Paradise Valley, a temperature where I could wear layers, where my bike seat didn't singe my butt, where I didn't worry about the welfare of little fluffy dogs on the street. It was a perfect evening, actually. If I could only tune out the sound of Kellie's pinched, snotty voice, I could focus on memorizing the passcode to her security system.

5-8-2-6-1, 5-8-2-6-1, 5-8-2-6-1.

The house was so well protected that she had to enter it each and every time she went through the door. The beauty of it was I didn't even have to ask. When I got up to get us some Coke Zeros, she told me the code outright. Five numbers and I was in. A nice little practice run.

Maybe I should have felt guilty, sitting in Kellie's hot tub as her guest, while daydreaming about robbing her blind. And a tiny little part of me did. It wasn't a very friendly thing to do. It certainly didn't fit into the Valley Prep code of conduct.

But then I reminded myself that this was Kellie Richardson, after all. As I learned a few short weeks ago, she lived to torment people. She'd bullied them every day from the comfort of this hot tub and laughed at their expense. And while the rest of us were studying hard, she was paying someone to do her work for her. Yup. She had what was coming to her.

And there were Mary, Sierra, and Alicia to think about—I could get them off the hook. And Jocelyn. I could give her the ultimate gift package after this job. Or cash for a tutor.

It wouldn't be all that easy to get in when no one was here, of course. There was a gate to contend with, and security cameras, and sensors. If Tre's complex seemed tough to crack, Kellie's house was like the Mount Everest of break-ins.

"This weekend has been so beat. I don't know what's going on, but it's like if I don't throw the party, it doesn't effing happen. I'm so sick of everyone mooching off me." She lifted her toes out of the water and examined her Barbie-pink pedicure. "Thank God I'm going up to UA next weekend. Chip said that the Fiji Islander is going to be the biggest party before winter break."

"What's that?" I asked, feigning interest as I trailed my hands through the swirling water. And who the hell was Chip? Not like it mattered.

"It's a frat party?" she half asked, as if she was questioning whether I was really that stupid. "Phi Gamma Delta? God, Willa. Sometimes it's like you came from another *planet*."

I forced out a phony laugh that, in another situation, might have been confused with the cluck of chickens going to slaughter. No biggie. It was easy to swallow my anger now that I had the code.

"*Any*way . . . I missed it last year. I had to go on some stupid spa vacation with my mom. I was so bummed. They get a ton of bands and build a huge hut and fill it with sand. I just bought a killer Missoni bikini to wear. I'd invite you but Chip said he only has a couple tickets left."

"Mmm," I said.

She narrowed her eyes and waved a hand in front of my face. "Hello? Am I talking to myself here?"

"No. I'm just listening."

Actually, I was trying to figure out how I'd scale her stone wall without anyone noticing.

"Well, you seem totally zoned out."

5-8-2-6-1, 5-8-2-6-1, 5-8-2-6-1.

"Sorry," I said, tuning in. I was going to have to pretend to care, at least as long as I sat here.

"Have you talked to Cherise at all?"

"A little bit," I said, stiffening at the mention of her. I definitely didn't want to go down this road.

"After the way she stormed out of Nikki's the other night, it really makes me wonder, you know? Like, who my real friends are."

"I'm sure she's your real friend," I said. I wasn't trying to kiss up. I genuinely believed Cherise cared about her. "She was just upset."

"I don't know. She's been so moody lately. No offense, but ever since you got here it's like I've seen this different side of her. I blame you, Willa." She laughed loudly, throwing her head back, and her diamond stud earrings glinted at me. "JK."

"Don't give up on her," I said. As much as I despised

Kellie, I wasn't here to drive a wedge between her and Cherise. Though I did hope that Cherise might come to her own conclusions someday and realize she didn't need the Glitterati.

"We'll see." She stretched her arms lazily overhead before plunging them back into the water. "Well, anyway, friend stuff is boring. Let's talk about Aidan Murphy. He was totally flirting with me before he got kicked out of VP. Like playing footsie with me under the table at the dining hall. Remember the day that sleaze Mary came to school in that tired gold dress?"

Oof. That was the thing about Kellie. She always knew how to get you where it counted. "He was?"

"Yeah, it was so cute. Actually, *he's* been looking supercute lately, don't you think? Sexy, even. I invited him over last night but I guess he was busy. Maybe he was grounded or something for whatever prank he pulled. I mean, I know he's not seeing anyone. Do you think he's seeing anyone?"

"Not that I know of," I said, gritting my teeth so hard I was probably going to need headgear. I was thinking of how he'd kissed me, which, of course, I'd never tell her. She would almost certainly ruin the memory for me, one way or another. *Not Aidan. Of all the guys she could tramp on . . .* "What about Chip?"

"What about him? We're not exclusive or anything. Ooh, I have an idea. Let's call Aidan and put him on speakerphone."

"I don't think so. That's kind of . . . middle school," I said, trying to appeal to her inner snob. In my experience, speakerphone was never a good idea. I didn't want to be pulled into Kellie's games. Not now. Or ever, really.

"Oh, come on. Don't be such a bitch, Willa. It'll be fun. Nikki and I do this all the time." She already had her phone out and was paging through for his number.

I cringed at the word *bitch*. If only she knew what I was really thinking. I had to play along if I didn't want her to suspect anything.

She dialed his number and clicked on the speaker button so the ringing echoed across the hot tub. I hugged my knees into my chest, anticipating all of the possible scenarios that could follow. What if he thought we were making fun of him? Or worse, what if he really *was* flirting with her? I'd feel like such a fool if I believed for one second that he and I shared something special, even though I had no idea what that "something" was. Maybe he wouldn't pick up. I hoped he wouldn't.

"Hello?" Aidan answered, his voice kind of soft, like he was waking up from a nap.

"Aid, it's me, Kellie," she crooned. I watched her face instantly go all flirty and fluttery, as if he were in the hot tub with us.

"Hey, Kellie."

Was he happy to hear from her? I couldn't tell.

"And Willa's here. We're in my hot tub," she trilled suggestively.

"Hey, Willa."

"Hey," I called out, trying to sound normal, even though I was resisting the temptation to dunk my head under the water.

Instead, I stared into the blue frothy abyss. I'd been savoring my memory of him from the day on the road, replaying it over and over like a tiny little movie in my head, and I didn't want to lose that good lucky feeling. But if it turned out he liked Kellie, it would all mean nothing.

"What are you up to?" Kellie asked. "Wanna come over?"

And now, a third weird possibility presented itself: What if he thought I was putting Kellie up to this because I was too shy to call him myself or something? Ugh, that would be horrible.

"I can't, Kell. I can't leave my house. And I'd invite you guys here but I'm not allowed any visitors." His voice was suspended in the air between us. I really missed him, I realized. I wished I could see him. Only not here and not now.

"Really? You're actually going to stay in?" Kellie said in disbelief. "I never thought you were the type to play by the rules."

"Yeah, well, it's kind of different this time," he said.

"Are you sure?" she pleaded. "Don't you want to see us? Two girls in our bikinis?"

That was it. I had to jump in. "C'mon, Kellie. We

shouldn't pressure him if he's already in trouble."

She shot me a dirty look and then pouted at the phone in her hand. "So when will you be free again?"

"I don't know," he said. "I'm pretty much grounded. But have fun. Talk to you later. Bye, Willa."

I breathed a sigh of relief as she hung up the phone. That was one awkward and potentially upsetting moment averted.

"That was lame," she said. Then she glared at me. "Why'd you have to start acting like his mother? I mean, he might have changed his mind if you hadn't said anything."

"I just felt like you were coming on a little too strong." Then I rushed to clarify myself. "I mean, he's the kind of guy who's into a challenge, so I thought you might want to tone it down."

The words were actually painful to say, they were so false. The idea that I would be trying to help fix up Kellie and Aidan was ludicrous. But my true feelings—about him and about her—were so dangerously close to the surface now, I needed to say whatever I could to try to shut down the conversation.

"Whatever." She let out a noisy breath from the back of her throat. "If I need your help, next time I'll ask."

She seemed to buy my excuse, and that restored peace, or at least quiet, to the hot tub. But there was something else bothering me. All along, I'd been stealing with what I liked to think was a good purpose in mind. Of course, Tre was right. The feeling of going after someone's stuff, of actually getting away with it, was a high in itself. But I'd never felt too strongly about my victims. I was stealing for people, not against them.

This time it was like I *had* to rip off Kellie. Like I needed to. I wanted her to know that she wasn't better than me, or Mary, or Sierra, or Alicia—or anyone else. And, okay, maybe I wanted to torture her a little. The question was: Was it worse to do it out of revenge? A thought flitted across my brain, something Tre had once said to me. "You always want to take your emotions out of it. Because as soon as you start to care, you make mistakes."

I could just walk away now. But why, when the biggest prize of all was right in front of me?

Nothing was clear anymore. Maybe it was the steam from the hot tub—it was all getting clouded up in my head and I was no longer sure I could tell right from wrong, or even what I should do next.

Kellie, meanwhile, was busy on her iPhone, and she burst out into laughter. "You should see what's on the Buzz today. There's an amazing blind item about someone having sex in the Fieldhouse weight room."

"Hmph," I said. How had she not noticed that I'd never shown any interest in the Buzz?

"And there's also a pic we got of Sierra and her new boyfriend hanging out at the mall. When we saw him the other day he looked so familiar to me, and then when I uploaded it, I realized it's totally our gardener Ignacio. The comments write themselves, really!"

She typed something furiously into the keypad with her thumbs, adding another comment, no doubt, to the post.

Then she shoved the phone in my face. Over the photo were the words *Dirty hands + scum of the earth = true love forever.*

My chest burned with fury as I glimpsed what had been written beneath by various posters. *Can you say gutter trash? The man doesn't speak English. Guess she likes to roll in the mud. Filthy is as filthy does. Does she steal his money, too?*

But that wasn't all. I scrolled down farther to see that there was a photo of Cherise. She was smiling her beautiful smile, oblivious to the nasty caption scrawled over it.

Have you seen me lately? I used to be cool but now I'm a thief-loving loser.

Any last shred of guilt I had floated away like an errant bubble, dancing on the surface of the hot water. I stood up and "accidentally" dropped the phone on the cement. I didn't bother to grab one of Kellie's towels before marching inside to grab my stuff. If I dripped on her floor, so be it.

I was sick of pretending. I was sick of playing along with this witch. Now it was time to do something.

TWENTY-ONE

IN A WAY, it was all too perfect. A Saturday evening, warm and still. Late enough to be dark but early enough that people were still out doing the things regular people do on Saturday nights. (Even for me, banditry was not exactly normal weekend recreation.)

I pulled my bike up to the mailbox at the gated entrance and looked up. Neat little lights lined up like candy buttons on the driveway. A few lights had been left on in the house, too, strategically, for security purposes, but I knew for a fact that Kellie was at UA, and her parents were in Europe.

Beyond the mansard roof was a perfect view of the mountains, rising cool and shadowy in the distance. I smiled, nervous but inspired. This was my first attempt at jacking a house, and I was basically starting at the top. Why mess around with a little rancher when I could go straight for a multimillion-dollar estate?

I tucked my bike under a puffy oleander bush to the right of the gate. It wasn't the greatest getaway vehicle, but without an accomplice it was going to have to do. I smoothed my hair back and pulled my hoodie over it. I was wearing a carefully chosen thieving outfit: black zip-up sweatshirt, gray jeans, and pink high-top Vans. Should I have been wearing all black? Probably. But even crooks have to have some fashion sense. Besides, they were the best shoes I had for running.

I looked up again. The house was strangely unfamiliar from this distance, like it could have been anybody's. Maybe I'd just never stopped to look at it quite this way. I thought of all the times I'd been here before: that party when I first met Tre; the night we watched movies sprawled out on the leather sofas in the gi-huge-ic media room; the time we snuck into her dad's wine cellar to sample champagne that probably cost five hundred dollars a bottle.

I thought of all the sick stuff in her closet, rows and rows of clothes and purses and shoes that had just been given to her, stuff she'd never even use, stuff she didn't even know she had.

At that particular moment she was probably three vodka tonics to the wind at the island party—whatever it was called. She'd be sucking face with Chip or some other frat guy who'd be forgotten as soon as her hangover hit and/or she met the next distraction with a six-pack.

And then I remembered the smug look on her face

when she discovered that Sierra was hooking up with her gardener. All the horrible things that had been posted online.

That was all I needed. I put on my gloves, hopped the gate with a running jump, and sprinted toward the house, making my movements quick and light like Tre had taught me.

Target: the back door.

Of course, the Richardson estate had several back doors. But the other day when I'd cased the joint, I'd found that the kitchen entry had the simplest lock—a standard moderate-security key-in-the-knob jammy. It was also, conveniently, the closest to the driveway. In and out.

I stood with my back to the stone edifice of the house, making myself as tiny as possible. With a flick of the wrist, I reached up to the security camera mounted above the door and wiped it with a smear of Vaseline-coated tissue I'd balled up in my pocket.

Now I was officially unspottable.

I set to work on the lock. It gave easy, with the quick swipe of a screwdriver in the jamb. I smiled to myself, feeling the satisfaction of my skills, my good planning, the righteousness of my mission. I was good at this. Really, really good.

Then it was just a matter of entering the code into the keypad, which disarmed the security system with two beeps. *5-8-2-6-1, baby.*

Inside the house was quiet—but not dead quiet. More like a vibrating silence that let you know people had been here not too long ago. The Richardsons had left for Italy a few days before. Florence, the housekeeper, was also on vacation, visiting family in Tucson. I flicked on my pocket flashlight for a better view. A few glasses and plates were piled up on the marble kitchen island—probably Kellie's. The appliances buzzed softly behind their camouflaged panels. I was tempted to grab a Coke Zero out of the fridge, but I knew that I couldn't risk it. Besides, I wasn't there to rob her parents.

Although I have to admit, the thought crossed my mind. Weren't they partially responsible for turning Kellie into the hollow shell of a person she was today?

Kellie's room was at the end of the left wing. I crept down the hall in the dark. Her door was, of course, unlocked. I turned on the flashlight again, directing it around the room to see what goodies she'd left for me. For someone with a live-in housekeeper, it was surprisingly disheveled. In the light's roving eye I spotted a pile of books and papers on the floor, discarded outfits on her bed, a jumble of makeup on her vanity—and then the dresser, carelessly strewn with jewelry.

"Jackpot," I said softly.

I grabbed handfuls of necklaces and bracelets studded with diamonds and rubies and emeralds, and a few pairs of dangling earrings. By the weight in my hands I knew they had to be real, and I was sure they were from Tiffany or some other fancy place. I decided to leave behind the gigantic studs I'd seen her wearing on the first day of school and many times since. For some reason, it felt like too much, like that would be going too far. They were kind of a signature Kellie item. Besides, I already had enough jewelry for a stretch Hummer full of debutantes.

On to the closet. I opened the door and looked down the long aisle of hanging clothes and the heels and boots and sandals lined up on shelves above them—everything that a no-limit credit card could buy. I eyed up the Prada purses hanging on the wall hooks, but decided they would take up too much room. Instead I grabbed a Hermès scarf and whatever cashmere I could find. The backpack was taking on a satisfying heft.

The closet smelled like Kellie's perfume—Guerlain Vol de Nuit, which was spicy and floral. It was like a ghost of her hovered over the racks, and I realized just how personal this space was. If Kellie had any private thoughts, this is where she had them. My conscience pulled at me a little—for invading her territory, for violating her trust.

But then I reminded myself that every item I was taking was going to be put to good use. They could get Jocelyn her tutor, and maybe some new shoes. Kellie would never miss them—and even if she did, they were all pretty much replaceable. Besides, she'd set herself up for this. All of those rumors she'd started, all of the cruel comments online, all of the times she'd gone on and on about the Busteds and how pathetic and skanky they were. *Look in the mirror,* I wanted to say.

But this—goodwill and revenge wrapped up together—was so much better.

Kellie's iPad and a brand-new laptop she'd shown me just last week were lying in a neat stack on her desk. I scooped them up, too. Who knew what sorts of nastiness were encoded in her computers' caches? That pretty much did it for my bag capacity.

I took one last look around the room to make sure I'd left things as I'd found them. It wasn't my style to ransack. But I did want to leave a signature of sorts. I stood in front of her mirror and picked up a lipstick from her vast collection.

I had to let Kellie know that it wasn't who she thought was behind this. So I wrote something she would know only I knew, spelling out the message in waxy fuchsia script on the glass:

> *Here's the latest Buzz. I'm not a Busted. But I know that we all need a little help sometimes, even if not all of us can pay a tutor to write our papers for us.*

In a way, it was my confession. I pointed my flashlight at the mirror and stood looking at the bold words, wondering if I had gone too far. The thing was, she would only know it was me if she remembered the night of her party, when she'd been totally plastered. And I seriously doubted she would choose to turn me in, because it would also potentially get her into trouble. And now I had Kellie's computers with evidence of all the Buzz bullying in my possession if I needed it. Besides, confessing would be worth it if it cleared Sierra's, Mary's, and Alicia's names. At this point, I had to do it.

As I lowered the flashlight, my gaze caught on a framed portrait hanging next to the mirror. Kellie and her mother on the tennis court, tanned and wearing even white smiles and unwrinkled shirts that looked like they'd never seen the outside of a Lacoste store, let alone a full match on an actual court. The resemblance between them was undeniable.

It reminded me of my own mom. Out of habit, I pulled on the bird pendant around my neck. A pang of sadness shot through me. We used to be so close—best friends, even, but that seemed like a long time ago, before we came to Paradise Valley. Now I was alone in more ways than one, just someone creeping through the dark unseen.

I sighed, gathered my stuff, and started toward the door. But I guess I'd paused too long because when I moved again, I must have tripped a motion sensor. The lights flipped on all at once, and then a sound that could only have been the alarm let loose in loud shrieks.

I froze.

Oh no oh no oh no.

In all the times I'd mentally practiced for this day, I'd had no idea that there was more than one security system. At this very moment, though, with the deafening noise burning my eardrums, it seemed stupidly obvious.

There was no time to panic, although that was exactly what I was doing. I threw the bag on my back and bolted down the hallway. The dark corridor was now strobing with flashing lights.

I just need to go back out the door I came in. In and out.

As I rounded the corner back through the breezeway, the alarm stopped momentarily. I heard myself panting, the clapping of my feet on the slate tile, and then, the distant whine of sirens. I doubled my pace, running through the library and the den and the dining room. But even as I ran I knew I was being sloppy, messing up the rugs, leaving more footprints.

I made it to the kitchen door and pulled on the knob. It was stuck. I tried the locks, but no go. How? I hadn't locked the door behind me when I came in—I was sure of that.

Okay, what now?

I wiped my brow with my sleeve. My heart rattled in my throat. The alarm started up again, slapping my brain into blank fear.

Think. Think! What had Tre said?

He'd said to run like hell.

I ran toward the front of the house. It would be okay to use the front door if I could just get out quickly—I calculated that I could run down the driveway in less than two minutes to get to my bike. I just needed those two minutes.

The huge wooden front door loomed ahead of me. I undid the bolts and grabbed the handle. It was locked, too. Not just locked—sealed. Here I'd thought I was all clever, outsmarting the Richardsons' security. I'd completely underestimated this system that now had me trapped inside.

The sirens were getting louder, which could only mean they were closer. I pulled out my screwdriver, figuring it was worth a try.

Please, please, please work.

My hands were sweaty and shaking but somehow, with a few turns of the wrist, I jiggered the mechanism to release. The screwdriver clattered to the floor, and I let it go.

Just as the door flew open, I saw the lights flashing up the driveway. A police car pulled in front of the house, screeching to a halt. I couldn't tell whether it was a real cop or a rent-a-cop but I didn't care, and I wasn't going to stick around and wait to see what happened next.

My speed surprised me. I was running faster than any sprint I'd ever done for Ms. Lonergan in gym class. Somehow, I felt airy, light. It had to be the adrenaline. My legs pumped and the air scratched against my throat.

"Stop!" a man yelled as I flew past and found my bike. "Stop right there!"

TWENTY-TWO

I KNEW SOMETHING was wrong when the bike stopped moving altogether. I must have been riding through the dark desert streets for twenty minutes, at least. But now it was like my wheels had lost traction, like the ground had turned to pudding. I hit the brake and I practically fell off. I got down on the hot pavement to see what the problem was.

It was obvious right away. My tire. The one that had blown the day Aidan gave me a ride home from school. The one that I had supposedly patched myself a few months earlier. *I should have taken him up on his offer and let him fix it,* I thought.

Yeah, well, I should have done a lot of things differently.

But there was no time now to dwell on it. I let the bike fall to the side of the road, quickly kissing it with my hand and hoping that this wasn't a final good-bye. I couldn't take it with me. It would only weigh me down.

Nothing to do now but run. I went off-road, running as hard as my legs would carry me over the thick brush. The terrain was bumpy, and full of hidden divots and big stones. I came down on a cactus and my ankle nearly gave out, but I recovered and kept going. I couldn't look back, not even when a car screeched to a halt in the distance and I heard footsteps on the trail behind me.

I kept on until I'd reached what must have been someone's backyard. I jumped an agave plant, hopped over some boulders, and then I was face-to-face with a stone wall. This was trespassing, but what choice did I have? I planted my palms on the rough stones and vaulted myself up, flinging my body over onto the lawn on the other side, and landing in a squat.

I would've congratulated myself on this gymnastic feat, except when I looked up, I had a face full of sprinkler water. Real nice.

I started to use my shirt to towel off, but there was no time. I could hear the footsteps behind me. And the shouting.

Move, I told myself. *Keep moving.*

I scrambled to my feet and resumed a fevered run over the yard, which seemed to stretch across infinity. The ground blurred beneath me until I hit another fence, which was taller and sharper than the last one, and bordered a golf course. For once I was happy to see a golf course—that was something I could work with, maybe. Especially if there were golf carts.

A dog barked in the distance and I prayed it wasn't loose and people-hungry. I wrapped my hands around the spires and tried to hoist myself up, but my palms slipped against the metal. My lungs hurt. My legs were tired. My hair and chest were damp from the sprinkler. I looked up into the pulsing stars, pleading silently for a miracle.

And that's when I felt the arms gripping me, pulling me down, and then the weight, like a 200-pound sack of stones, throwing me to the ground, face-first. A knee pressed on my back, and my arms were pinned together behind me in a relentlessly tight grip.

"We've been looking for you, little girl," I heard him say. Then there was the cool grasp of metal encircling my wrists, locking together with a click. "You're under arrest."

If you ever wanted to know what happens after you get tackled by a middle-aged cop as you try to flee the scene of a robbery, here's a little glimpse: When he removed his knee from my back, I was struggling to breathe, the wind knocked out of me. I tried to stand up, which was nearly impossible with my hands cuffed behind my back.

At that point, I believe the cops were reading me my rights, but I could barely hear them over my own gasps. I was led back to the car, firm grip on my arm. Then they shoved me in the backseat.

They drove through darkness, headlights sweeping

the road in front of us. The chill of the car's air-conditioning encased me and it felt like a morgue. I wished I was out in the naturally warm air, and not crammed into this bizarrely small space behind a bulletproof glass divider.

As we rolled on, I grappled with the reality of what was happening. Was it really possible that this was me, in the backseat of a cop car? I had only my senses to prove it. The smooth plastic of the seats, the smell of old coffee and cigarettes and aftershave, the sounds of the sirens. The cops ignored me most of the way, talking only to each other and into their radios. I stared out the smudged window, watching the normally vibrant skyline of cacti and rock formations dull into smears of black.

It felt like we were driving forever—until we weren't. We parked in front of a sprawling white building. Paradise Valley Juvenile Detention Center.

It looked newly built, a box stacked on top of another box, surrounded by gravel and small plantings that had barely started to sprout. The parking lot was lit by greenish fluorescent lights.

The policeman who'd pulled me off the fence, Officer Carmichael, and the one who was driving the car, whose name I never got, escorted me in by the elbows. Carmichael was fortysomething, with black hair and a well-toned physique, while his partner was younger and scrawnier, with a bad case of acne.

Inside, a grumpy older woman in a brown uniform

stood behind the front desk. She pushed a bunch of papers in front of me for signing. She was rude, and I had a brief flash that people were only going to be rude to me from here on out.

Then the two cops brought me down a hallway to a big office with lots of cubicles. They introduced me to Officer Daniels, who would be my intake probation officer. Daniels was a big, intimidatingly red-faced guy, chins spilling over the front of his uniform. He looked like he was built for punishing people.

He told me to have a seat in front of his desk. By the time I looked up at his extra-large scowl, I was no longer in shock. It all got real.

I was in custody. This was going on my permanent record. I closed my eyes and opened them again, but the same scene remained. I was trapped. I trembled like an animal in a crate.

They'd uncuffed me and were allowing me to sit there unrestrained, but in the eyes of the law—the particular ones staring at me just then were icy blue and very judgmental—this was only a courtesy, a temporary reprieve. I was a menace to society and they wanted me under control.

If only I could just explain, maybe they would see that it wasn't that bad. But I was too afraid to speak out of turn. My mouth was dried up like a neglected houseplant.

"We're going to go through what's called a screening

process, so I need to ask you some questions," he said.

It was a long list. He asked me if I was intoxicated. If I was depressed. If I had any prior felonies. If I had ever been in a violent incident. If I'd ever run away from home. If I owned or carried a firearm. I laughed nervously at the last one. *Of course not, who did he think I was?*

One look at his dead-serious face and I remembered.

He made some more notes on his sheet and then typed some things into his computer. I tried not to let my eyes wander around too much. Just by being here I felt like I was taking in criminal vibes as much as I was giving them out—it was like guilt by osmosis. Had this happened to Tre, too? Or Aidan?

Daniels coughed. "I'm going to call your mother now, Willa."

He dialed her number on his desk phone. It was Saturday night. I had no idea what she was doing. Whatever it had been was about to be interrupted by a call from the police telling her that her daughter had just been arrested for a break-in.

Hot, raw fear surged into my throat as I waited. I felt like I was staring down an abyss of the unknown, and it was dark as hell. How would she handle this? It wasn't a call anyone wanted to get—there was no way around that. I had a feeling that Daniels wasn't the type to sugarcoat, either. Having to sit here and listen to this conversation would be unbearable. I looked down at my shoes, wishing I could close my eyes until it was over.

But she wasn't picking up, because Daniels frowned and hung up the receiver.

"No answer. I'll have to try again."

Well, that was okay, I thought. I was in no rush to have that confrontation. But then worry seeped into the edges of my thoughts. If she wasn't home, where was she? Out with that guy again? Was she all right? What if something happened to her and I was in here? I would never know.

"Will I get to go home tonight?" I asked, suddenly picturing the worst.

"Don't think so," Daniels said, clicking and unclicking a pen. "We have to finish the screening process and hold you until we can get a hearing. And tomorrow's Sunday. Not much gets done around here then."

A horrible, intense shiver crept through me. I was spending the night. In lockdown. Possibly two. And then a hearing? What would happen then?

Daniels pushed his chair out from his desk. "Do you want some water? Some coffee?"

"Water, please," I croaked, and my voice sounded like I'd already been locked up in isolation for forty years.

He stepped away. I surveyed the room, all the cops in uniform coming and going from their cubicles. There had to be at least a dozen of them sitting around at their desks, and then there were the civilians, like me, who had been taken in. A few feet away, a tall wild-haired guy with a visible scar on his chin was still cuffed and looking anxiously around the room, twitching like he was high on something. Another girl was wearing thigh-high boots and a leather skirt. I was pretty sure I knew what she was in for. We were all innocent until proven guilty, supposedly, but I immediately assumed they were all guilty of something, as they probably did when they looked at me.

In the detention center it didn't matter that I had a 3.8 GPA or that I thought I was trying to help people. No one here would care. I could see that now.

Daniels came back with a damp cone-shaped cup from the cooler. I took it from him, and noticed that my hand was shaking. I drank the water quickly and collapsed the paper in my hand. My wrists were sore and red where the cuffs had been.

"So then what happens?" I asked him.

He shrugged. "I don't know. We have to wait and see."

I thought of Tre. "Will I be sent to boot camp?"

He looked at me with interest. "Are you confessing?"

"I want to talk to a lawyer. They said I had the right to. Can I talk to a lawyer?"

"Sure." He handed me the phone. "Be my guest."

I looked up at him with hesitation, realizing that I had no idea who to call. "I don't actually have a lawyer."

"Here's a list with some names." He pushed a piece of paper in front of me. "These are court-appointed attorneys."

I glanced at the list and then back at the phone. What would I even say to a lawyer? *Hello? My name's Willa and I'm inquiring about your thief-representation services. . . .*

Maybe I didn't want a court-appointed attorney. Maybe I needed someone expensive and big-time to handle my case. I tried to remember everything I'd seen on lawyer shows.

I was only fifteen years old. How the hell was I supposed to know what to do? I looked up at Daniels, who was watching me expectantly with just a hint of a smile on his face. I had no clue.

I wanted someone to tell me what to do. I tried to think of who else I could call. Tre was no good, because I couldn't call attention to him. Cherise wouldn't have any advice, and she probably wouldn't be all that thrilled to hear I'd been ripping off her friends. But maybe Aidan would. Maybe talking to him, just knowing he was out there, would calm me down. All of a sudden I ached to hear his voice. It was worth a try. I dialed his number and he answered on the second ring.

"Aidan," I gasped when he answered. "I need your help."

"Willa? Where are you?"

"I'm at the station. I got taken in. What do I do?"

"What happened?" His voice sharpened with concern. "Did they call your mom?"

"It's a long story," I said, looking up at Daniels. "I can't talk about it right now. My mom wasn't home."

"Look, don't do anything, Willa. Just stay quiet until your mom gets there."

"Okay," I said, biting my lip.

"It's going to be okay," he said, his tone soothing and clear. "I promise you. Just hold tight. If you need anything at all, I'm here for you."

I wished he were here *with* me so I could wrap my arms around him.

"Thanks," I said. "That means a lot right now."

I hung up the phone and sat back in my chair, looking down. The cuff marks on my wrists looked a bit raised now, like *o*-shaped welts. I tried to close my eyes and let Aidan's words, the sound of his voice, wash over me.

"That was your lawyer, eh?" Daniels asked, raising a doubtful eyebrow.

I wasn't going to give him the satisfaction of knowing.

Minutes ticked by. Sitting there doing nothing was starting to feel like torture. This was how they got you. I knew Aidan was right. I had to stay quiet. I tried to steel up my face, make it expressionless so Daniels couldn't read what I was thinking. But his knowing, almost-mocking way of talking to me made me really nervous.

He got up again and moved some files around. When he came back, he said, "You know, this isn't like the adult criminal system. If you confess on the record it's actually going to make things easier."

I knew what he was trying to do. I pursed my lips

together and tried to drown out his voice. *Don't listen. He's going to trick you.*

"We have all kinds of evidence that it was you, Willa. Including the backpack of stolen goods you dropped."

I didn't say anything, just kept staring down, anxiously willing my brain into blankness. I imagined what he saw in front of him, a scared young girl who was in way over her head.

"It's up to you, really. But it'll save us all a lot of time if you just admit it."

Again, I stayed mute.

"A lot of people have been looking for you. You've had a good run, you know? Whatever you were doing, you did it well—I mean you stole a lot of things and you gave away a lot of things. You also got people talking."

Don't look at him. Tune him out.

"But one thing people in this town don't like is someone who runs away from responsibility. And the more you run, the harder it gets. You can't live a lie forever. It gets to be a burden." He stopped talking and stared at me hard.

My eyes traveled upward from the bottom of the desk to where his hands were resting on its surface. And then to his face, which was unshaven and pudgy, but, I could see now, not entirely angry.

I heard the truth in what he was saying. It had been hard for all these weeks to be two people at once. In the beginning it had been thrilling to help those girls, but maybe, over time, I'd lost sight of that. Maybe I'd focused too much on the stealing part, like Tre had said. The thing was, I'd always known deep down that I couldn't keep going like I had. Sooner or later I would be caught. And sooner had turned out to be now.

"I mean, if I was you, and I believed in what I was doing, I'd probably want people to know. You had your reasons. You're not a bad person. Why not stand behind what you've done? Be an adult about it."

"Fine," I burst out. "I get it. It was me, okay? Are you happy?"

Then, for the first time since I'd been taken in, I started crying. Daniels didn't say anything further. He let me sit there for what felt like a half hour, crying and letting it all sink in.

On top of everything else, all the worry and disappointment and regret, was the little voice in my head repeating what Aidan had said on the phone. I was supposed to be quiet. I'd screwed up. Majorly. And now I would probably never see him again.

Daniels handed me another cup of water. It was so cold that it hurt my teeth. I gulped it quickly, then put my head down between my arms and felt the tears run off the sides of my face into my sleeves.

I'd confessed. It was all over.

Sometime before midnight—by then, I'd lost track of time, just listening to the police radios drone around the cubicles—my mom arrived at the center. I could hear her coming before I saw her, her familiar footsteps treading lightly and quickly on the tiled floor.

"She's here for Willa Fox," I heard the grumpy woman from the front desk say.

I sat up and turned toward her. My mom headed in my direction, her half-buttoned jacket flapping open, her face drawn up in distress. She didn't look at me and I almost didn't care—I was so happy to see her. I wanted to jump onto her back like I'd done as a little girl and have her carry me out of there on piggyback. I was way too big for that now, of course, and it would be a ridiculous thing to do in this situation. Besides, they were detaining me. I was stuck here.

"Hello, officer." Her tone was cool and formal, but I detected a little huskiness in her voice.

Daniels shook her hand and gestured for her to have a seat in the chair next to me.

"So what do we need to do now?" she asked, all business.

"I just need you to sign a few forms. We'll review the paperwork and her past record and have a hearing on Monday, most likely."

My mom cleared her throat. "Will she have to—serve time?"

"We will refer the matter to a probation officer and a judge," Daniels replied as he shoved his hands in his pants pockets. "It's really going to depend on how they view the seriousness of the crimes. In the meantime, you might want to think about getting her a lawyer."

My mom finished signing the papers.

"I'll give you two a few minutes to talk," Daniels said, walking away from his cubicle.

"I cannot *believe* what you've done," my mom said very quietly when he'd walked away. Now she was staring right at me and I could feel a kind of fire in her eyes. "I could kill you right now, Willa. I really could."

I had never seen her so furious. I'd never heard her say anything so violent. She was a yoga-loving pacifist by nature. "Mom, wait. Let me tell you my side of the story. Please?"

"No! I don't want to hear your explanations." She drew her lips back to bare her teeth. "And I don't want to hear any excuses. You've broken the law. You've jeopardized your future, everything we've worked so hard for."

I could feel my lower lip quivering. "I wasn't trying to—I had good intentions."

She held up a hand to silence me. "What'd I just say? Are you listening to me at all? These are *crimes* you've committed. They've been all over the news. Do you have any concept how *serious* this is?"

I swallowed hard and opened my mouth to answer her, but nothing came out.

"You're young—you have no clue, Willa. But everything you do in life has a consequence. We have to keep living with our consequences. And what you've done . . .

you may as well have just thrown everything away. I just can't believe how reckless and irresponsible you've been."

Her words sliced through me. I'd always felt like she was on my side, like it was the two of us against the world. But this time it wasn't. It was all accusations. She didn't even want to hear my perspective. Like she'd already decided I was guilty!

And something in me turned sour then. I needed her again, and again she wasn't there for me. "I guess I'd thought you'd at least try to understand, but forget it."

"And what do I need to understand here? How do you expect me to be okay with this?"

"It's not like you were a model teenager," I snapped.

"I got *pregnant*. It's very different from breaking and entering, stealing people's personal property," she said, narrowing her eyes at me. "What I did wasn't against the law. It wasn't hurting other people."

"I wasn't hurting people, either!"

"But you were. You were deceitful. I mean, what upsets me most are the *lies*—that you've been leading a double life all this time. I thought we trusted each other."

"You're one to talk," I said, gathering my arms up into my chest.

"What's that supposed to mean?"

"Oh, come on. Double life, Mom? You're the queen of it!"

My mom let out a frustrated sigh. "I don't know what you're talking about."

We were fighting in harsh whispers, staring each other down but trying not to make a scene. It was beyond late. There were only a few people wandering around the intake area at this point, and most of the officers had gone home. It felt like she couldn't leave until the conversation reached some plateau or we reached some kind of understanding. But we were clearly going in a different direction. And there were no barriers now. I had to put an end to this hypocrisy: We were both going to have to tell the truth.

"Mom, I saw you at Target, okay? You were meeting that guy there."

She clapped a hand over her mouth in surprise. "You followed me?" Her expression collapsed into disbelief. "You actually *followed me*? What the hell?"

"Who is he?" I demanded. "No more lies. We moved here for him, right?"

Silence from her end now as she stared me down, still shaking her head. She wasn't budging.

I went further. "I just wish you'd shut up about my future—it's never been about me. Just be honest for once—"

"I'll be honest when I can trust you."

"And what about me trusting you? You'd been so mysterious, never telling me where you were going. I had my suspicions."

She reached over and grabbed me by the shoulders, shaking me. "You think this is some kind of game, to spy on me and make up stories? There's no affair, okay? I told you that."

I had nothing left to lose. The question flared through me and spun out into the air like a Roman candle. "Is he my father? Tell me the truth."

"I'm leaving." She stood up and slung her purse over her shoulder.

"Where are you going?" I asked.

"Home. We're finished talking here. You've got a crazy way of seeing things, Willa. You've just been arrested and you're blaming *me* for *your* problems, accusing me of lying to you." She was halfway down the hallway and yelling over her shoulder. "You have no idea what's going on. *None!*"

There was nothing I could say to stop her as she stormed toward the exit, moving back out into the night. I stood there, limp and helpless. She was a free person. I, on the other hand, wasn't going anywhere.

TWENTY-THREE

THE NEXT MORNING, a "counselor"—in juvenile hall, this is what they called the people in uniform telling us what to do—woke me up and told me I had visitors.

I was still wearing the hall-issued sweatshirt, underwear, and scrub pants they'd given me when they'd booked me—my real clothes had been stored in a paper bag on a shelf at the front desk—but I had to put on my laceless blue shoes, which they'd made me leave outside the door of my tiny gray cell.

I had not slept at all. Instead, I spent the night on the thin mattress rearranging cinder blocks like Tetris in my mind, trying to replay the night's events, wondering what I could have done differently, wishing I could take it all back and start over. I wondered what people at school knew about my arrest. Surely, by now, Kellie and her family knew. Which meant Cherise and Nikki did, too. Maybe Tre. Maybe even the entire student body.

Mostly, though, I thought about my mom. The cold way she'd looked at me in the station. Somewhere on the cellblock was the distant sound of a tap dripping, and with each drop I felt my heart slowly breaking into little pieces. I ached inside with regret and longing.

Not helping was the glass window in my cell, which was there for the staff to look in on me. It also let in the light from the hallway, keeping me awake and reminding me where I was. In the system. An object of scorn, cast out by society.

The whole point of juvie, of course, was to make you feel remorse about what you'd done, and they'd designed it brilliantly. Before I could meet my visitors, I had to have my designated shower in the girls' bathroom, which was in an open row of spigots with no walls or privacy. Then I had to have my state of Arizona–funded breakfast: a small bowl of tasteless cereal and a squat little plastic cup of juice with a foil top, the kind they gave you after blood donations. Then I was allowed to go back through the hallway, down to the visitor's area, which was where I came in the night before. I was led from one destination to the next by different counselors, but none of them even looked at me or introduced themselves.

My mom and the lawyer she'd found for me were waiting on plastic bucket seats in the hallway. The lawyer was here to talk to me about my case. I wanted desperately to be alone with my mom but there was no time for that now.

Christopher Siegel, Esq., stood up, introduced himself, and gave me an abbreviated smile, teeth contrasting with his tanned face, silver hair combed neatly from a part to his ears. He pumped my hand in his giant, Italian-suit-sleeved one, and then got down to business right away. He explained how the hearing would go down and he gave me instructions on what to say and how to act. All I had to do was be very quiet and polite, he said. I had to call the judge "sir" or "Your Honor." I shouldn't speak at all unless I was asked a question. He asked me whether I had confessed to the crime, and I told him what I had told Daniels.

He nodded diplomatically. "Not too good."

Siegel said there were a few options: They could hold me in detention—anywhere for a few months to a couple of years, depending on how seriously they decided to treat the crime. They could also send me to a boot camp, like the one Tre had been to, or they could send me to counseling and put me on house arrest with one of those ankle bracelets celebrities got when they were arrested for DUI.

I chewed on the inside of my mouth, feeling the weight of what he was telling me sink in. I didn't know which option to hope for. They all sounded pretty awful, but after my one night in juvie I was certain I didn't want to be staying there for any length of time.

"Is there any way I can just go home while they figure this out? Pay a fine or something?" I asked, my voice cracking a bit. I wanted to sleep in my own bed. I wanted to talk to Tre. I wanted to talk to Cherise. And most of all, I wanted to talk to Aidan.

"No, you have to wait here for the time being," Siegel said. "We really don't know what they'll do. Every case is different. Sometimes they want to make an example out of you. And this has been very high-profile. You've made the cops look stupid. So you should be prepared for the worst."

My mom was dressed in her nicest suit with panty hose and pumps, even, but with her patchy skin and red eyes, she looked even more haggard and worn down than she'd been looking lately, if that was possible. She'd just been sitting there silently the whole time I talked to Siegel—it looked like she was staring into space—but when she turned her head I could see the flash of tears in her eyes. I wanted to hug her but Siegel was sitting between us. Besides, just then I wasn't sure if she'd let me.

After a half hour, the visiting time was up and they had to leave. The counselor came to take me back to my cell. I stood, watching them go, my mom looking smaller as she disappeared down the hallway.

"C'mon," the counselor said gruffly, leading me away.

Inside my cell, I went back to staring at the walls and tried to sleep, but there was a loud buzzing sound from the fluorescent lights overhead. I was exhausted, I realized.

The tears came then, shaking my body with sobs. I

curled up in a ball and cried. My life was pretty much over. There was no going back now. I'd ruined everything.

I thought back to my first day riding my bike to school, taking in the stark beauty of the landscape. In here I could only see the sky in twenty-minute intervals, as I learned when they let me out for a walk in the afternoon. There were about ten kids altogether and we walked around the building in circles while a counselor watched us. I didn't talk to anyone else—I was too scared. At the same time, I felt hollowed out by my crying jag. A darker, more despairing sensation took over. Was this going to be the way I experienced fresh air from now on? How would I survive it?

When our time was up, a bell rang and we were lined up and ordered back inside. Sometime in the evening I was brought my dinner, a dry chicken leg and some canned peas.

And then it was another long, long, long night. Alone. Waiting. For what, I had no idea. I was too scared to hope for anything. My luck had clearly run out.

In the morning, we sat in the corridor outside the courtroom for three hours, though in the last two days my whole concept of time had shifted. It could have been ten minutes or a month. Siegel, in a different suit, with a shiny green tie, went over a few more things with me and then we waited and waited.

Finally, the double doors opened and we went inside. My mom, Siegel, and I sat down behind a small table in the front of the room. The judge, cloaked in a black robe with a matching black beard and bushy graying eyebrows, was seated behind a wooden bench. Behind him were the American and Arizona flags. He was holding a stack of papers and the sign on his desk said THE HONORABLE FLOYD L. PRENDERGAST.

"Willa Fox, you're here because of an arrest on Saturday, correct?"

I nodded, gulping down a rising lump in my throat.

"I'm looking over your records here. It says you were taken in because of a breaking-and-entering incident, and that you are suspected of as many as six other robberies and thefts over the past several months."

"Yes," I said, steadying myself, trying to be strong. My mind was flashing over the separate incidents—my visits to the pawnshop; my trips to the mall. Even as I was owning up to them, it was like watching a montage from a movie—it all seemed so distant now.

"It also said that you confessed to these crimes," he said, squinting over his wire-framed oval glasses.

"I did," I said.

I felt Siegel nudging me.

"Your Honor," I added.

"Do you have anything to say about it?"

"Just that I'm really, really, really sorry for what I've done." I closed my eyes and tried to summon my composure, but a sob was just lingering beneath the surface—I could feel it.

"And why did you do these things?"

I squeezed my hands together and took a deep breath. "Your Honor, when I came here, to Paradise Valley, I was so excited to have this luxurious life," I said, my voice quaking a little. "I looked around and I could see so much beauty surrounding me. For the first time I was part of the other half and I thought this was the way everyone should be able to live."

I paused, remembering how I'd felt those early days, riding my bike around town, walking through the school campus, sleeping in my cushy bed. Like I was safe—but more than that. Like the future was wide open to me. I looked up and saw that he was listening intently.

"And then I noticed that there were kids who had nothing, or next to nothing, and they were just trying to have their shot, too. But some of the rich kids wouldn't give the poorer ones a chance. They ignored them, or excluded them, or tortured them with online bullying."

The judge nodded, urging me on.

I took another deep breath and continued. "So I had this idea, to make things more equal. I would spread the wealth around and level the playing field for the less fortunate kids. And maybe show everyone how arbitrary it was. That we're just born into a situation, but that it didn't have to define them. In short, Your Honor, I just thought I was helping people."

His expression was a blank, lost in the craggy lines of his face. I couldn't tell if he was hearing what I was saying, but just the force of his presence looming over me made my words sound ridiculous, my voice small and squeaky. I wanted to run away.

"But I realize now that it was a stupid idea, and that I wasn't really helping anyone. I was actually doing the opposite."

Prendergast leaned over his folded arms. "As we like to say here in the halls of justice, 'Two wrongs don't make a right.'"

"No, sir," I said mournfully.

Judge Prendergast turned to my lawyer. "Do you have anything to say on your client's behalf?"

"Just that we request you take into account that Willa has no prior record, Your Honor. We feel that she is a smart, capable person who is simply guilty of poor judgment in this instance."

"I would say six robberies is a bit more than poor judgment," the judge countered.

"With all due respect, Your Honor, my client did have good motivations, however misguided her decisions were."

Prendergast waved a hand, as if dismissing what Siegel was saying. "Actions are the bottom line, aren't they? I mean, we don't prosecute thoughts or ideas in the courtroom, do we?"

"No, Your Honor."

He cleared his throat and pointed to the papers. "In cases like this, Willa, where the defendant has no record, is generally well behaved, and gets higher marks on the screening at the justice center, we like to treat the incident as an aberration. We don't charge them with a crime but we put them on probation, and ask them to perform some community service."

I looked at my mom and then at Siegel to read their reactions, but neither was giving anything away. Both were just listening attentively to Judge Prendergast. I turned back to do the same, feeling a tiny bit of optimism blooming inside of me. At the same time, I wanted to keep those thoughts in check. Prendergast could say anything next.

He removed his glasses and rubbed his eyes with the heels of his palms. "Now, look. This case has received a lot of media attention. My office has been fielding calls from the press all morning. If I let you off without serving time, there are going to be people who will be after me, asking why I wasn't helping protect their community, why I was letting an admitted criminal free. So I need you to promise me, Willa, that if we let you go home today, you'll be a model citizen from here on out."

I nodded fiercely. "Yes, sir. I will show you—and everyone else—that I deserve a second chance. And that I'm ready to make a new start and make it right."

"And I'm going to need you to repay everyone you stole from. Every cent of it. My understanding is that the damages are in the thousands. That will be one of your probation requirements."

"I can do that, Your Honor." How, I really had no idea. But I would find a way. Anything but spend another night here.

"Okay, then. I'm sentencing you to one hundred hours of community service and one year of probation. Your probation officer will tell you how you can fulfill your service requirement and how to proceed with your meetings," he said as he signed a piece of paper.

I looked at my mom, and her eyes, softening in tears, met mine. She grabbed my arm and squeezed it. I felt, for an instant, at least, like we were on the same team again, that maybe I hadn't lost her after all.

Prendergast straightened his stack of papers. "You're free to go now. But remember what I said. Stay out of trouble."

Siegel had arranged for a car to drive us home. On the way out of the building, he told us we were lucky, that this was the best possible scenario we could have asked for. That Prendergast was more than fair. Now I just had to scrounge up the money for restitution and follow the rules of probation, which meant staying away from drugs and alcohol, staying away from known criminals, and not leaving the state without my probation officer's permission. After a year, my record would be clear.

He walked us to the car and then headed back into

the building, where he had another case to see to.

In the backseat of the car, my mom seemed relieved—I gleaned this from her body language, but not from her words because she still wasn't saying anything.

That is, until we were halfway down Morning Glory and we saw the throng of people trailing down the driveway, jostling for position. Their cars, painted with the names of various news channels, clogged up the street, double- and triple-parked in rows—some were mounted with satellite dishes. A few of the neighbors had come out of their houses to watch.

"No no no," my mom said, shaking her head and looking like she was going to cry. "No way. This isn't happening."

She paid the driver and instructed him to stop several yards away, in front of a neighbor's house. "You can leave us off here."

She gestured for me to go in through the back but even as we headed in that direction, some of the media people spotted us and started running toward us in a wild herd.

A TV reporter I recognized from one of the local stations was in front, shoving a microphone in my face.

"Channel Five News. So what happened in court today, Willa?"

Then the questions and the people asking them came thick and fast from all sides, like popcorn rattling around in a microwave bag.

"Did you confess to the crimes?"

"*The Arizona Daily Star* is calling you the Sly Fox, do you have any comment on that?"

"Why'd you do it?"

"What was the sentence?"

"What'd the judge say today?"

"Are you sorry, Sly Fox? This is your chance to address the public!"

My mom pulled my hood over my face. She put her arm around me, pulling me tightly to her, and guided me toward the front door.

I peeked out from underneath my sweatshirt so I didn't trip and I caught another glimpse of the scene. There were at least six cameras, some hoisted on shoulders and others mounted on tripods. Raised hands holding digital recorders. Microphones dangling off long poles. People wearing badges, carrying shoulder bags.

Flashes went off. The crowd rippled as we passed through, shouting more questions that were overlapping in one loud, manic web of sound.

I didn't know what to think, and there wasn't much time to. Off to the side I could see a few people holding signs in support. FREE WILLA! THE SLY FOX LIVES. And others, not so supportive: JUSTICE FOR PARADISE VALLEY NOW. ADULT CRIMES = ADULT PUNISHMENT. HEY, MAINSTREAM MEDIA—STOP GLORIFYING CRIME.

They were all here for me? Weren't there any murders in this town? Any corrupt politicians to cover? I was strangely flattered. Somehow, without even trying, I'd become a celebrity.

But before I could revel in the attention, my mom had pulled me into the house. She slammed the door behind us. Inside, she began closing blinds and locking doors.

"Don't just stand there, Willa," she snapped. "Help me, for chrissakes!"

I tried to help, dashing around from room to room, making sure no one could see or get in. By then, some of them had set up their cameras in the back by the pool. They had the house under surveillance from every angle.

My mom was pacing back and forth. "I need you to go get your phone and give it to me."

I did as she asked and handed it to her, heaving my shoulders in disappointment. I'd been hoping to call Aidan as soon as I got home—to let him know how it all turned out and to thank him again for helping to calm me down. Also, to hear his sexy voice. Now it might be a while before I could talk to him.

"What are you doing with that?" I asked her, timid.

"As you might have guessed, you're going to be grounded indefinitely. Besides, now that we're a media freak show, I need to change our numbers."

"Aren't you overreacting a little with the privacy? It's a small town. They can find us if they want to, wherever we go."

She whipped around and narrowed her eyes at me. They flashed in anger. "Don't you understand? This is a living nightmare. The entire national press is outside. They know where we live now. And we can't even leave if we want to, not without breaking your probation. We're so screwed."

"I don't understand," I said. "I thought the lawyer said we were lucky with the ruling. And I thought you wanted to stay here."

"Not anymore, I don't."

She went into her bedroom and slammed the door. Inside I could hear her shuffling around, moving heavy things.

I knocked on her door. She didn't answer, so I knocked again.

"Go away," she called. "I can't deal with you right now."

She'd shut me out.

What did I expect? This was all my fault. I was getting exactly what I deserved. Even if the court had let me off the hook, she had every right to punish me. I'd not only broken the law, but I'd embarrassed her. She was ashamed to be my mother.

But this was the worst punishment I could imagine, maybe worse than being locked up in juvie. I couldn't stand it that she wouldn't talk to me. She was all I had, the only person I could count on in the whole world.

All those hours in the cell, I'd been thinking about her. Remembering when I was a little kid, how she'd sit with me in the library and we'd read dozens of books at a time, staying until it got dark, leaving only when there was nothing good left to read. How she helped me fix up my bike, finding the vintage seat for me on eBay and surprising me with it. And how she'd once made me a birthday-cake castle out of ice-cream cones when I was in a medieval phase, painstakingly gluing on chocolate shingles with sugar syrup for hours.

She had taken care of me all these years by herself, starting when she was only just a little older than I was now. I couldn't imagine having a baby at this age. It couldn't have been easy.

She was obviously really furious with me. But I knew she loved me. She'd brought the lawyer, which must have cost a fortune. She could've just left me in juvie, which is what I probably deserved.

I sat on my bed and stared at the ceiling, knowing that trying to read or watch a movie would be useless at this point. Every now and then I would look out the window to see if the reporters were still out there. By nightfall, a few cars had left, but most of them were still there. I could see the occasionally blinking lights of cameras floating around like fireflies in the yard. They were like little glimmers of hope—reminding me that there were people out there who cared about me.

How long would we be trapped in here? I wondered. When they let me out of lockup, I hadn't expected that I might be imprisoned in my own home. It could go on for days like this, and what if my mom was still avoiding me? The idea was terrifying.

I just needed her to forgive me. I needed things to be right between us again. We had to go back—not just to the way we were before I got arrested, but to the way we were before we moved here. I didn't know what that would take, but I was prepared to do anything.

I went out into the hallway and knocked on my mom's door again. "Are you in there?" I asked.

Nothing.

But I could hear some thumping, like she was still moving things around. Maybe reorganizing her closet. She sometimes did that during times of stress.

I slumped down outside her door on the carpeted floor, pulled my knees up to my chest, and listened for a while, feeling helpless.

"I'm sorry," I said into the crack of the door. "I know you hate me right now, and I don't blame you. I really screwed up. And you're right. There's just no excuse for what I did."

I took in a deep breath and let it out. "And I'm sorry for the other night—I didn't mean to accuse you or blame you for anything. I know it's not your fault at all. It's me. I take full responsibility for my actions. I'm also sorry for following you. It was a stupid idea. And it was an invasion of your privacy. I just let my imagination get the best of me. And I'm sorry I lied to you. I'm just sorry in general, I guess."

As I let the list of my wrongs rattle off into silence, I

could hear that she had stopped moving around. Maybe she was sleeping by now. Or just thinking about what I'd said. But what if something had happened to her?

"Mom?" I said, suddenly panicking. "Are you okay in there?"

"Yes," she said, her voice husky. "I'm fine."

"Okay. Good."

"How are you?" Her voice was thin but threaded with genuine concern.

"I'm okay." I took it as a good sign that she was asking. "I was just wondering. Do you think you can ever forgive me?"

"Maybe," she said softly. "But not tonight. It's been a really long day for both of us and I'd just like to sleep now. So maybe you should go back to your room. We can talk more tomorrow, okay?"

"Fair enough," I said into the door. "Well, good night . . . ?"

I didn't like the idea of going to sleep with everything still unresolved, but at least we were talking to each other civilly. Talking at all had to be a step in the right direction.

"Good night," she said. Or at least that's what I think she said. It was kind of muffled.

I shut out the light overhead. Then I started back down the hallway to my room, fumbling my way through the dark.

TWENTY-FOUR

IF THIS WERE any normal Tuesday morning at eleven A.M., I'd be in third-period French. Of course, life was not normal at all, and I was just waking up. I'd been suspended from school until Thursday. There had been official calls for my mom and me. Mr. Page had told me over the phone how disappointed he was, which of course made me feel worse. Valley Prep still had to bring my case before an internal disciplinary board to see whether I would be expelled for my crimes. They told us it might be "disruptive," under the circumstances, if I came back right away. The hearing was scheduled for Friday.

I knew I was lucky. I was in no hurry to face everyone at Valley Prep. Another day or two at home was just fine by me. Since I'd been back, I'd savored every moment of normalcy, from my own pajamas to the ability to sleep in darkness.

My mom was at the kitchen table as usual, with a copy of *Modern Painters* and her cup of tea in front of her. She'd cleaned at some point, because there were no dishes in the sink and the counters looked freshly wiped. The sun streamed in through the back windows, planting squares of light around the room. I paused in the doorway, watching her read. Things seemed brighter now in the light of day. Like a fresh start.

She looked up at me. "This is still your kitchen, you know. The water's probably hot enough for tea."

That was something. I put an Earl Grey bag in a mug and poured water into it. Then I sat down in my normal spot across from her. She was fully dressed in a striped tunic and slim jeans, and her hair was pulled back in a ponytail.

"How'd you sleep?" she asked flatly.

"Pretty good," I said. "My room here is like the Ritz-Carlton compared to the juvie cell."

Total silence. And then I regretted bringing it up in that way, cracking a joke. She would think I was making light of the situation, not taking it seriously.

But it's not like it wasn't on both of our minds. Was I supposed to pretend it hadn't happened?

"I mean, I was tired from being there," I backpedaled. "I didn't sleep much."

"Yeah, well. I can't imagine it was too comfortable." Translation: *I'm not really interested in feeling sorry for you right now, Willa.*

I focused on my tea, which was developing an oily sheen on the surface. I'd left the bag in too long. I took a sip and it was strong, almost bitter.

I thought we might be able to get at least some kind of peaceable silent tea-sipping thing going, but then my mom pulled her chair away from the table and stood up. She moved toward the sink and set her cup down in the basin. Then she folded up her magazine into thirds and stuck it under her arm.

"Are you going somewhere?" I asked.

"Yes," she said. "Out. I'll be back later."

So this was our new arrangement. Like two strangers rooming together.

I heard the laundry door squeak open and shut with a hollow clap. Then there was the rumble of the garage door opening.

I couldn't wonder where she was going. I wasn't going to pry anymore. She was setting the terms here and it was my job to simply accept them. It was going to take a while to build up trust between us again. That was okay, I thought. I would do whatever was necessary.

Not wanting to sit at the table alone, staring at her empty seat, I picked up my tea and went back to my bedroom.

There was some business to attend to today. I had to check in with Daniels and set up a meeting. I needed to start thinking about a plan to get some money so I could pay everyone back. Asking my mom was out of the question. I'd probably need to get some kind of legitimate job. A job they could give a fifteen-year-old confessed thief that would pay more than minimum wage and was within walkable distance. It sounded like a lot to ask.

I also needed to talk to Cherise. It had been days now, and I was sure she'd heard about everything that had happened. I had to come clean with her. But I didn't have my phone, so I went online.

I checked my email first to see if she'd written, and I almost fell off my chair.

I had eight hundred and fifty-two emails in my inbox—the last one being a message from the account server that I had run out of storage room.

Most were names I didn't recognize. As I briefly ran through them, I gleaned that they were from all over the country, people who had heard the story. Some of them were mean and accusatory, calling me a crook, a scoundrel, a liar. In this category were a few messages from Kellie and Nikki that I couldn't bring myself to open.

But my heart lifted when I saw that most of them were actually supportive, with subject lines like *my hero, the new Robin Hood,* and *Sly Fox rules.* There were a couple requests from reporters, from *People* magazine and TMZ. One agent from a Hollywood firm had written, asking if they could represent me and my story. I had approximately one hundred and sixty-three new Facebook friend requests.

I noticed a message from msantiago@gmail.com. Mary! I clicked it open.

> *Hey Willa,*
>
> *I heard you're in trouble and you're probably not even reading email but I felt like I should write on behalf of Alicia and Sierra and myself and thank you. For the last few weeks, I was wondering who was behind that new stuff. You should know that it made us really happy, even though we kind of knew it was too good to be true. So thank you so much for all that you have done, Willa. You risked your life for us and we will never forget that. The Sly Fox has some huge fans around here.*
>
> *See you soon (I hope),*
>
> *Mary*

Happiness, true happiness—something I hadn't felt in days—surged through me, and my heart felt like it was going to burst. This is what it had been all about. It hadn't been a waste. And maybe, just maybe, it had even been worth it.

I logged on to IM. Cherise happened to be online just then—my third good sign in the last twenty-four hours. Maybe these were omens of hope.

Hey, I messaged her.

MiZZJackson: Hey.

Willa1997: You're not in school?

MiZZJackson: Home sick.

Willa1997: So, I guess you heard some things?

MiZZJackson: Yes.

We paused, and I watched my cursor blinking in a blank box before I figured out what to say. I was afraid if I waited too long she might log off.

Willa1997: So you know everything?

MiZZJackson: I can't believe that was you. Why didn't you tell me?

Willa1997: I don't know. I didn't tell anyone.

MiZZJackson: I was next, wasn't I?

Willa1997: No! Never. Not you.

MiZZJackson: How am I supposed to believe that?

Willa1997: Because it's true. You're my friend.

MiZZJackson: So what's the difference? Why them?

Willa1997: They were so mean. You saw the stuff they did.

MiZZJackson: So they deserved to be robbed?

Willa1997: I just wanted to make things fair. I messed up.

MiZZJackson: Yeah, you really did. You lied to me. To all of us. I feel like I took you in and helped you and introduced you to everyone and you practically spit on me.

Willa1997: I never meant to hurt you. I'm sorry. I really am.

MiZZJackson: But are you? Even if you could take it back I doubt Kellie and Nikki would ever forgive you.

Kellie and Nikki were never really my friends, anyway, I wanted to say. Cherise was the only one I really cared about.

Willa1997: What about you?
MiZZJackson: You've put me in a bad position now. I mean, you don't know how many years I spent trying to be accepted by these guys. Years, Willa. I'm finally part of the crew and now you want me to go down with you because you made a stupid mistake? I don't think so. How do I know you won't just turn around and start stealing from me?

My heart sank. I knew I couldn't just convince her with words. It was going to take much more to show her I meant it.

Willa1997: I know I have to make it up to you.
MiZZJackson: It's not just that. Kellie has already made my life hell for what I said the other day. You saw her post about me, didn't you?
Willa1997: Yeah. I saw it.
MiZZJackson: If I still hang out with you, it's over for me.
Willa1997: But is she really worth it, Cherise? I think you're too good for her. For them.
MiZZJackson: Look, you have no idea, okay? You're just the new girl.

I winced. The words glared at me from the screen, sharp and dismissive. Okay, so maybe this messaging thing wasn't helping. Maybe I needed another tactic.

Willa1997: Can we talk about this in person? It's kind of hard over IM and my mom took my phone away.
MiZZJackson: I don't think so. I don't think my parents are going to let me see you anymore.

The light feeling I'd had after reading my emails had drained out of me like helium from a balloon. I really liked Cherise's mom. I wanted her to like me again. I wanted Cherise to like me again.

Willa1997: What can I do?
MiZZJackson: Nothing. I'm done, Willa.
Willa1997: If that's what you want.
MiZZJackson: Yeah. It is.

Okay, I started to type, but she had already logged off.

I signed off and sank back down onto my mattress, reeling with hurt. From my bed, I could see that there were still reporters outside, a full twenty-four hours later. I didn't know what to think. How was it that the people who knew me best were the ones who were turning their backs on me? I mean, my own mom wasn't speaking to me. And now Cherise. Yet the people who didn't know me at all were the ones sticking by me.

Maybe, I thought, I should just embrace the whole Sly Fox thing. She was much more popular than Willa right now.

Sometime in the night—it was dark, and I was asleep—I heard a window opening. It took a few moments for it to register that this was a real noise and not just the sounds in my dreams. I sat up and grabbed for a robe.

"Mom?" I called. But no one answered.

Pulling the ties around my waist, I made my way down the hall to the front door. Until I hit something.

It felt like I walked into a body, a man's body, and I screamed as we made impact.

"Whoa," the man said.

"Who are you and what are you doing in here?" Dark images flashed through my head. I thought maybe it was a reporter sneaking in, and the idea chilled me to the bone. Why couldn't they just leave us alone? My mom had been right about the media after all.

"Hey," he said, grabbing my wrists. "Calm down. It's just me. Tre."

"Oh my God." I clutched at my chest, trying to catch my breath. My eyes adjusted to the darkness and I could make out his frame, and then the sculpted angles of his cheekbones and the long lines of his leather jacket and jeans.

"I just wanted to check on you. Wanted to make sure you were okay." He had stuffed his hands in the pockets of his jacket. I'd had no idea that he knew where I lived, but he'd obviously used one of his signature moves on my house. "Sorry it's so late. Did I wake you?"

Once my near–heart attack subsided, I had to smile. I was thrilled to see him.

"Yeah, but it's okay," I said. "Come in."

"Are you sure?"

"Yeah." One good thing about being arrested is that practically any other act of rebellion, like letting a guy break into my house at two on a Wednesday morning, seemed absurdly innocent.

I led him into the living room and he sat down on the couch. I didn't bother turning the light on, as a little pale light from the street was leaking into the room. I sat next to him in the violet shadows.

"How are you?" I asked.

"Eh, not bad. You know." He laughed a little. "Sorry for the late hour, but with my record and everything, I had to sneak in here. In case anyone was watching."

I remembered what the lawyer had told me about not associating with other criminals. We could probably both get in a lot of trouble for hanging out, but just then I didn't really care. I wasn't about to turn him away.

"I'm glad you're here," I said, patting him on the knee. "It's been a rough few days."

"You wanna talk about it?"

My eyes welled up with hot tears. I realized that in all this time, no one had really been all that interested in my side of the story, or how I felt. They were all focusing on the bad stuff. What I'd done. He was the first one to look beyond that.

"I don't know. It was just—scary. Getting cuffed and dragged into the station. I was really freaked out. I didn't know what was happening."

He nodded. "And they're pretty nice to girls in there. At least compared to guys like me."

"It was horrible. You don't even realize how good you have it until—"

"Until they want to take it all away. Yeah."

He got it. He had been there. I exhaled. Just exchanging a few words with him helped me shake off the heavy feelings I'd been shouldering—the guilt, the fear, the shame. He wasn't judging me at all. He was simply here beside me.

I slouched down on the couch, putting a fat white pillow behind my neck. "Can I ask you something?"

"Go ahead." He folded his arms across his chest.

"Why are you being so nice to me? You took a big risk in coming here."

"Want me to egg your house or something?" He laughed.

"No, no, no. Just, you didn't think what I did was wrong?"

"Maybe I did at first. But I've come to see that your heart was in the right place. I mean, you had your reasons and they were actually kind of ethical at the core—unlike me." He shrugged. "I was just causing trouble for thrills."

"Yeah, but did you get hate mail?"

He laughed. "When someone finds out his Ferrari has gone for a cruise through the barrio, he's not gonna send you flowers. Believe me."

I sighed. "I don't know if I can go back to Prep. Even if they let me go back, they're going to torture me."

"Not necessarily. There are lots of people who think you gave the Glitterati what was coming to them."

"Maybe." I wasn't sure it was going to be so easy. But maybe knowing Tre was at least behind me—even if he couldn't associate with me in public—would help a little bit.

"So you have to do community service?" He stretched his long legs out in front of him.

"Yeah," I said. "I start tomorrow morning at the animal shelter. Of all the options they gave me it sounded like the most tolerable. I've never had any pets, but I figured maybe I could bond with a Labrador or something."

"It beats picking up trash like our friend Murphy."

I felt my spine straighten. What was Aidan doing right now? When would I see him again?

"He said you called him," Tre said softly. "He said you were really freaked out."

"I was," I said, remembering Aidan's voice on the phone the other night, how strong and caring he'd been.

"A lot of us were worried but I know you'll be fine,

Willa. You'll get through this," he said, standing up. "Well, I should probably get going."

"You sure?"

"It's late. But I'm glad you're okay. If you need anything, give me a call."

"Okay," I said, hugging him. The vaguely sweet smell of his leather jacket mingled with the scent of his aftershave, which was just a little spicy, like pepper. I hadn't realized before how strong his arms were.

He was a good friend. I wondered idly if he was still with his girl. She was lucky, whoever she was.

We pulled apart, and I walked him to the door.

"Your mom must be a heavy sleeper," he said as he stepped out into the night and got into his car.

My mom. She couldn't be sleeping through all this. Not through my scream, at least.

I peered out and saw her car wasn't in the driveway. I looked in the garage and it wasn't there, either. It was now three A.M. and she had been out since midmorning. Worry gripped me violently. Where could she be? I grabbed the house phone and dialed her number.

No answer. No voice-mail greeting. Of course: She was going to get us new phones. Her old one was disconnected.

I sat back down on the living room sofa, facing the front windows that overlooked the street. It was dark and quiet as always. I wrapped a throw around me and waited. Every time a passing car spread its light across the room I stood up and looked out the window, but none of them was her.

At five thirty, I was back in the kitchen with the cordless phone, getting ready to call the police. I tried to think about what I would tell them. I wasn't sure, after my own run-in with the law, that they would believe me or take me seriously. Besides, what if it turned out to be nothing?

Just then, the key turned in the lock and my mom came through the door.

"Where've you been?" I practically yelled.

"I had to figure a few things out," she said. She took a deep breath and placed her handbag on the counter. She seemed calmer, more purposeful than she'd been in the past few days, but small and young and vulnerable at the same time. She sat down at the table, pulled her hair out of its band, and folded her hands in front of her.

"Are you okay? What's going on?" I was nearly hyperventilating, even though she was home safe with me.

"Everything is fine," she said gently. "I've been thinking about what you did, and I have to say something that I should have said much earlier. No matter what, I love you, Willa. You know that. I love you unconditionally. And I know you were just trying to do something good. It was stupid, for sure."

I sat down next to her and draped my arm over her shoulder. "I know."

"But I want you to know that I can forgive you. It's

definitely going to change our lives and our plans for the future. But we'll get through this."

"I hope so," I said, feeling my own voice break up. I was so scared that we would never be able to move past this moment.

"I've always tried to raise you to be responsible, you know? I wanted you to have good values. Maybe, in a way, I gave you too much freedom. I didn't give you enough boundaries where you needed them."

I could see the pain in her face and realized that maybe what she had been grappling with wasn't so much the anger at me—though I knew that was there—but some kind of guilt that she had done something wrong.

"No," I said. "It's not your fault. Don't blame yourself for what I've done."

"But I've only wanted the best for you. And I still do. I've really wanted you to be self-sufficient and independent and smart and strong." Her eyes shone with tears. "You are. This thing—this was wrong, but I know that in general you can take care of yourself and make good decisions."

She stood up and I did too. She put her arms around me and kissed me on both cheeks—with force, almost.

"I love you, Mom."

"I love you so," she said into my hair. Then she pulled away. "We should go to bed. The sun is coming up already. We'll be feeling the pain tomorrow."

"I have to report to community service," I said.

"That's right. What time?"

"Noon."

"That's not too bad," she said, smiling. It was the first time I'd seen her smile in days, it felt like. "Well, get some sleep."

"Good night," I said.

Back in bed, I realized that in the midst of all that had happened, I'd never asked her what we were going to do for Thanksgiving. It was only a few weeks away. Now that she had forgiven me and things were better, I wondered if we could start planning for the holiday. It would be like clearing the slate. When I woke up, I would offer to make a pie, or some stuffing.

I had things to be thankful for now, definitely: There was my mom, there was Tre, and there was Aidan. I wasn't alone. The thought cheered me a little as I drifted off to sleep.

TWENTY-FIVE

I'D NEVER BEEN so excited as I was on my way to the animal shelter to report for community-service duty. Okay, maybe that was an overstatement, but I was genuinely looking forward to it—not only was I going to get out of the house and interact with other humans, and thus have a reason to shower, I was also going to play with cute animals. It was the beginning of the rest of my completely legal, totally rule-obeying life. *Bring it on,* I thought as I hopped out of the car and waved good-bye to my mom.

It was amazing how much you could crave the little things after being locked up, how much you could enjoy your freedom when you were back in the world.

The animal shelter was a 1950s brick building with columns, set off from the street and the rest of the town by its old-school architecture. I practically bounced up the stone steps that connected the sidewalk to the entrance. I felt like I was entering a place where I was safe—a place where all the hubbub about Sly Fox didn't matter.

Inside, I was directed beyond the front hall with its desk and little waiting area to a meeting room, where about ten people were gathered on folding metal chairs. Most of them were older, like senior-citizen older, but there were a few people in their twenties. I wondered if any of them were here for community-service requirements like I was or if they were just here out of the goodness of their hearts.

A woman in a polo shirt embroidered with the shelter logo stood at the front of the room. She was about forty or so, with short brown hair that was pulled back into a barrette. She introduced herself as Jan and told us she was the volunteer coordinator. She asked us to go around the room and introduce ourselves.

This took a few minutes, and everyone smiled at one another politely. When it was my turn, I just said my first name and prayed that no one would recognize me from the news. Maybe it was my imagination but I thought I saw two women react, exchanging a glance. So maybe the Sly Fox thing would follow me in here. I had to face facts: Unless I moved away, this would probably be happening for a while.

"Welcome, everyone. I appreciate you coming in today and I look forward to having you work here with us at the shelter. How many of you have been here before?"

A few people raised their hands.

"How many of you have worked in any shelter before?"

As Jan was talking, I heard the door behind me open as someone entered the room.

"Have a seat," Jan said to the new person. "We're just getting started. And your name is?"

"Aidan."

Aidan?!

I spun around and saw that it was indeed the Aidan Murphy I knew. What was *he* doing here? I actually gasped.

He saw me staring at him and he smiled before coming over to the empty seat next to me. He looked almost embarrassed. "Hey, Colorado."

OMG. OMG. The room instantly brightened as if all the lightbulbs had been blasted with a giant energy surge.

I wanted to stand up and applaud his entrance. Instead, I smiled widely and said, "Hey."

Was he getting hotter by the day, or was that my imagination?

"You two know each other, I see. I was just about to start telling everyone a little more about what we do here at Mountainside and how you volunteers can help us."

He sat down next to me. "Tre told me I'd find you here," he whispered. "I thought we could serve out our time together—you know, make it a party."

He was so close to me, I could feel his breath on my ear—just like the other day. . . . My heart quickened with the sensation.

I tried to focus on what Jan was saying. She explained the various roles we might be able to take on: administrative assistant, cat or dog buddy, or cleanup patrol.

"We'll start you with one of these, but you'll rotate through all of them in the time you're with us," Jan said.

"How are you?" Aidan whispered.

"Okay, I guess." *Better now that you're here*. "You?"

"Okay," he said. "Criminal system's a bitch, huh?"

I nodded.

"One of the problems we face here is finding homes for these animals," Jan said. "If you're in the front office, you'll be helping us work with potential adopters. Keep in mind that we're competing with pet stores and with dog breeders. People usually come here as a last resort, or if they can't really afford to buy a pet. Has anyone here gotten an animal from a shelter before?"

One woman raised her hand.

"How about the rest of you? Where did you get your pets?"

"I adopted my cat from a friend," another woman said. "He was depressed and peeing in her house so she needed to give him away."

"My mom used to breed dogs," Aidan said to the room. "Little fluffy ones. People would travel all the way across the state to buy them. She would show them, too. It was like a hobby. For years I tried to convince her to stop—I told her there were so many animals out there without homes, and she was making it worse."

He was an animal-rights advocate? The surprises never ended with this guy.

Jan nodded. "We find that in this affluent area, a shelter dog can be a tough sell. Right now we're just at capacity here. So if you know anyone who's looking to foster animals, please let me know."

Jan said that the rest of the day would be spent touring the facility, so we all got up out of our seats and she opened a pair of double doors to show us where the animals were kept.

We passed by a row of cats in their cages—some chubby with fuzzy little faces, others sleek and majestic. There were cute little bunnies and a few hamsters and gerbils. Then it was on to the biggest section of the shelter, the dogs. I was trying to pay attention to the animals but with Aidan so close to me, I was having a hard time concentrating. I could feel the charged air between us with every step.

As we walked down the row of cages, the dogs rushed forward to greet us, leaping up to stick their paws and noses through the wire.

"Hey, guy," Aidan said, stopping in front of a cage to let a beagle lick his fingers.

"He likes you," I said.

"You think so?" he said, his face earnest as he leaned

in. I felt my insides melt a little, watching him comfort the small dog. He was stroking his head now, murmuring, "It's gonna be okay, buddy. We got you."

I stood there by him while he moved on to the next one, a mangy-looking terrier mix. It was not a very cute dog, but he gave it the same dose of love as he had to the first one. He seemed lost in his own little world, talking to the dog and letting it lick his hand.

After a few minutes, he looked up, self-conscious. "What?" he asked.

"I'm just watching you," I said. "I didn't know you could be so . . . sweet."

His mouth slowly curled into a smile. "I told you . . . we're like caramels."

Later, after we'd finished orientation, Aidan and I walked out together to the front steps.

"So you're a celebrity," he said. "I couldn't turn on the news the past few weeks without hearing about you. You were everywhere. It was awesome. Who knew you were such a badass?"

"I'm not, really," I demurred. "Well, maybe slightly badass."

"I heard you were carrying out a suitcase of cash from the Richardsons' safe. And that you were shot at four times during the chase."

"False. Where'd you hear that?" I asked. But I didn't have to.

"The Buzz, of course. The only news source of record in the Valley. I heard you dug your way out of the juvie cell with a bendy straw and some Starbursts." He grinned. "Actually, I made that one up myself."

"Nice," I said. "But what about you?"

"What about me?"

"How'd you finally persuade them to kick you out? How'd you end up here?"

His face clouded over and I felt a wall come up. "I told you, Colorado. I don't really want to talk about it."

"But you know all about me now," I insisted. Why the secrecy? It was like Tre all over again. Or my mom. I couldn't stand these big mysteries—not from people I cared about.

"Believe me, you don't need to know. It's not that interesting a story. Not like yours, anyway." He stared off into the distance.

I watched him closely. He looked the same as he always had, the same shaggy hair and amazing eyes and everything else, but also subtly different. He was more reserved, or more humbled. Or something.

And he was acting differently, too. He'd always been a bit like a puppy himself, bounding back whenever I shooed him away, but now I could see that something was going on for him. Something hard.

I decided to let it be and change the subject. "How's that terminal illness treating you? Still dying?"

It took him a second, but he recovered quickly. "Eh,

so-so. But we're all dying, right?"

"It's true, from a Buddhist standpoint." I sighed. "I don't know how we'll be able to stay here with these animals week after week. It's kind of depressing."

"Well, someone needs to help these little guys."

"They shouldn't be locked up like that," I said. "It goes against their nature."

"No, they should be free." His eyes lit up with an idea. "We could do it, you know. Let them out."

Was he insane? "What, just break in here and open the cages?"

He shrugged. "Why not?"

"I don't think so. I mean, it's a nice fantasy, though."

"It wouldn't be that hard. You know how to do that stuff, right? Like pick locks and things?" He pantomimed a break-in with an imaginary doorknob.

"Aidan, my days of breaking and entering are over," I said.

"That's what they all say. But once the criminal life is in you, it's hard to go straight." He had the goofy smile on again, and I was relieved to see it come back. Aidan was just not Aidan without it. "I guess I should roll. How are you getting home?"

"I need to call my mom. Can I borrow your phone?"

"Sure," he said, handing me his Droid.

I dialed the number to the house. But there was no answer. It just kept ringing. She must have disconnected the house voice mail, too. This no-cell-phone, anti-press policy was driving me crazy. Was I supposed to contact her via carrier pigeon?

"She's not there." I handed him the phone.

"I can give you a ride, if you want." Our fingertips touched around the phone. My body instantly went hot.

"I can walk . . . " My voice trailed off as I met his eyes. It was my old stubbornness talking—not my heart.

"It's at least six miles," he said. Then he shrugged. "I can only kidnap a girl once, you know. Then it starts to get a little shady."

He started down the steps to the parking lot. I watched his lights flare as he unlocked his car. I looked around. It was getting dark. All the other volunteers had left. It was evening now, and they all probably had families to get home to, meals to cook. I could be waiting here for a long time. And I didn't want to watch him drive away. I didn't want him to leave at all.

"Wait!" I called out after him. "I'm coming."

He was just standing there with his hands on his hips, smiling at me as he watched me approach.

"That is, if the offer still stands." I exhaled as I caught up with him.

"Are you kidding? After everything they said about you? It would be my privilege to take you home. You're a living legend, Sly Fox!"

I shook my head, smiling. "Just call me Willa, okay?"

TWENTY-SIX

TO HIS CREDIT, Aidan drove pretty safely all the way to my house. And though he did insist on wearing his NASCAR sunglasses in the falling dusk, I was too busy thinking about other things to get hung up on the cheese factor. Like the fact that he'd actually come to the shelter for me—though I couldn't quite believe it was for my sake. I was going to have to double-check this with Tre when I got home.

Then there was the little matter of his hand on the gearshift, inches away from me. And the inside of the car, which was practically a cloud of his scent. Under these conditions, it was hard to form sentences.

"We should count ourselves lucky we didn't have to go to that pre-holiday luncheon yesterday," he said, changing lanes. "It's really one of the lamest things you could imagine. They make everyone do these poetry readings and then we all have to say a weird little prayer."

"You're luckier than me," I said. "You don't have to go back there at all."

"Maybe so," he said. "Your street is here, right?"

"Yeah," I said. *He remembered.*

Okay, freaky. Settle down.

He shook his head with sympathy as he turned onto my street. "Let's just say Kellie's not too happy with you right now. But if you could handle juvie, you can handle her," Aidan said. "You're a tough girl, right?"

"Oh yeah." I gave him two thumbs-up. If anything, juvie had shown me exactly how not-tough I was.

He pulled up into my driveway. "Well, Colorado, maybe I'll see you around at the shelter."

"Yeah," I said. "I guess I'll be there next Monday."

"Me too. I've got nothing else going on these days." He laughed, but it was not a particularly joyous laugh.

"Thanks for coming today. And for your help the other night, of course. And thanks for the ride."

He gave me a look, like he was detecting sarcasm.

"No, I mean it this time. I would've been standing there all night. And you drove very nicely." I glanced up at him, shy all of a sudden.

"I've been working on it, like I said I would." His eyes darted away from me, back to the windshield. I looked at his profile, the jagged geometry of his face.

"I appreciate that. And so do the agave plants," I said, pausing. Was I supposed to hug him? Kiss him?

Shake his hand? I was trying to read his cues, but one thing I was learning about Aidan Murphy was that he didn't always give off the clearest signals. "Well, have a good night."

He turned back toward me and his face was smooth and serious. "You too, Willa."

I unclicked my seat belt. He unclicked his, and leaned over to my side of the car.

I had been anticipating this moment for a long time, ever since the day he first drove me home. And if I was going to be honest with myself, probably long before that.

My breath stopped as he moved closer. I let my eyes close, and then . . .

. . . nothing.

When I looked again, his lips were inches away from mine. Frozen. "What's wrong?" I asked, my heart jangling in my tonsils.

"Nothing. It just looks like your front door is open."

I craned my neck behind me and saw the slant of light coming from the front of the house.

"That's weird," I said.

"Maybe your mom left it that way?"

"Yeah, maybe. Maybe she just walked in." But I looked back to the driveway and saw her car wasn't there. It could have been in the garage, but then she would have gone in the house through the adjoining door, and not the front.

"You look worried. Can I walk you to the door?" he asked.

"No, no," I said, embarrassed. The kissing moment had clearly passed, and I was positive I'd looked like an idiot with my lips all puckered up. No wonder he'd held back. "I'm fine."

Aidan must have sensed my unease, because he left the car in park. "I'll wait until you go in," he said. "Just in case."

"Thanks. I'm sure it's nothing." I wasn't sure at all, but after he had gone on and on about what a badass I was, I felt like I had a reputation to uphold.

I went up to the door, which was cracked about four inches, and pushed it fully open.

"Mom?" I called.

My voice didn't so much echo as hover.

Right away, I could see that everything was wrong. The living-room chairs and sofa were upturned like tipped cows, exposing the staples of their upholstery seams and the pads under their feet. The glass on the poster over the sofa was smashed in; a cobweb of cracks now covered the image of the forest I'd loved so much. My mom's hand-stitched pillows were thrown on the floor and looked like they'd been stomped on.

What the hell? I moved frantically through the house.

In the kitchen, the floor was littered with broken plates, glasses, boxes of food. A pool of milk was forming under the refrigerator where a carton had been dumped. All the appliances had been bashed in with a hammer or a baseball bat, it looked like. Several of the cabinet doors were hanging off their hinges.

Everything had been destroyed so thoroughly I didn't need to go in the other rooms to know that they probably looked much the same.

Our beautiful house. Completely trashed.

A chill danced up my spine, along with a sickening thought. This was the Glitterati's revenge. It had to be. They'd found out I'd gotten out of jail and they'd come here to pay me back for my crimes themselves.

My mom wasn't here, clearly. We needed help. Or at the very least, a witness. I went back to the front step and called out to Aidan.

"Can you come in here? I need you to see something."

At the sound of my voice, the pantry closet creaked open. Footsteps clattered behind me.

Oh my God. Someone was in the house. Fear blazed through me like sparks swallowing a fuse.

I spun around on my heels and caught a glimpse of the person's back, a flash of flannel shirt, dashing out of the kitchen. Just when I caught up with what was going on, the intruder flung open the sliding glass door and was now running out into the backyard.

I took off after him. I could hear Aidan yelling for me as I sprinted through the house and outside to the patio. But by the time I got out there, he'd already leapt over the fence into a neighbor's yard.

Aidan was beside me, leaning in, his face full of alarm. "What the hell just happened?"

"Someone just trashed my house!" I gasped. "He got away!"

"Let's follow him," he said, grabbing my hand. "We can still find him if we hurry."

We charged back to his car. Aidan reversed in a rocket blast down the driveway, sharply turned out, then accelerated forward into full-throttle speed down Morning Glory, all very calmly, like this was something he did every day.

"How will we find him?" I said, my heart pounding. "I don't even know which way he was headed."

We hit the cul-de-sac and Aidan deftly turned the car around. "Note the Mercedes's superior turning radius. Where does your yard lead to?" he asked.

"It's another street back there. Sierra Vista Road."

He pulled out onto the main road and turned down Sierra Vista, where the walls of cacti on either side of the road seemed to be closing in on us. Zooming past in the opposite direction was a gold Chevy Tahoe.

I only got a blinking eyeful of the driver, but I thought I could see a plaid shirt. "That's him, I think!"

Aidan slammed on the brakes and made a U-turn. Seeing us, the Tahoe picked up speed and we both careened out onto the main road, Aidan's car following by about twenty yards.

"Where's he going?" I asked.

"No idea. Do you know that guy?"

"I think it must be the Glitterati."

"What? That guy? I've never seen him before."

"I mean, they put him up to it," I said as I thought it through. I couldn't actually picture Kellie and Nikki stomping on my living room couch. "They hired him or something. They had to. They'd never do something like this themselves."

"He's heading toward town, it looks like." Aidan stared hard at the car in front of us. "You really think it's them?"

"Ever heard of an eye for an eye?"

"In the bible. And in action movies when someone is about to get a limb amputated," he said with a sidelong glance.

"My point exactly."

"I don't know, Willa." Aidan sounded skeptical.

"Why not?"

"Just, that's a little extreme, even for them."

"Okay, then," I said. "Who else would be breaking into my house and ransacking our stuff? If you've got any other ideas, I'd love to hear them."

"Do you have any other enemies?"

By now, with the Sly Fox story on the national news, I could have enemies in fifty states and Puerto Rico. From the emails, at least, it seemed like I had just as many fans, though. And who would go so far as to do something like this? This person would've had to have our house under surveillance to know when we'd be out. That made us a mark. With the thought came a wave of nausea and dizziness so strong that I covered my mouth and hunched over.

"Are you okay?" he asked.

I nodded, trying to pull myself together. I took some deep breaths. There was no time to feel anything. We had to get this guy.

Aidan yanked on the gearshift and the car jolted onward. The race-car getup was starting to make more sense in this context. "All I'm saying is we shouldn't jump to conclusions. It could be anyone, really. A local vigilante. A competing thief. The mafia."

"The mafia? In Paradise Valley?"

"They're everywhere," he said. "Trust me."

"But it doesn't make any sense."

We were heading toward the business district of the Valley, which meant we were hitting thicker traffic. It was nearing rush hour. Everyone had somewhere to go. The momentum on the road slowed as people changed lanes, and other cars kept threatening to come in between us and the Tahoe. More cars meant more obstacles and more potential to mess up.

"Don't lose him!" I shouted.

"Get his license plate number just in case we do. Did you get his license plate number?"

"No. Do you have your phone?"

He dug into his pocket and tossed it over to me. I opened up a memo page and typed in the number on the Tahoe, which had California plates. That reminded me of the car Cherise and I had seen in the Target parking lot.

Which belonged to the guy my mom had met there. The one she clearly didn't want us to see her with. Could this have something to do with her?

No. This was Kellie and Nikki, maybe Drew. California wasn't that far away, I reasoned. There were lots of people driving around Arizona with California plates. Kellie herself was always going to some spa in Santa Barbara. If they'd hired someone, the guy could have easily come from there.

"So what are we going to do when we catch him?" he asked.

"Call the cops. I don't know."

"Just supposing we do that. How will we restrain him until they get here?"

I pictured it like a book I read once where the hero followed the bad guy to his safe house in the woods. In the story, they'd taken the air out of the tires so he couldn't escape.

Only we were in the middle of the desert. There were no woods around. For all we knew, this guy could keep on driving back to California, or back to his mom's house for dinner.

"You're strong, right?" I asked.

He didn't laugh. "Sorry, Willa. There's no way I'm gonna wrestle with some guy who just trashed your house."

I clucked my tongue with annoyance. Why was he turning back into a spoiled pretty boy—now, of all times?! "It's probably some frat kid. If you're too scared, I can do it myself."

"I *am* scared. Dude probably has a gun. Besides, if I were you, I wouldn't be so quick to pull the cops into anything right now."

"Just forget it. I'll figure it out." My voice was high and indignant.

"Look, Willa, I'm not saying we should give up."

I clutched at the door handle as we careened around a curve. "Then what do you suggest we do?"

"I don't know. I need to think about this." He chewed on his lip. "We can't just throw ourselves into a combat situation, though. We need some backup. Some security."

I considered his point. It was true that we didn't have any kung fu moves. We didn't have weapons. We didn't have booby traps. All I knew how to do was pick pockets and break into places, and all Aidan knew was how to break down computers and score big on standardized math tests—none of which was much help right now. As much as I hated to admit it, Aidan was right. We needed a better plan.

We passed some gas stations and a shopping plaza

with a half-full parking lot. It was your typical suburban landscape, but the blue light of the November dusk—which was almost blinding in its sudden dimness—made it all seem ominous and unfamiliar. Within minutes it would be fully dark, and people started turning on their lights.

A VW Beetle to our left signaled to get into our lane, then aggressively pulled in front of us just as we were hitting a light.

"Dah!" Aidan blurted out.

The light turned yellow and the Beetle stopped, effectively trapping us.

The Tahoe sped off, leaving a few little puffs of exhaust that quickly evaporated into the evening air. And with it, our best hopes of finding out who was after me.

Aidan pounded the steering wheel in frustration. "Now what?"

On my side of the car I pressed my lips together, feeling the blood drain out of them. "Just take me home," I said.

"Are you sure you want to go back there?"

I nodded. I stared ahead at the road, feeling more certain now in my gut. It was the crooked part of me, the part of me that could see a goal ahead and break down all the little barriers along the way. The fear and the dread had passed over; now there was just focus.

We would head back in the direction of my wrecked

house. I'd regroup. I'd start cleaning everything up. With or without anyone's help, I would make sure that the Glitterati hadn't gotten the last word.

Yes, I'd started this thing. But the game had changed. I was sure of that now.

And I wasn't the type to give up that easily.

EPILOGUE

SO I'M NOT totally up on all the etiquette in a situation like this, but what exactly are you supposed to talk about on the ride home after a quasi-thug who just trashed your house and led you on a ten-mile car chase escapes into the night?

I got nothing, people.

I mean, at that point, Aidan and I may as well have been two zombies—well, two zombies in a luxury SUV. Up until the guy got away, there'd been this huge wave of adrenaline surging between us. Now it was barely a crackle. I could see it in Aidan's face, the way his lids were hanging heavy over his eyes, the way his breath had deepened. My own head felt crispy, the beginnings of a headache crossed with a spacey emptiness. We were burnt out.

Aidan reached over and turned up the radio, playing more of his doom metal. That felt appropriate, at least. I looked out the window without really looking. The moon had popped up and it was full and bright and exposed, almost vulnerable out there all by itself in the enormous open sky, dangling over the sharp peaks of the mountains. I shivered a little, thinking of what lay in store at home.

I just needed a shower, maybe, then a cup of tea. And then I'd figure out what to do with the mess. It would be fine, I told myself. I wasn't terribly convincing at that particular moment—but I wasn't such a great listener just then, either.

Aidan eased the car onto Sierra Vista and then onto Morning Glory. My street was quiet, no real activity except for a car passing us in the opposite direction.

A silver Nissan, I saw as it went by. With California plates. Like the one . . .

My heart lurched.

No, it couldn't be.

My mother's mystery man.

I started calculating the possibilities. If there were a quota on how many weird things could happen in a day, I'd already hit it with the above-mentioned car chase and house-trashing.

So this was simply a coincidence. Right? Or maybe I was imagining things.

"What's wrong?" Aidan asked, suddenly, turning toward me. He must have sensed the internal struggle I was having with my runaway brain. Either that or the way my knuckles had gone white on the passenger-side door handle.

"It's nothing," I said. "I'm just—I think my nerves are just shot. It's been a bizarre day."

"Well, I won't argue with you there." He shook his head and pulled into my driveway. Then he smiled, his eyes twinkling a bit as he shifted the car into park. "You really know how to liven up a Wednesday afternoon."

"Oh, this?" I said, waving a hand through the air ever so casually. "This was nothing. You should see what I do on Thursdays."

"Can I at least help you clean up?"

"No, that's okay. My mom will be here soon." I unbuckled my seat belt and let it slide into its retracted position. I had a funny feeling that she and I might get into another fight about keeping secrets. I definitely didn't want Aidan to be around for that. "But thanks for helping today—with everything."

Again with an etiquette quandary: How do you thank someone for possibly risking their life for you? It was impossible.

Best thing to do was get out of the car quickly, before we could have another awkward moment. Because, of course, in the middle of everything, I still hadn't managed to forget the cringe-worthy botched kiss. Um, yeah. No chance of that. That was the kind of thing that would probably haunt me until I was fifty.

I sighed to myself and waved to him through the open passenger window.

Maybe it really wasn't meant to be.

He waved back and reversed his Mercedes out of the

driveway. Tiny pin-dot beginnings of tears welled up in my eyes. I was just overwhelmed, I told myself. Just tired.

And as I started up the walk, true exhaustion sank in—I could feel it hanging all over me like a heavy coat. I got out my key. Then I remembered that in our haste to catch the intruder we'd probably just left the door open. Not like it mattered, because everything inside the house was ruined anyway.

Still, a shiver ran through me—what if someone else was in there?

No. There's a quota, remember?

Just then, my eye caught on a corner of white paper tucked under the front door. I reached down to grab it.

It was a calling card. *Special Agent Jeremy Corbin,* it said on the front. Federal Bureau of Investigation, United States Department of Justice. Above the name was an official-looking embossed gold and blue shield, and below it, an address and phone number in Los Angeles.

Why was the FBI here? Had they known about the break-in, or were they here for something else? And when? I wondered. Had we missed the card when we came into the house earlier? It was possible, I guess.

I turned it over in my hand. On the opposite side, scrawled in blue ink, was a note:

Willa, I know you're in trouble. And I can help you. Call me if you need anything. JC

No, it hadn't been there before at all. Somebody had left it moments ago. I knew because I'd just seen him driving away from my house.

Mom's mystery man and Special Agent Corbin were one and the same.

But what did *he* have to do with any of this?

Before I could register the shock of learning my mom had been talking to the FBI, I heard brakes screeching and the sound of a car door flinging open. I looked up, startled, my heart pounding yet again.

It was Aidan, bounding up the driveway, his hair flying in a blond halo, his sneakers slapping against the pavement. I watched him run toward me, my jaw dropping.

"What is it?" I gasped, terrified that something else had happened. "What's wrong?"

"I forgot something," he said, stopping in front of me and staring straight into my eyes. He grabbed my shoulders, and my already-racing heartbeat doubled its RPM.

I felt his lips first, pulling gently on mine as we found each other, drew away, and reconnected in soft pulses. His arms wrapped around my neck, his open hand cradling the back of my head. His chest pressed against me, firm and sturdy. Then his mouth—insistent, yet warm and enveloping. The herbal, sweet smell of him, the tangle of his hair in my fingers.

After a moment, I realized my eyes were still open, staring in disbelief, but now I let them close.

I sank into the kiss, letting it all go—my fears and worries, the unanswered questions, the whole crazy day, and the crazy days before it. This moment was the only one that mattered, wasn't it? Aidan was here with me, closer than he'd ever been. And for now, everything else was just going to have to wait.

ACKNOWLEDGMENTS

GREAT BIG PARADISE Valley–mansion-size thanks to the following people:

My partner in crime Claudia Gabel, who totally made this book possible from start to finish, shaping multiple drafts and smoothly guiding the manuscript down the halls of HarperCollins. Your wisdom and bubbly enthusiasm have made this process a joy.

My agent Leigh Feldman, who got me into the big leagues and offered equal amounts of straight talk and encouragement along the way. Also, sturgeon. You rock.

Gracious publisher Katherine Tegen, cover designers Amy Ryan, Joel Tippie, and Torborg Davern, photographer Howard Huang, editorial assistant Katie Bignell, and the rest of the team at HarperCollins for their support, savvy, and hard work.

My parents, Zella and Stephen, who gave me the crazy idea that I could be anything I wanted to be when I grew up. Susannah and Aubrey, who are the best sisters and best friends a girl could ask for. My late grandmother Rose, who always said there was a little larceny in everyone. (She was talking about swiping rolls from restaurants, but hey.)

And my husband, Jesse, for reading and commenting, assisting with research, offering pep talks, disrupting me when I needed disrupting, and loving me in the best possible way. Aidan Murphy's got nothing on you.

Willa Fox was told to stay out of trouble. In fact, it was an order from a juvenile court judge.

However, that was before her house was ransacked and her mother disappeared. . . .

Turn the page for a sneak peek at how her adventure continues in

PROLOGUE

"JUST GO!" AIDAN yelled.

There wasn't time to sort it out. I had to jump. The man was right behind us now, yelling. Aidan was depending on me, and we were in this together. I inhaled big gulps of air like I was about to dive underwater. Counted *one, two, three* . . .

As my feet left the wooden planks, cold air rushed around my face, so sharp it was almost a burning sensation. My arms flapped uselessly at my sides. I wasn't flying. I was falling.

On the way down there was nothing but nothing. Air. A painful silence. For minutes, it seemed.

Then my feet jammed hard, and I landed in a heavy squat, snow crunching all around my sneakers, my bones thrumming from the impact.

Three seconds later, Aidan fell beside me, flinging bits of crystalline ice.

We looked at each other and then up.

The man had disappeared somewhere inside the house. He was coming down or calling the cops. He could report us. He probably would report us. My heart was in my throat, hard and whole as a jawbreaker.

Okay, so this break-in had been a bad idea. Aidan was right. We'd pushed our luck a little too far. If only—

Don't think.

Aidan was on his feet. I got up, too. And we ran like hell.

On the other side of the building was our stolen car, but we both knew it was too risky to go that way. We didn't need to say it out loud. In all the days we'd been on the road together we developed a silent language. We had to head for the trees, even though it was impossible to gauge how deep they were or what lay beyond them.

Aidan was like a lightning bolt, several paces ahead, the reflective strip on his bag catching the bright white around us. He turned around and urged me on. It frustrated me that he was naturally faster. I pushed as hard as I could to keep up with him. My ankle was sore from the fall and the pain rang out with every step, but I couldn't pay attention to that now.

Our rhythm was steady for a few moments: the sound of our shoes swallowed up in the blue holes of the snow, punctuated by the bag flapping on my back and my own heavy breathing.

Keep going, Willa.

The cold air raged through my lungs. Gravity had us racing down the slope of a hill, legs rubber-banding our bodies onward into the thicket of pale-barked branches. The last bit of daylight was sputtering out in purple splashes on the sky but the world bleached out to a blur between my now-frozen eyelashes.

In the distance I heard the sound of a car starting. And was that a siren, too? Maybe I was imagining the siren part.

The déjà vu hit then, so powerful I almost lost my balance: I'd been here before, and not just in my head. The night I broke into Kellie's house. Chased by cops. Busted.

I couldn't do that again. I *wouldn't*.

Please, I thought. *Just let us get out of here.*

I closed my eyes as I wished and kept running, foolishly. I knew I could trip on the twigs scattered over the snowy ground or run into a tree, but I had to play by the wishing rules.

Never mind that I'd broken every other rule in the book. I probably didn't deserve to get out of this.

"Willa!"

I opened my eyes and saw what Aidan was pointing to, lights and flashes of blue glass ahead.

Through the trees, a tall building loomed in front of us, its wings like open arms welcoming us back to civilization. Groups of tourists hovered on the sidewalk around it. Stateline, Nevada's casinos and hotels. Surely we could get lost in a crowd like this.

It was our light at the end of the tunnel. Our neon, blinking light. Maybe my wish was going to come true after all. Maybe I really was lucky.

We just. Had. To run. A little farther.

Soon, we'd be on blacktop again. I sped up, anticipating its hard support.

My legs were caked in snow. I could see us mirrored in the side of the enormous building, our bodies dark and distorted, emerging from the woods like figures from a nightmare. But this wasn't a nightmare. This was our life. Our life on the lam.

ONE

THE SAFE WAS empty.

As in vacant. Cleaned out. Filled with nothing.

My fists opened and closed at my sides. Shock blotted out the rest of the room, the wreckage of my mom's closet, even Aidan standing next to me.

"The money's gone," I said out loud finally, the words at once both obvious and foreign on my tongue. I was referring to my mom's painting fortune, the money we were supposed to be living on, and though Aidan probably had no idea what I was talking about specifically, he could see that in the most general terms this was all very, very bad.

I could only stare into the flat silver void of the open metal box, as if by staring I might psychically fill it back up, the green bills in their neat little rubber-banded stacks, flying in reverse through the room and landing in soft thumps. As if I could go back in time to a moment where the money, as far as I knew, was still in the safe.

And why stop there, really? While I was at it, I would've liked to unsee all of the chaos of my ransacked house. Fling my mom's clothes onto their hangers, her scarves and underwear and socks swishing into place in closed-up drawers, send the sheets sailing to the ceiling so they could land on the bed, flat and even and unwrinkled. The downy snow of feathers on the carpet floating up and into the mattress slits, which would knit themselves back together seamlessly. The shattered bits of the ceramic lamp reassembling into wholeness.

Then my room: My books filing one by one in an airborne arc onto the shelves. The tangled heap of clothing and makeup and shoes on the floor unknotting and separating into the carefully organized arrangement I'd once maintained. The spilled nail polish whirring a pink stream into its little bottle.

Us too. Aidan and me scrambling backward, sucked down the hallway, the expressions of surprise at each new bit of destruction falling off our faces like discarded masks. Our cries of dismay garbling demonically into our throats. The breath refilling our lungs. The front door swinging open and pulling us back out into the Arizona dusk.

Aidan and me, kissing, just outside the house. That's where I'd have to stop.

Our first kiss. His arms encircling me. The herbal smell of his soap. His fingers threading through my hair.

That one perfect meeting of our lips and breath and skin.

Sure, there were lots of moments leading up to the kiss that I would've liked to forget. Glimpsing the flannel-shirted intruder dashing out my back door. The two of us chasing him across town in Aidan's car, to no avail. Me returning, dejected, to see what had become of my house, sure that this had been all my fault. My comeuppance for messing with the Glitterati. Hell, I'd erase the last three months if I could.

But not if it meant losing those crazy perfect few seconds of Aidan bounding up the driveway. Coming back for me. The sudden thrashing of my heart as he neared. The unexpected warmth of his mouth. No one ever forgot their first kiss, did they?

And he was still *here*. Only now he was looking at me with a furrowed brow.

"I don't know, Willa," Aidan said softly. "This doesn't look like the work of the Glitterati."

His voice, deep and buttery, broke through my thoughts, and I reluctantly tumbled back to the present moment. The one where nothing was making sense. The one where my house was wrecked, the money was gone, and my only theory about who was behind this was full of holes.

"No," I said. "It really doesn't."

I paced around the shredded remains of my mom's room as we tried to talk it through. This was Wednesday evening of what was officially already the longest day of my life. The longest week, if you—*shudder*—counted back to my nights in juvie. It seemed impossible that only hours ago Aidan and I had met up at the animal shelter where we were both doing community service. We'd of course had no idea when Aidan dropped me off that we'd find the house like this, or go on a car chase, or any of the rest of it.

"I could imagine Nikki or Kellie hiring someone to come in and mess stuff up, mess with your head, but I don't think they'd go this far," Aidan said, still puzzling it out. "Why would they break into your mother's safe?"

I had no good answer. He knew Nikki and Kellie and Cherise, aka the Glitterati, better than I. He'd been going to school with them forever. For a short time, when I first started Valley Prep in the fall, I'd been part of the clique. Before I'd started stealing from Nikki and Kellie. (Yes, it sounds bad, I know. But I was trying to help the girls they were bullying. Anyway, I'd gotten busted breaking into Kellie's house, and that's what landed me in juvie.)

"Nikki and Kellie don't need the money, that's for sure," I said, gnawing on my thumb. And while they were willing to go illegal in all the usual teenage ways—drinking, smoking pot—I couldn't imagine them risking their trust-fund futures to take money they didn't need. Even if it meant getting back at me for what I'd done. But if it wasn't them, then who?

Maybe I had other enemies. Cherise, my supposed best friend, had disowned me when she found out I'd been stealing from the others. The entire population of Paradise Valley knew about my thieving. It had been on TV, in the papers. (The whole serial-theft thing had really made a splash, which goes to show you that these rich towns are kind of lacking in the news department.) So it could have been anyone, really.

Something else was bothering me. I walked back into the closet and knelt down for another look. It was empty, yes, but unharmed. The lock on the safe hadn't been picked or burned out or busted in any way.

How could that be? I drew in a breath and felt my heart pulse through it.

"It was opened by the combination," I said.

Aidan folded his arms across his chest. "So Plaid Shirt had to have known it."

"Only my mom had it, though. Unless . . ."

. . . They'd found it somewhere else. With a start, I dashed down the hall to my mom's office-slash-painting-studio-slash-inner-sanctum. The one room we hadn't checked out yet.

Plaid Shirt had been in here, too. It was obvious from the computer monitor that was smashed and the hard drive that looked like it had been hit repeatedly with a hammer. The file cabinets were open, though they were still mostly empty from the other day when I'd watched my mom destroy old papers in a shredding binge. Sickened, I went to the closet where she kept her paintings and slid open the louvered doors.

Empty.

Aidan came to stand next to me.

"They took her paintings, too," I said.

He pinched his chin. "Anyone you know that would be after her art? I'm sure that's the kind of question a cop would ask."

"They could be worth a lot of money, but I don't know who would know that," I said. My mom had supposedly sold some of her work at auction, which was how we could afford this fancy place, the exclusive zip code, the elite school. The thing was, I was pretty sure she'd lied about selling those paintings—just a few days ago I found all of them in that closet. And if *that* was the case, then I had no idea where that money actually came from.

"Collector? Art thief? Whoever he was, he knew what he was looking for," Aidan said.

We walked back through the house into the kitchen and I tried to see it through a thief's eyes. (Maybe not so much of a stretch.) Full shelves of dishes and glasses had been tossed and trampled. Some of the cabinet doors were hanging off their hinges. He'd even unloaded our refrigerator. Which was just tacky, in my opinion.

"He must have," I said. "I just don't know why he had to pulverize every last piece of tableware."

All I knew for sure was that the first beautiful house

we'd ever lived in was ruined.

But it was almost like all the destruction, all the wreckage around the house was some kind of subterfuge to distract us from the robbery. Like he'd wanted it to look like it was sabotage. I had to admit that it was a pretty smart approach—one that I wish I'd thought of in my own thieving days. Whoever Mr. Plaid Shirt was, he was good. A pro.

"He wanted to scare you."

He'd been watching us. A wave of dizziness hit, and I felt behind me for the stable support of the wall. I could no longer look at the situation like a fellow thief. I could only see it as a victim. This wasn't just a prank by some kid. This was a criminal in another league of criminals. If scaring me was what he wanted, he'd accomplished his mission. And whatever this thing was, it was much bigger than I'd thought.